MANTIS GREEN

Farah Ysvette Mourad Vera

MANTIS GREEN

Farah Ysvette Mourad Vera

TABLE OF CONTENTS

MANTIS GREEN

MANTIS GREEN

Para Ita.

PRELUDE

A change in light urged the hermit crabs to retreat from the shore to their crevices in the roots of the buttonwood trees of Fort Jefferson.

Before morning, a mythic shadow exited the mote, searching for breakfast.

Nearby,

a stirring in a patch of sand,

bubbling up, as if boiling.

Green sea turtle hatchlings burst through the fine white sand and waddled quickly towards the water.

They successfully evaded a sleepy pelican, who struggled to keep its eyes open and focused on a spot in the water, facing the other side of the beach.

From its perch on a slippery wood piling, the bird watched a fish too large to eat. Eventually, the fish would signal the arrival of a school of gulp-able morsels, and the two would snack on a few.

Most of the sea turtles had made it into the water by

now, half a dozen way ahead of the bale, following a deeper blue.

This was Day One.

MORNING

Sunlight spilled over a small horizon, washing over a handful of structures atop a pint-sized moon called Mantis Green. A rotting orange lay alone in the flooding light, no insects invited to feast on what remained of its food. The light crawled up a door and beamed through the stained glass, casting colored shadows on the terra-cotta tiles of a lifeless parlor. The air too still, the dust too settled. A wave of particles flew in from the side, cutting through the light, with a creak of the floorboards in the adjacent room. A shadow darted past the swelling light. Blue and gold and red stretching up the walls, as their color faded. Where they merged, the light was pristine and pure. At the corner, they split up again. Blue and yellow blended into green and unfurled down to the base of a large rectangle—perfect enough to be a masterful sculpture on display, but which in this case, had been repurposed as a kitchen table. Pressed tightly against the edge facing the green light was a figure, head tilted down, a thin shine in the eyes like egg whites.

9

MANTIS GREEN

Gallia Sinlava didn't like people, but throughout her five decades of life, she had been an anthropologist, sociologist, psychologist, essayist, painter, and nurse. Her hair was short, her eyes were big, and her skin a toasted coat. She was the last to bear the family name and gladly so. Her life ended soon after she moved to Mantis Green, one of the luxury satellites orbiting Earth.

Gallia stood in her kitchen, cleaning the fold of her arm, preparing to give herself a shot of a milky substance. Next to her, a green liquid collected in a cordial glass: fresh juiced barley grass. Her creation and morning ritual. It had been featured in a few health and culinary publications back on the surface and remained one of her company's best-selling products. She had also attempted to partner with her preferred barley grass seller, a pair of hairy smart-farming brothers, who turned out to be "unbearable bores hung up on their social resentment." The thought of meeting others like them discouraged her, and in the end, she partnered with no one.

"It's a free world. People can choose to purchase or grow their own greens."

"Let's go with that."

"What?"

"We'll encourage the 'Grow Your Own' method. Folks can get their tools from us and we don't have to worry about all the extra controls for edibles. It's good."

She went along with the project manager's suggestions. Consumer products were her least favorite thing, but a lot of the company's revenue came from there, and she needed that money to fund her research and other nonprofit branches. And yes—although she hated to think of it this way—she had an expensive lifestyle, which was highlighted in an absurd color the moment she decided to move to her own planet, where (as she put it during a particular interview) she could finally "breathe clean air" and arrive healthy at her old age.

"I believe the air is everything. When we talk about longevity, we talk about food and sleep and exercise... and all along we're breathing in and out."

"So you're offering yourself up."

"In a way, yes."

"That's wonderful."

"Yes."

"Thank you."

"Thank *you*."

There was an uncomfortable pause before the reporter moved on to the next set of questions, mostly about Gallia's daily schedule on Mantis Green, how time worked up there, whether she would miss it... She would not.

Here, on this rock, by herself. That's how she had always wanted it to be. On Earth, she had wanted to be alone more than anything, to get away from the crowds and their clouds of dust. On Mantis Green, the air was clean, the light was smooth, day and night were a choice, and time seemed irrelevant.

As scheduled, artificial night gave way to morning. The crystals in the synthetic atmosphere turned at different angles to wrangle the right amount of light. Filter globules in the next layers colored the light to reflect it more appropriately. A yellow morning light, crisp and clean, reached the windows of the house, as Gallia prepared to dive into her day. *Her day, at last.*

The process of distilling barley grass didn't amplify the nutrients or enhance the flavor; its function was purely meditative. The juice was distilled slowly, hypnotically, following (now simulated) gravity's pull, filling the air with a vibrant and sweet aroma. The machine had three clear spherical chambers, each one larger than the one before it. In the first, the fresh squeeze of barley grass collected from the extracting mechanism. The second contained chilled water. The contents of the first two chambers were then vaporized and mixed on their way to the third chamber, whose surface was etched with faint lines in the shapes of continents (but not the true shapes of America, Africa, Europe, etc.) It was a strictly nonpartisan design, whose purpose was to evoke an ideal Earth, at the peak of its natural potential, without pre-determined limitations or attachments to its past or present geography; a cleaned-up picture of home, a feeling of serenity, settled thoughts. Mantis Green itself had been designed to emulate this pristine Earthly state, although it was more a matter of aesthetic than anything else. In reality, Mantis Green was rather unstable and generated a considerable amount of waste.

The juice collected in a glass, drop after drop falling one by one from the spout. The first drop was success, climax, results, closure. Some consumers chose to watch each drop thereafter as well, many claiming a deeper effect of the practice on their mood or mindset, and in more fervent cases a measurable effect on their adrenal health. An article had been written years back about a man who swore that counting drops had cured him of a severe autoimmune condition. He had been cured, indeed, but the article suggested it was due to an improved lifestyle overall, which incorporated better air and diet, and a significant decrease in stress. It is possible that counting drops can trigger a desire to make and maintain such changes, the way other spiritual and wellness practices do. Gallia, a hardened cynic, gave up early. Two or three drops were satisfaction enough.

She took the syringe off its stand and plunged the needle into her arm, pushing the milky substance into her body. It was a complex blend of vitamins, minerals, herbs, anti-depressants, and a mild derivative of LSD. Then, she took off her white rayon robe, drank the barley grass and pressed a lime green button on the bulky wooden counter. The windows began to expand down to the floor and up to the ceiling, like the house's eyes were opening. The shutters shrank into themselves quietly. A blend of vitamins and sunscreen swirled inside the glass. Natural sunlight filtered though the synthetic atmosphere and penetrated the room, as Gallia stood with her arms outstretched in the warm yellow-lit space, eyes closed. A soft music emerged from the heavy silence, lightening up the soundscape and thus alleviating the can-like pressure of the room. A xylophone dialed side to side in gentle balanced steps of rhythm. A timer lit up on the counter and tic-toc'd, just barely in sync with the music. And on this particular day, a set of little footsteps broke up the tempo. It was a cautious young owl walking into the room. This was Giancarlo, the only other animal on Mantis Green. He was coming in for some filtered sunlight.

This side of the impressive manor on Mantis Green faced Earth at all times. Gallia would sit at the table, after her sunbath, until the "early afternoon," which was marked less by the slight shifting angle of the light crystals, than by the moment she'd start to feel hungry. The high-noon quality of the light could be overwhelming some days, and when that happened, Gallia moved to the back of the house for some shade. There, we had built her a long lemonade porch overlooking the stars, which appeared different from the way they did on

Earth, more vibrant but somehow less disarming. Anyway, it was better than staring down at Earth on the other side. To Gallia, the cobalt peacefulness of it was dishonest, the perfection of its curve a mirage. She rejected almost any exchange of looks between Earth and herself. Time and time again, she found herself looking down at the ground as she passed an observation spot.

Most satellites were constructed as indoor oases, but Mantis Green emphasized "the outdoors." The docking station was, of course, enclosed and simple. Gray, bare and functional. But as the gate opened, a lush little yard lay ahead. You'd step off the station to find a terra-cotta path that wound up through a field of bamboo and horsetail. The smell of earth and chlorophyll was of notable strength, and there was a thin haze that hung in the air and swirled visibly as you moved through it. As the plants became more sparse, the terra-cotta broke up into stones, and then into smaller rocks until it was sand deposited at the base of a massive front door. Gallia had specifically requested this entrance to the house, although she only used it a few times.

The magnificent door was flanked on both sides by olive trees. It was partly made of wood, salvaged from a Caribbean shipwreck, which Gallia had personally bought and kept in storage for nearly two decades. Gallia liked to reuse. She liked thinking about the stories and emotions encrusted in objects on their second or third life. However, she refused to donate her body after death, which meant it would have to be retrieved from Mantis Green and shipped back to Earth, rather than being composted locally, with the rest of the rock. Waste.

The front door opened to an inner courtyard, where the terra-cotta resumed after another sandy patch. There were benches, geometric sculptures hidden behind layers of ferns, and an orange grove on the side closest to Earth, with an enormous weeping willow at its center. You wouldn't notice it right away, but there were often lots of rotten flowers, orange blossoms mainly—and even the fruits themselves—on the floor. There were no birds or bees to scavenge around Mantis Green, so the plants lived half lives.

Waste.

We had installed a dozen air-conditioning oscillators in the inner courtyard, to make the air mimic the effects of the breeze. Just one of those things Gallia never noticed. It played right into her illusion, but she had not once expressed appreciation for it. Maybe she did notice, privately. Or maybe it was just *so* seamless that she couldn't notice. I don't know.

There was a small network of trails to explore and lots of spaces to plant more things, including two underground astroculture labs. However, Gallia seemed insecure about her ability (or maybe just unwilling) to actually tend to a garden, so we hired a homestead officer with a botany background for her. His name was Covas Lundledge, and he would come onto the surface periodically, as authorized by Gallia, to harvest and care for the plants.

Covas was a practical man. His parents had suffered in their old age. While young, they had lived spontaneously, pursuing transient passions and following their curiosity. But as time pressed down on them, they had struggled to survive aging and illness and poverty. He had made a point of compromising as often as necessary to avoid such hardship in the winter of his own life, although he wants you to know that he did not resent his parents' choices and was grateful to them for all they had imparted on him in life and in death.

The entrance to the lower-level labs was through an elevator by the weeping willow, near the front door of the house, which was a hefty thing. We thought it was silly to install a full fledged door with bolts and whatnot, so we had initially chosen a wrought iron gate. It had to be replaced, of course, once Gallia requested the storm system, to avoid water getting into the foyer. The final product had been built by an artisanal contractor we hired, out of some shipwreck debris from Gallia's collection with stained glass inlays. It was a gorgeous work with an unfortunate side effect. Gallia was prone to hallucinations and stained glass turned out to be an especially potent trigger. She had mentioned her predisposition to spontaneously conjure psychedelic imagery only in passing, during one of our design meetings. One of our consultants had suggested using stained glass on the fireplace.

"I'll end up roasting myself trying to hug whatever comes out of it."

Gallia paired her comment with a manufactured laugh to lighten the mood, but no one joined in. We were all too slow to catch on, I suppose. Or maybe we all noticed her running off, out of reach, and refused to venture in after her. I did find her word choice peculiar. Why would she choose to gift a welcoming gesture to such an aggressive apparition? We all buried the moment quickly, and in the end, she agreed to a similar design. I overheard Sylvia, her estate administrator, suggest to her in private that she should request all stained glass be eliminated from the plans, but Gallia refused and insisted that she did not want to appear too picky or weak. They fought for a while. I think I was the only one to witness it. Gallia did not appreciate the unsolicited concern. She kept the stained glass concept, but I was able to quietly steer everyone in favor of simple geometric shapes instead of more defined imagery. Both the fireplace and the front door were adorned with the custom-made glass. But based on what we found in her diary, it seems that she saw plenty in the shapes, during her episodes.

From Gallia's journal:

"At first they're just gray shadows. The colors come later, as the shapes start to shift away from each other. They become enlarged and infected, and I try to hide before they see me."

One night, she sat by the fire, TV on, drinking wine. The sofa was too far, so she moved down to the ground. Flashes of light from the TV pierced the space between her and the fire, often, making her look up. She was tired; eyes closed, head tilted back, pressure on her spine. Vertigo set in. As soon as she felt herself spinning uncomfortably fast, she opened her eyes, tried to focus on a corner of the room, blinked a whole lot. Nothing. Still spinning. She looked straight ahead at the fire, the stained glass above it. She touched it. Caramel light, sweet enough to eat. A yellow salvation. Comfort. But when the fire flickered, a familiar haunt appeared: a blue-green claw, grabbing her hair, inhaling her life, feeding its own soul with it. In the end, it rejected her, cast her in a dry red bath. She felt hot, suffocating. Run away. Get away from this thing. A beast after her. Hungry, indiscriminate, violent. The claws on the wall, the red behind her, the yellow above and out of reach. Coming from the front door, another set of assaults. More red. Brighter blue, meaner green. No yellow light to save her. Overtaken by the rest. She closed her eyes and surrendered to the spin. She spun until she found a dream to wake into.

19

MANTIS GREEN

She awoke on the floor hours later, bathed in multicolored light coming through the door at the front of the house, overturned glass in a dark sticky puddle of wine by her hand. She had made it through the night and was now sitting up in the spacious parlor. In there, we had placed a divan and a small marble coffee table with a wooden ashtray on it (her specific request). On days like this, Gallia would pull a pack of cigarettes from behind a pillow on the divan. Why she went through the trouble of hiding them, like a child would, is beyond me. She would smoke one—or in some cases, half of one —checking the stillness of her hand every few seconds, waiting for it to stop trembling, replaying her thoughts from the previous night, staring at the colors in the glass, wishing they would swirl into each other and settle into a neutral amber.

Leave me alone. The differences…

Gallia had trouble in the "mornings." Her dreams were often unpleasant and they bled into her waking mood. She'd have to spend a good long while thinking it all through, interviewing herself to make sure she was okay, checking her hands until they were visibly settled. Health is important.

The most important. I must be healthy to live well and that means my dreams too. If I'm not healthy, I don't function.

On days like this, she'd skip the barley grass. On days like this and after Giancarlo's death, every day altogether.

When order has run out, there's no use trying to summon it back. It won't come. It'll only run faster and further. Heal. Know you're sick and heal. I'm sick. I need to breathe. I need to sit. I need some sun. I need some air. An orange. A coffee. Some water. Some sleep. A swim. The pool.

Splash. On days like this, Gallia would go into the cave and swim the mood away. By the end, she behaved like an otter: active and playful and floating a lot. Fully nude. Happy. Why she didn't do it more often, I don't know. She had a habit of forgetting what was available to her on Mantis Green. She had a whole planet to herself but still insisted on staying locked up inside the house.

She returned to the parlor after swimming and her hairs would stand on point with the change in temperature. Her mood had also changed, lightened up, cooled off, *whatever is supposed to happen*, she thought. The parlor opened directly into the office on the left and the living room on the right. The office was small and had a fake chimney. We had even installed a scentaur—a powerful scent simulator—that was programmed to emit the smell of burning wood whenever the "fire" was on. Gallia preferred the real fireplace in the living room, of course, even though having it on made the atmosphere heavy, despite the robust filters we had built in to control the effects of the smoke. She never worked in the office at all, anyway. It became a "banishment" room, where she dumped things she didn't want around anymore.

21

The living room featured a massive window facing the courtyard. A narrow pebble road went behind the weeping willow, all the way to the "horizon." There, we built a dip in the road, a cliff illusion that led to a stairwell feeding into a set of excavated spaces, the "cave." In there were three major rooms. First, there was a reading room with a fully stocked pantry and bathroom. If she wished, she could have lived in this room for days. Just past it, there was a "hot spring" that eventually flowed into the pool. We built it as an alternative way to get to the final stage of the luxurious triple-chambered grotto, the nap room. The nap room was perfectly quiet, completely sans echo. The entire room was covered with layered cork in the shape of organic waves with embedded crevices and channels that absorbed extraneous sounds. In there, we had set up a bed, a sofa, a hammock and a sleeping pod.

It was no surprise to us that Gallia spent a great deal of time in this hideaway. She worried about visitors.

They stare before making themselves known. They stare and they lurk.

She wanted more than anything to be hidden and alone. Covas was least fond of this trait of hers. As Gallia's homestead, he was in charge of monitoring her stability and that of the rock's. For the most part, he could just record his observations from afar, especially since the security program we had implemented had a sensitive notification system. It delivered him a detailed report twice a day and provided a live feed of general metrics in between reports, including thermal readings, gas emission and oxygen levels, pollution, gravitational stability, pressure, and all the other usual things. However, if Gallia was in the cave or in the courtyard, the system would transmit an alert of unusually low levels of added carbon dioxide inside the environment. These blind spots were meant to be quiet spaces, so we had not installed the same 24/7 sensors there, since they emitted a low "buzzing sound" that Gallia claimed she could hear and disliked very much. For the record, the buzzing came from the humidity filters, which were needed to regulate the environment in order to avoid static electricity or mold problems in the cave. Anyway, sometimes Covas had no choice but to call the enigmatic sovereign of the little planet and endure the cold and austere reaction she projected at him.

"Miss Gallia." He would say into the intercom, knowing there might be no answer for a couple hours. He would repeat the greeting every 30 or 60 minutes until he got a response. Then, he would ask how she was feeling.

"Good" would immediately wave him away. But if there was any trouble, he ought to know, and luckily it seemed like Gallia was willing to volunteer this information more often than not. Trash was a frequent complaint, and so was,

"Is the delivery here yet? They're late again."

In the beginning, she may have been right, since the process was far from streamlined. But as the days progressed, and she renounced the concept of time, she was often just plain wrong. Everyone around her tried to anticipate her impatience, but it was a hard thing to judge, so the endeavor was seldom fruitful.

Gallia disliked being checked on, but she expected prompt assistance always. She also knew that should something happen, it was important to have someone looking for her.

If a rock falls on my head while I'm in the pool or if I slip in the grove, I want them to find me quickly.

To assuage this very present fear of hers, we installed panic buttons all over the place. All she had to do was press the closest one and a whole team of people would be immediately notified. Gallia had purchased a deluxe emergency plan that included a support team of fifty people, who rotated positions and were available at all hours.

Death had been after her for a long time, she felt. Always, it seemed. And eventually it would arrive on Mantis Green and take her. The dread was stronger than any desire for survival she could have felt. She was instinctually suicidal but had rejected having control over her own life a long time ago, so she felt that it wasn't her place to make the choice. She chose instead to "live well" and do everything that was expected of her. She helped others, supported fashionable moral vendettas, and pretended to form her own strained but popular opinions about things. Others reacted favorably enough, so she felt validated and moved on. It wasn't until the Auroral Marionette went up that she started thinking about what she wanted for herself.

To rest, to be left alone, in peace, away from it all. To live as if I were dead and to not matter anymore. I want to walk free. I want no one looking at me. I want them to leave me alone. This world has too many voices, too many thoughts, too much reproach.

She was a terrific complainer. Even in all her self-righteous glory, this woman refused to tolerate any discomfort or inconvenience. Whether it had always been that way or not, I don't know, but I guess it gave Sylvia and the rest of the Sinlava army a raison d'être.

Speaking of Sylvia, it seems she had entered a difficult space in her own life, having no one to look after every minute. She lived in a tri-loft downtown. At one point, she had considered moving away somewhere less dense, but the next day, she knew she would never be happy without her city comforts, so she abandoned the idea. She enjoyed herself that day, having realized that she loved the masses of bodies flowing through the streets, the clouds of gasses hanging over their heads, the smells and flavors of all the things entangled in the air. She appreciated removing the day's historical residue from her skin every night in the shower. And she loved waking up to hear the radio describe the dramatics that awaited each morning, the changes in weather, the fluctuating dangers to watch for, the anxiety and excitement, the worry or anticipation about things to come. Then, going to sleep not knowing what new events would be taking place, upon waking again. Sylvia loved this. Gallia did not.

From Gallia's writing on Mantis Green, it seems that she mostly slept on the hammock in the nap room. She suffered from night terrors (naturally), and I think she liked the instability of the hammock because it was more likely to wake her fast, once she started clenching and shifting around. I know the feeling well, and it's the reason I prefer hammocks during tumultuous times.

I'm fairly certain that she never slept in the bed. Sometimes I wish I could have seen her dreams. They must have been vivid and terrifying. But there's no use in indulging in morbid daydreams about someone else's hell. I know my own dreams. They speak real, unadorned language.

My name, if it matters, is Milian Sieglund. Gallia Sinlava's life affected my own in a strange way, and I thought I'd share my side, in case anyone's interested or encrusted in a similar place or situation and wants company.

She proved to be an eternally displeased customer. No

matter what attempts I made at dazzling flair or ease of functionality, to fulfill her requests, she never approved anything without a crinkle between her eyebrows. And yet, we spent more money, time and effort on this rock than any of the others on the Auroral Marionette. In hindsight, we can see the mistakes we all (together) made, although Rotari would love to deflect any and all accountability, on the basis of this being *my* project, while working under their umbrella. It burns me up, though, that *she* will never see. Her prime privilege was to bypass her own accountability, when the remorse should have thrown her into a painful trance, a Saint-Médard-style convulsion, visions, stigmata and all. If anything of hers remains, I wish daily that it can have some knowledge of all this. But I don't know that justice is that natural.

As much as I miss Earth and people as a whole, I don't miss the devaluation of responsibility I witnessed during my last years there. I don't miss embracing blame, or the political games that ensure my demise and insure the business of places like Rotari and people like Gallia Sinlava. I don't miss Rotari, and although I hope to return, I doubt I can ever "go home" again. I suppose in that sense, Gallia and I were the same, and probably how we found each other.

Gallia got exactly what she wanted, and most importantly, what she needed. And I suppose we can say the same about me.

Back in his childhood home on a distant little planet, as he continued to swirl inside this collection of thoughts and memories about Gallia Sinlava on Mantis Green, Milian began to feel sick. He took his deceased mother's skull and went to the bathroom to puke. He fell asleep resting his head on the toilet's tank, his mother's head nestled in his arms, her right parietal bone scraping against the porcelain with each breath he took.

He dreamt of Mantis Green. He dreamt that it had been built for his mother, and as soon as she arrived, the walls compressed and took her in, in essence, and left no trace of her as he knew her. All that remained was an eerie feeling of her presence. Her agony. Her breathing in all the air, making it stale, depleting it of oxygen. Embalming the plants and the walls and the furniture and every detail of the structures with her sighs, her gloom and her pain. It hurt to be absorbed by a house and Milian felt it.

OPPORTUNITY

My first meeting with Gallia was on a sunny day. I remember because she arrived with her face covered in a pasty coat of sunscreen. We had never met before, although I had spoken to the people in her office several times while I was a junior consultant at the ASP (Autonomous Sustainability Project). The Sinlavas were one of the most influential families in what they called the "big green" market, the most powerful industry to emerge in the last fifty years. The family had sponsored several large-scale public projects in a span of four decades. Andrea Sinlava—Gallia's grandmother—had built the first coast-to-coast sani-culture link system, which was essentially a continuous rendering facility that turned compostable garbage into rich soil and delivered it directly to the farms. The concept was far from innovative, but Andrea had an amiable personality. After several proposals, it had been her candid input that brought the plans to fruition:

"We should pop some pipes down there. They can do the work."

MANTIS GREEN

Most of Andrea's projects started off this way. People assumed she was making a joke or commenting absently, but she was dead serious. And she had been thinking it through for a long time before speaking on the subject at all.

She was a loud bombastic spectacle of a woman, an unlikely matriarch: a middle child, no formal academic recognition beyond a completion diploma from a local college (which she accomplished as a favor to a family friend seeking to mentor her), a history of odd jobs and a short-lived experience writing poetry and painting on newsprint with cheap watercolors.

She wasn't a thinker, or a business genius. She was an Olympic-level shot-putter, who infamously refused to join the Olympic team. They asked, but she refused to take a drug test, on principle, and urged the other athletes to do the same.

"We gotta go back to trusting sometime. Drug addicts are obvious. The legal bureaucracy is a distraction to athletes. I, for one, have no desire to play games in this court."

Those were her words outside the courthouse on a cold afternoon in Mexico City.

She also enjoyed swimming, but mostly when engaged in racing someone or something. Story goes that Andrea liked to swim in the swamp in Florida, hoping to one day race an alligator. She got her wish once and lost her left toes in the process.

After several years campaigning for the implementation of her pipe system in places like California and Oregon, a progressive politician from Bolivia contacted her to bring it to her country. After Bolivia became the first country to efficiently and successfully recycle their trash back into food at the national level, other countries in Latin America put in their bids for Andrea's piping method. Germany and China joined in, then the Middle East, Africa and the rest of Europe. Here and there, independent cities in the US started implementing the system, and soon the Andrea pipe networks became commonplace all over the world. Any fish scale wrapper or paper coffee filter that went down your garbage shoot was guaranteed to end up part of an odorous mixture at some farmer's compost well, at no extra fee and no extra burden to you (or the farmer... eventually). At first, it was a wholly privately-owned enterprise, and the Sinlavas made an obscene fortune. They would have been royalty for a hundred years at least, except for that on her deathbed, Andrea sold the networks to the governments themselves and then donated the money to local conservation groups in each place. She dedicated all donations the same way:

"To my children. Enjoy."

No one asked her what that meant. It could have been a dark joke, or it could have been a gift to help the world be better for her children. Andrea Sinlava had died a saint or a prankster. The children need not worry, of course. The family had their hands in everything, and they were bound to have a surplus of money for four generations, at least.

The Sinlavas were as popular as they were generous. With their support, we designed places like the Hydrodomes of Toscana and the Cloudi Generators of the Gulf of Mexico... and also the ones in the North Atlantic coast unfortunately, which unleashed a tempest of headlines that included: "Ecosystem permanently damaged," "80% of industries in Maine capsize as a result of Cloudi technology," and "Good-bye, Lobster Tails!"

The Maine disaster had occurred during my first few months as an independent contractor working for Rotari, a design and architecture firm based in New York that called its top executives, "Dream Makers." Those magical beings designed homes for the eccentric and conceived of commercial places like The Wells—yes, that garish chain of underwater malls. Still, they helped me update my legal status from student to skilled worker, so I tried to remain grateful. After all, they didn't just provide flashy structures for socialites and shoppers, but were industry leaders in alternative architecture. Rotari was one of the first to promote widespread underwater dwelling, and also the first to capitalize on universal orbital tourism. They also manufactured all their own, patented, core building materials.

Gallia came to my office after having received an invitation to the Auroral Park dedication, to be held at the newly unveiled Stratos Station in the Auroral Marionette. She had followed the development closely and wanted to commission a satellite for herself. Until now, most of the existing satellites were small rocks, anchored close to the ring, and most of them were vacation homes. Gallia wanted a detachable *moon* for herself. I offered some coaxial condo options over the Pacific ocean, which afforded a more isolated sensation. But she *despised* the Pacific and was,

"Not looking for a vacation home. I'm leaving for good, and I don't want to have to be so guarded all the time. I heard what happened to those people on that side with the climbers."

"Oh, that was a complete misunderstanding..."

Some outlets had spread an incorrect report of a break-in at one of the satellites the previous month. It had turned out to be a surprise party for a young singer, which his security team had not been notified of. Unfortunately, some of the guests had arrived drunk and a big fight had broken out. The press had branded it a "Security breach in the heavens!" It doesn't take much to frighten some folks with money.

"Please. I understand. Can you just indulge me and present a design in a couple months?"

"I'll have it in a couple weeks," I said.

MANTIS GREEN

I called a daily brainstorming meeting with my team to come up with a book of designs for Gallia. Every day, the "team" was new, and the people who had the best ideas the day before were gone. Some would be back on rotation within several cycles, but others were simply tossed other ways by the turnaround wheel. It was very difficult to make the leap between contractor and staff, not to mention securing a full work visa, if you happened to be born outside of Earth, like many of us at Rotari.

I had been lucky to be a part of one of the last generations to benefit from a forward-thinking system, before the next flavor of nationalism creeped into every corner of the dear little planet. It was still possible to arrange for short contractual visas, with the caveat that no "limited foreign contractor" may overstay their position within a team to the point of becoming indispensable to the project. Rotari played it safe and kept participation to a daily rotation. This game of musical chairs had begun as an alternative to complete prohibition of foreign contractors. The standard industry argument in favor of foreign workers had been cross-training and skill development, which promotes progress on Earth as well as developing planets. When agreement proved impossible, the compromise became to allow for temporary outsourcing, as long as the "provable objective" was time-bound education and professional development.

"There's not a relevant enough requirement for it—in fact, it may be detrimental to our own development, in the long run."

Justice C. Hayward Combs had been much criticized for his remarks on the matter, as he'd done everything in his power to shut down the compromise. Despite his firm objection, the decision stood, and so here I was with my mockery of a team, and I was thankful nonetheless. Combs had also wanted to lift a ban on a naturalization retraction bill that would reverse citizenship for any non-refugees, which meant *me*. Had it not been for my brother's hastiness, we may have been refugees after all. If we had stayed home for a few more months, we would have been fleeing, hidden, in the same cargo ships as some of our neighbors, and then perhaps he would still be alive, or we may both be dead. Anyway, we'd be up for review regardless, and our fluctuating legal status on Earth would remain a thing of identity for us, something unknown to my Earth-born colleagues.

I had requested for certain people to be granted an extended position on the project, but my application had to be "submitted, in writing, for review." The review process took an average of 60 to 90 days (or more, depending on the length of the contract, past Earth/US employment history, place of origin, etc.), since it involved a change of legal status. Rotari took its compliance and legal standards very seriously, and while they would never outwardly discourage originality or withhold due acknowledgment, they did maintain a rigid bureaucracy about their controls, to mitigate any possible risks to their reputation and profit. There were many a fee associated with sponsoring a foreign contractor for an extended visa. Denials were common and often sealed with,

"It's a matter of precedent," or

"We think it's an exciting prospect that requires further review. Thank you for bringing it to our attention."

You're welcome.

Nonetheless, Rotari did have a penchant for instigating and capitalizing on new cultural and social trends, which is how they got away with hiring so many external workers in the first place, even if they had to abide by the stringent non-Earthling regulations imposed on them by the law, which had been tightening up more and more with the changes in politics around the world.

While working for Rotari, I witnessed the inverse relationship between what consumers wanted and what they thought they wanted. Just as their sympathies toward people from other corners of the universe narrowed in scope and strength, their cravings for foreign imports diversified and expanded exponentially. Hot plumanda desserts—a fluffy, foamy, overly sweet, utterly dull-flavored, unnecessarily large, soup bowl type thing to dip your biscuits into—from Acacia

Tii were available as special items in bistros across the world; people everywhere were manufacturing underwear in bulk out of chasni fibre, imported from mines deep within a dark star that was outside of our own galaxy; and the exotic pet markets had hundreds of new animals and plants to offer every new breeding season. So much for returning to "made here on Earth," and so much for saving on import costs, and so much for reviving true-Earth manufacturing and bringing the "true human spirit" back from its "liberal grave" as one US official put it.

This hunger for foreign fare at home had only grown since I came to the little planet, so much so that some cities had assimilated alien foods into their own regional spreads. Conversely, it had also launched things like the "Earth diet" into popularity—you guessed it, eat only foods from Earth and you'll look completely unlike yourself in no time at all. Almost anyone was willing to break the diet of course, for a toast to the new year, with a glass of extra sparkly Natora champagne, an effervescent delight made from wildflowers harvested on a dwarf planet trailing Neptune's orbit.

Natora champagne was certified as *farmed, harvested and manufactured remotely by China*. The Chinese had invested in remote agriculture all over the place. They had devised a way to harvest locally through bots. Then, the bots would harvest samples and transmit their genetic data to a lab in Beijing, where they could be reconstructed and reproduced. They had OI and MI versions of most products. OI stood for "One Iteration," which meant they had copied the data from one sample only and cloned it exactly over and over again, one size fits all. MI was like the organic brother of OI. It stood for "Multiple Iteration," which meant they had copied dozens, in some cases hundreds, of samples and reproduced them, and then, on top of that, plugged in different values for variables like color, sweetness, softness, etc. This provided customers with an illusion of choice, and it allowed sellers to charge a premium on top of the regular price for the products. The debate was the same: how much more nutrition are you getting for the extra dollar?

I preferred the illusion to the one-size-fits-all, at least in terms of food and textiles, but not when it came down to art supplies. Rotari liked to buy MI everything, which meant our illustrators could never find the same shade of green twice. As a result, all of the artwork from our illustrators at Rotari (including the stand-in child's mango popsicle) had to be superimposed or "heathered," just in case. Lucky for us, most clients preferred this. They liked that we didn't just "splash on a color and call it a day."

We took pride in our artwork at Rotari and held several shows every year, some of them in major museums around the world. A permanent collection of our architectural drawings and maquettes was kept at the Boamne in downtown Los Angeles. They rotated the items in and out of their vault every few months, but I don't think they could have shown them all in one year; three, maybe. I never saw any of my drawings on display—I suspect because they weren't vivacious enough to be displayed as "art"—but my maquette for our precious little Earth belt is kept between the entrance and the gift shop year-round. Only "Rotari" is credited on the tiny placard at the base of the glass. It can be photographed from outside, and it's kept lit even when the museum is closed. Or anyway, that's how it used to be.

If the sunshine has left before, I am ignorant to that fact. I knew, most likely, that I would never see that type of sun again. It didn't matter that I could bask in orange glows and yellow mists and green waterfalls of sunlight on my home planet or elsewhere out in the galactic neighborhood of ours, or even if I ever got the money and the time, the full artificial splendor of those exoplanets and stars where the Chinese were making a fortune harvesting cloneable produce. I assumed there must be a good quality of replicated sunlight there. Even if I could find an approximation somewhere nearby, the struggle of immigration paperwork all over again was unappealing enough to make me want to drift aboard an asteroid until I died. But I didn't do that. And anyway, I have to finish telling you how I got to this place.

Dancing in a shirt without underwear on, it would seem. I let my guard down, as you say. All this vastness and all cultures express themselves in terms of war.

I was the happiest I've ever been when my PMs at Rotari agreed to hear my idea for the Auroral Marionette. It was a shorter meeting than I expected, on a day replete with weather. The concept was so obvious, they couldn't believe we hadn't done it yet. Ain't that always the case. The one difference was, that unlike those drifting satellite hotels and cruisers, the Marionette would be visible from Earth. Rotari would be the first to give the sky a skyline, the first to find a new place to build a massive city technically still *on Earth*.

Gorgeous. Congratulations. Can't wait. The PMs exited the room, thanking me and wishing me well with the development.

"We'll send the proposal to scheduling and go from there."

"Thanks, Anaiida."

"Of course. Thank *you*."

Anaiida had been my senior PM since I started working at Rotari and had been the one to write my recommendation for a permanent visa (when that was still an option). She had been born in an Earth territory on a dwarf planet much like mine, but which was much closer to Earth. Her mother had moved there shortly after an economic collapse in her colony on Mars, where *her* parents had landed after fleeing political persecution in their home star, where they had fought for re-liberation after an oppressive imperial government from the other side of the galaxy had overtaken and subjugated the natives. Now we were both at Rotari, discussing the birth of my own little version of a colony.

"They're gonna get involved, so you better plan for it right off the bat."

"I guess so."

"It's gonna be a thing for immigration services all over."

"Well, I don't know how feasible it's really gonna be—
"

"People always find a way. They have to."

No rebuttal from me. I had done it, just as she had. We had to account for a proper customs complex that would handle traffic between Earth, the Marionette and everywhere else. Initially, it was bundled with the rest of the services: travel security, law enforcement, fire department, paramedics and everything else. But it did seem like a good idea to separate them from everything else. Anyway, we'd have plenty of space to accommodate a research facility or whatever else they wanted. Government buildings can be modest, when they need to be. What we both worried about—although neither of us wanted to say it—was that we would be forced to give up a third of the ring for immigration use. Surely someone would suggest it along the way. Like a border wall around the planet, where all incoming had to stop before touching the surface.

We would end up posting for independence from Earth, like we'd done with a couple of the other satellite properties. We'd comply with universal law and cooperate with Earth law, in good faith, but the destination would not be legally considered Earth. It would just be the Auroral Marionette. Posting for independence was a decades-long ordeal, but better we do it from the beginning than try to secede from Earth later. This way, we had grounds to refuse government use of our pre-independent land, which was also private property. If they wanted a building or a refugee zone, they needed to get our approval first. Meanwhile, our skyline around the Earth would provide stellar hospitality to anyone, regardless of their immigration status on the planet.

Soon we'd be crawling with people of all kinds, from all parts of the galaxy. From that vantage point, it was a nice picture.

But the crowds would annoy me. I was sure of that. They'd have a taste of the sublime far-awayness and then immediately try to point out their hometown. Many would leave unchanged. Others would stay awhile, in their new idea of luxury, pampered into oblivion, with a new status symbol to flash down there: a satellite rock (available for rent or purchase, just give us a call for the tour of your life!), never once glancing down at those poor suckers back there on the surface. Mudskippers.

I ended up working almost alone on designing Mantis Green, a satellite unlike all the others. It wasn't a station-like vessel, but rather a planet with a "core" and an "atmosphere" that opened up to face the Earth and space. Inside the "core" were the server room and data center. If we had started growing bonafide planets, Rotari would have really become God. And I would have been its prophet. And I would have been tragically terminated.

I'd arrive at the conference center before the sun came up, to gather my thoughts and courage. I'd spend three hours at least just drawing and sketching different rooms and working out the scale and layout for all the structures. By the time people started trickling into the office, I was brewing the second pot of coffee. And by the time I entered my first meeting, my hands were too shaky to take notes.

"You were discussing it yesterday—"

"I'm sorry, Aram. I don't remember that."

"Well, let me refresh your memory, then…"

They'd put all kinds of ideas in front of me and I couldn't bother to focus on them knowing they'd all be frankensteined tomorrow, just like they were doing to yesterday's mash-ups. The newcomers always reviewed notes from the previous meetings, and offered their take on the ideas. A lot of this work was more advertising than development. Some of them had a reason for it: they wanted to get into PR. PR was a highly competitive department, and one of the only ones that was exempt from the temporary contract rules. To work in PR, you had to have a unique feature that couldn't be taught, which most times just translated into some kind of striking beauty or exotic charm. It was celebrity work. Shallow but promising citizenship.

Every once in a while, when we agreed on something, I used it as an anchor for me and my "team." And for a little bit, I got the hang of it and we tried to build on the previous set of details each day until we had some meat on our bone, as they say. On and on it went, like lining up grains of rice to make a fence.

Two and a half weeks after Gallia's visit, I called her up to present the designs. The presenter on that day was a young but passionless woman in a steel gray sweater, whose tone and timbre didn't favor our embellishments at all. She had either miscalculated or was simply unprepared. Gallia rejected all of the designs because they were either "too cold and compound-like" or "strange." Each one.

"Absurd." That's what she whispered as she left the

meeting.

She had re-stated, with an excess of words, that she wanted a "natural manor" with courtyards and caverns, molded details on the walls, a variety of outdoor recreation spaces, etc. Most of our plans included some configuration of those requirements already. But we had no desire to argue with her, so we fused a couple of the designs and rearranged some of the cosmetic details and readied to present again. This time, we asked for a meeting with the presenter, which was denied, since presenters could not be pre-assigned until the morning of the meeting, based on availability. When the day came the following week, we had the very same presenter, but this time she wore a forest green blouse and expressed herself in a completely different manner, lively and in vogue. Gallia chose one immediately and without much comment. We thanked the presenter and went upstairs to discuss the contract with Gallia. Within two hours, we all signed it and sent it up for processing. I saw Gallia smile—not at me or my team, just a spontaneous and relieved reaction—as she shook my hand.

I delivered a copy of the meeting record to the "team" as part of their project review and thanked them for their efforts.

CLOUDI IN MAINE

When it happened, I was away on vacation, readying my backpack for a ten-mile hike down to Havasupai Falls in the Grand Canyon, which I'd been trying to visit for nearly 4 years.

The opening ceremony was set for Memorial Day, to cinch off the spring and start generating moisture during the summer and fall. The sky was gorgeously clear on Friday morning, perfect for hosting the maiden run of the Cloudi generators. Masses of people were at work still, fulfilling the half day of nonsense that they owed their employers. Subliminal messaging on behalf of the clutching fists of government and the more privileged: *Don't forget your place… but we will have a reward for you when you clock out.* Also could be for security reasons, I suppose. Or perhaps all current members of government are so old that they need to be at dinner by two (brunch was at seven). I don't know what to hit them with, anymore. Forgive me.

People would flock to Bar Harbor all weekend from all over the area to witness the new technology in action. As early as 7am, the air was already infused with barbecue smoke and salt. I was back at my apartment, reluctantly watching the live broadcast of the event from the corner of my eye. I had thought of calling, after awaking with an uneasy feeling, to propose some more long-term testing. A week at the most. They could still announce it and have their party. But people would have complained. Nothing would have gone wrong and the hesitation would have cost Rotari some reputation money. I thought, nevermind, and went to sleep.

"Money doesn't multiply like we do, you know." I heard someone saying that to someone else at my father's funeral. The memory had popped into my head, suddenly. I had felt profoundly ashamed that day, even as an eavesdropper.

I put the memory out of my mind. The scheduling of this thing didn't allow for proper calibration, especially with the colder months leading up to it. Of course it didn't help that the November elections were likely to result in reduced funding for the coming year's climate control projects, but it would have certainly been less costly to delay the fanfare until my team was sufficiently comfortable with the system's performance. They wouldn't want to hear it. We had already pushed it for nearly six months, and from afar, it all seemed to be in the right place. As soon as we hit a short streak of successful tests, we threw our hands up in the air and let them have it. We had tested and retested. It was good. And it wasn't. It would be. But then it wouldn't be. If evenness denotes equilibrium, then let's rest, at last.

The event itself was very smooth. All in attendance were pleased with the small puffy clouds that issued forth from the generator and mottled the skies. The Cloudi were a tremendous success, so far.

For nearly two months, the area enjoyed an almost natural humidity. On misty mornings, coffee happened outside, while inspecting the rare sight of dew on cars and trees. During the day, crowds were out enjoying the intermittent sun by the shore. Now that its rays were filtered through a reliable parade of clouds, its unpleasant brightness and heat were diffused. For a few nights, they even had some warm wind and gentle thunderstorms, which brought a lot of people out onto their porches. They watched the lightning and rain over the ocean and eventually went to sleep in their hammocks or benches or swings, lulled into dream states by the manufactured magnificence of Rotari's rolling thunder.

Just when it seemed like we had done everything right, a torrent of rain and hail birthed a massive knot of twisters shrouded in hurricane winds. The monster fed off the Atlantic and grew to cover most of the eastern US, thinning out over

Ohio, Kentucky and North Carolina, and part of the southeast of Canada, with Nova Scotia, New Brunswick and Southern Quebec at the center, dispersing over the area just west of Toronto. It was like an eyepatch on the world, like a space giant had thrown a wet sock at the planet. The ocean was whipped up until the sand was on top. And I can't even explain how many islands disappeared and how many others formed in the coming four months, but needless to say, the area was in a prolonged state of emergency, with recovery efforts ongoing. The storm (if we can call it that) had been "contained" by our team, as far as the generators were concerned, but the tempests raging on had been naturally occurring, so there wasn't much we could do without causing more trouble. We had to stop scratching the bite and let it heal on its own.

I'd never get to see those bright blue falls, after all.

In between frantic calls, I managed to book a flight to the disaster scene. A lot of the disaster recovery process turned out to be therapy services, anger management and grief counseling for my entourage at Rotari. I didn't get to speak to a single actual victim, but I sure hope someone did. Once on the ground, I only managed about twelve hours of sleep over seventeen days and lost my voice twice. The cleanup was hard but straightforward. It was the investigation and related sea of paperwork that was the most exhausting. Much of my experience on Earth involved an obscene amount of paperwork that I never got used to.

The area was a surreal sight. Buildings and boats were integrated into each other. Sea life and land life lay atop one another, lifeless. The sky was green for days—my first days in hell. It was cold and wet and the air thick as a sandwich.

Rotari had been in a good place at the time, so they were able to compensate the states and provinces for most of the damages and even make some improvements to the area that had long been neglected by the local governments. They came out on top, after proving to be far more generous than the elected officials.

People trusted and respected Rotari. No surprise there. They allowed me to stay on, after two very practical regulatory incident reviews. After all, the response to the Maine incident had had the fortuitous side effect of earning Rotari public trust needed to get the Auroral Marionette approved. They kept me on. I still owned a hundred percent of the design for the Marionette, since the paperwork hadn't yet been finalized :)

When I got home, I slept for what seemed like a week. In reality, it was ten hours. In comparison, it felt like days, for sure. I awoke with a dry throat and aching feet.

I spent three weeks by myself, putting together designs

for proposed components of the Marionette. I mapped out the station first, since it would take up the most space. I also added some of the vacation clusters and doodled on some of the education and entertainment center. I was eager to share my work, at the end of my time alone, but I didn't want to be pushy after the Northeastern chaos we'd just been through. Just when I was about to put in a request for a work session, Anaiida called me. We had been given the opportunity to present a proposal for the Auroral Marionette to an executive committee that would then (hopefully) take it to the C16 Summit to gauge the global response to the project before formally requesting permits.

"Better now that it's coming from one head instead of thirty. It'll be easier on them, too."

"How so?"

"I don't know. It's that sort of "Genius Author" thing. If no one likes it, they can blame one guy and be done."

"I'll take it."

We emphasized a lean framework that would allow for change over time. Rotari was keen on versatility. The Auroral Marionette proposal was a one-headed idea that was aware of the company's signature sensibility. And they loved it.

It was my biggest project, so I quietly thanked the Cloudi mess in Maine for indirectly affording me the chance to undertake it. The other two associates assigned to my team dropped off the project's current specifications and I was left alone to play with my rocks. The station came first, of course, then Sondras Alluma, the main hub, which would primarily be a shopping and entertainment center. Sondras Alluma would evolve into a micro-metropolis with its own culture and values, our most successful piece of the Marionette.

It was larger than all the other rocks, but still walkable within a couple of hours. The structures on it were simple hive-like cubbies, each one with a unique purpose. A colorful rock, and quite pleasant to wander. From the station, a mono-rail went there and back. The arrival chamber led to a grassy walkway through a glass "wow" tunnel that offered a peek at the approaching landscape.

The first set of hive cubbies were painted in warm neu-tral shades with details in bright azure blue and creamy pastel orange. Everything on the rock was brand new, but the chalky decor made it feel home-made and lived-in. The cubbies var-ied in size and were connected by a network of escalators and people movers. Most were retail spaces stacked atop one an-other, with the exception of a handful of cubbies on the back side that were used for daily operations and were closed to the public. This is where we housed the storage, stock rooms, garbage, etc. Next door were the Police, Customer Service and Urgent Care cubbies.

Beyond this first set of spaces was a plaza that split off

into four major roads, each one sprouting small clusters of buildings designed to look naturally mismatched, all containing businesses on the lower level and apartments above that. The little delta also spilled into restaurant row and an exclusive boutique promenade. The other road contained hotels and entertainment, a more late-night arrondissement. Sondras Alluma could comfortably hold about 400,000 people at a time, most of them day-trippers that traveled between the main station and Earth, or Marionette tourists, who took the shuttles between Sondras Alluma and one of the more exclusive retreat rocks on the ring. There was also a section for pedal-shuttles under construction that would eventually allow self-guided ring tours around the world. Last I heard, the liability discussion had nearly killed the idea altogether, but the way Rotari worked, I believed they would eventually—with or without "incidents"—launch the attraction as an overpriced little loop that would be featured in every must list, regardless of the questionable value it offered wealthy travelers. Still, for someone whose feet have never stepped off the surface, the first-time sensation of "cycling" on a small part of the orbit would likely be well worth it. It was an illusion of course, but a nice one.

I think I could have enjoyed such a thing, once upon a time, before I set foot on Earth. But what I had wanted more than anything was to be a part of the daily unglamorous mess of the surface, to disappear successfully into its overcrowded commotion, under its blanket steeped in many odors and flavors. To be part of the infusion.

Farah Ysvette Mourad Vera

SHOWERING WITH A SPIDER

On the first day back in my hometown, I took a shower as soon as I got to the house. I'd had an old friend steal the key to the house from my aunt, so that she wouldn't know I had arrived. We didn't have problems between us, but I wasn't prepared to suddenly reconnect with someone whose world was now foreign to me. She would surely resent any (inevitable) difference in my character.

One of the first things I thought of, when I found out for sure that I wouldn't be able to avoid being returned to this planet, was how I planned to hide in the house for at least a few days, perhaps leave at odd hours in some kind of costume, a religious habit maybe. People here had a blind reverence for what they called "the faithful." If I posed as one, maybe it would deter people from approaching me on my pilgrimage through the *all good given world.*

"All good given world," a shy but proud exclamation, as I walked, from those who felt like they had fulfilled their pilgrimage requirement already. Mostly, it was older people, though I had some presumptuous young ones approach me to say it, too.

My first night, unable to sleep, I stayed awake listening to an argument between two people next door. They had different recollections of a recent event. One of them felt abandoned, the other one burdened. When I was a kid, they had a rooster in the backyard. I stared at some dark gray spots on the ceiling over my bed, directly above each of the three light bulbs on the lamp. That can't be a good sign. I wondered if the rooster next door minded the yelling, since it had to be up at dawn. How much sleep does a chicken need, in order to have a productive day?

I got up to take a shower. Same old moldy ceiling, looking fresh of course. My mother had only died a day and a half ago. I had planned to surprise her. Once I found out—after some more proper reactions—I had to confess to my aunt that I'd asked a friend of mine to steal her copy of the house keys.

"I can't believe you had me robbed."

"More like pick-pocketed."

"The keys were never in my pockets, Milian. You had someone come to my house and pick my lock and steal my property—well, the property of your mother."

"It wasn't like that."

My friend had snuck in through the bathroom window.

She was very careful not to damage anything or get anything dirty. My aunt was obsessive about her house. Everything in its place always. Once, she caught me having snacked on a handful of jelly beans from a jar she kept on a bookshelf in the hallway. It was a big jar and I only had a few. How could she notice? I'd been staying with her for a few days, while my mother was at a retreat after my father's passing. My aunt came home from work and took a shower. She emerged from the steamy room, wrapped in a towel and said to me,

"Milian, did you have some jelly beans?"

I was taught not to lie because the truth always comes out in the end.

"I did. I'm sorry."

"It's ok. Next time, ask me first, please."

That was it. She just didn't like people sneaking around, touching her things without her permission. Initially, I was going to have my friend put the keys back after I got into the house, but obviously that was no longer necessary.

Anyway, on my first day back, I showered with a spider. It watched *me* more closely than I watched *it*. I had to recall how to share space with insects, here. There were many, and they were seen as a sign of luck.

"Be grateful. Someone likes your company."

My grandmother used to tell me that, every time I saw a bug, like an ant or a roach. Once, I had ants crawling all over my breakfast. They were on the underside of every slice of plantain on my plate. My grandmother laughed and said it again and again, each time like she'd never said it before.

This place was big on socializing at all times, even with bugs. The only ones I didn't mind were sunnybugs. Biologically, they were completely different from fireflies, but they looked exactly the same. I used to watch them zig-zagging through the orange fog in the early mornings. Little dots that shine: all living things in the universe seem to respond the same way to them.

I hadn't seen a spider since I was a kid, because they'd been mostly wiped out everywhere except my planet and a couple others. One of those massive unexplained die-offs. There were labs everywhere now devoted to their conservation, some of them were the same labs that routinely rehabilitated different bee species and even polar bears on Earth.

This spider's tiny body was swelled up, so I knew it didn't want me for sustenance. My father had taught me about how spiders eat. I thought eye contact would deter it from coming any closer, but instead I think it thought I was taunting it. After it saw me looking at it like that, it slid several feet down the wall from the ceiling to my eye line, like one of those action heroes in movies. Good thing they can't crawl through air. But they can swing. And that's what it did. It swung back and forth, up to a few inches off my nose. It wanted to approach me (and it wanted my dignity crashed and burned). It looked right at me, so I knew the intention was authentic and meaningful. Did it intend to inject some poison in me?

I've never been afraid of spiders, I don't think, but this one wanted something. When it came dancing for me, I truly wished to kill it but didn't have the courage. After the confrontation, I told myself that I had made a good choice—an ethical choice—not to kill it, even if it had meant to bite me, and no, I had no way of proving that was its intention. It lunged toward me a few more times, and when I waved my hand at it, it got into a fixed stance, ready to pounce. I had to close my eyes and turn my back on it, to shower properly. Each time I turned back around to look at it, it looked bigger. I had misjudged its size, maybe. It came defiantly towards me. Now, was it still the same… or had it grown again? Every time I looked at its eyes, I was prepared to scream (the last true defense, I guess). It didn't grow anymore (never "grew" at all). When I went to pull the curtains back, the spider tried to jump onto the fabric and ended up sliding down the other side of the wall. I let out a pathetic yelp. The spider scurried away beneath the floorboards. I can't say why I was so intimidated, but I guess the spider must be proud of its influence on a big dumb animal like me. The same thing had happened with a man on a train once. He wanted something from me. I could see it in his eyes. Everywhere I went, his gaze followed me. And he continued to move closer. I got off two stops early, out of fear. He watched me as the train pulled out of the station and into the dark tunnel ahead. This man and this spider. Both after me. So clear in their eyes that they expected something and only I could give it. Maybe they got it.

"What is 'Us,' if we can't say we love 'Them?' Who will bring 'You' into being? How? Can we say, out loud,

[Mumbling Crowd joining in]
I want progress.
I believe in transformation,
as you do.
I know my future is bright
and my past is ruins.
Good given."

The sound of "good given" gave me goosebumps. What a hideous pair of words, sound-wise. Like an accent too lazy to assert itself.

The church was right down the street; a small pink building with three separate chambers, connected by a tiny garden in the middle. I'd forgotten how boisterous that crowd could be in the morning. I tried to look outside, but the fog was still too thick. Through it, I could only see the warm yellow glow of the sun rising somewhere. And I didn't have to be anywhere, so I went back to sleep, hoping to wake up when the fog had dissipated. Even as a native, I couldn't remember at all what time the air usually cleared. And I didn't remember this song from the church, either. Good given.

I had a dream about a bird I accidentally killed as a child. It was laying on its side, stretching its eye muscles to look back at me, its beak wide open, a raspy and raw moan brimming over the back of its tongue. It was so loud. Much more than just a distress call. This went beyond distress. There was anger and betrayal and condemnation, punishment. For me. I felt panic. Regret; the kind that makes you have to right the wrongs. The thing that makes you quit on patience. Starving eyes on a pile of sweets. I gave into panic like a delightful indulgence.

PREPARING TO MIGRATE

Sylvia Dynes was Gallia's estate administrator. She had lived with, and worked for, Gallia since she could remember. As a matter of fact, Gallia had been present at her birth. Her mother had worked for the Sinlavas for fifteen years and had been Gallia's confidante for the last five.

Sylvia had been born on a night preceding a big party at the house. Gallia had made herself available to help with the delivery, recognizing the experience as an impressive conversation starter for the following night. She had been absolutely right, and guests had praised Gallia's bravery and willingness to help. Many of them had sent gifts in the days that followed, some even for Sylvia and her mother.

When she was old enough, Sylvia was sent to a nearby boarding school. Gallia had started suffering from migraines and the child's noise had been "identified as a trigger." At the end of each week, her mother picked her up and brought her home for the weekend. Gallia was usually busy and out of the house, so there weren't many conflicts about this arrangement, but the few that arose sometimes escalated into ugly fights.

The most severe happened on a weekend when Gallia found herself bed ridden with a migraine and a cold. She had treated herself prematurely for several ailments she didn't actually have, which had only exacerbated the simple seasonal cold she had acquired, most likely at a press conference the previous week. She'd caught it from someone after a lecture she had given at the C16 Summit, a semi-annual forum for climate technology discussions involving the sixteen leading world wellness associations.

The event planners had wanted to emphasize and celebrate the progress that had been made in recent years, as a result of the Summit's efforts. Gallia found the attitude distasteful, and she made her opinion known, immediately, to the hungry press upon arrival.

"We've lost more moisture in the air over places like the Everglades than ever before. If you look at the new photographs, you can see it looks more like patches of discarded mulch than swampland."

Everyone paired her comments with the same award-winning photo of the landscape. It was a wide overhead view of the Big Cypress swamp, a thick web of dried twigs and husks covering most of it, everything that had once been green was now the same chalky brown that had become so familiar in the rest of the Americas. It showed a much more dire situation than the previous award-winning photograph from a few years before. In that one, the water was still visible, but there was an alarming amount of dead mangroves throughout. The photographer had been invited to the Summit that year. He had received many compliments on having captured the colors of the deadly drought. The second photographer had not been invited. She wasn't as well-known and lived in a "troubled" country, so securing entry paperwork for her would have been too much hassle.

"It's no longer a place for life to thrive and we haven't done anything to correct it. This is not progress. We have spent far too much time on urban luxury agro and not enough time protecting and reviving the very things that keep this planet breathing. Small boutique farms cannot replace miles of forests and swampland or restore stability to the ocean. We have big ticket items still that continue to be ignored."

It wasn't a shock that Gallia felt this way. She was merely articulating a string of trendy complaints, but bringing it up at the Summit had created some tension among the Earth-saving elite. The overall sentiment was that Gallia's criticism had put a damper on the night; that instead of celebrating, she had taken the opportunity to scold everyone, as if to place herself above everyone else. They weren't wrong. She thrived on the idea. To mask her vanity, she had spent part of the night gathering signatures and asking for money to fund a deep-sea cleanup the following month. And after the party, she had called a press conference to discuss her plans. In the end, she won. She got a lot of press, public praise and the reluctant support of her peers at the lavish event.

Her impromptu scheme had been a huge success. However, she regretted the interviews that followed her speech, almost immediately. Aside from knowing that the cameras were all aimed at her at unflattering angles, the lighting was terrible, the sound noisy and full of distractions, and to top it off, she had spotted a shower of mist exploding from each reporter's mouth every time they talked. In many cases, she felt saliva landing on her cheeks and nose, possibly even her mouth.

I am eating their bodily fluids, she thought, revolted and regretting the series of actions she had taken to land herself in this predicament.

Gallia had many strange phobias, including an issue breathing outside air and speaking to others in person. The latter is explained above. The former stemmed from an experience in her teens.

She had been a dedicated triathlete and was preparing to try out for the Olympic team. One day, she found herself running right through the St Patrick's Day parade in Key West. It wasn't until she thought she could taste beer inside her nose, that she had the fateful thought.

"Parts of the air I am breathing have run through other people's lungs and stomachs, or worse..." She ran faster, trying to hold her breath until she had gotten far away from the crowd. Then, she breathed heavily into her shirt, but it occurred to her that her shirt was porous and therefore penetrable by other people's germs and particles.

From that point on, she ran and biked with a dust mask on. She also gave up swimming, because there was no way to bypass the contamination in the water. A couple months after St. Patricks Day, Gallia became violently ill. Her parents told the doctors about her running mask and they hypothesized that germs could have been trapped inside the mask, developing and thriving in there, which meant she could have been breathing in more infectious air through the mask than without it. Nice try, though.

"It could have been a fungus, even. Do you still have it?"

She did. She brought it in and they performed a series of tests but found nothing to support the doctor's guess. Nonetheless, that was enough to turn Gallia off the mask. Well, that and the painful gasps for air she endured for over two weeks at the hospital. It had all been psychosomatic and she was prescribed sugar pills to end the farce.

Gallia's weird phobia of previously breathed air had endured for decades, but she was able to rationalize it better as she got older and found that breathing it in didn't always have an adverse effect on her health. And anyway, over the years, she had devised a daily cleansing system to take care of any toxin or foreign organism that might find its way inside her body. She trusted this system and was convinced she had invented the perfect lifestyle for good health, until the day she picked up a cold from a reporter after her heroic ultimatum at the C16 Summit.

Her concern about the illness had quickly escalated.

Something with my blood maybe, an infection, some kind of new pathogen, a rare deficiency.

She studied her symptoms, performed extensive lab tests on her blood, urine, and feces. Lack of sleep made matters much worse. She started treating her symptoms one by one, but each time she took something to treat one, another one worsened. She developed a terrible migraine over the next day and a half and just as the symptoms reached their collective worst, it was time for little Sylvia to come home for the weekend.

Sylvia and her mother arrived near dark, just as Gallia was trying to relax after an hour of dry heaving and other flavors of unpleasantness. It was almost dinner time, but Sylvia wasn't hungry and on this particular day, she was especially angry about having to sit down to eat instead of playing in her mother's room. She yelled for release and when her mother refused, she yelled even louder.

"Stop her!" Gallia screamed at Sylvia's mother. She thought of threatening to end their contract, effectively putting them out on the street with nothing to their name except a stingy severance package, but she quickly recognized this as unnecessarily cruel and complicated. Instead, she expressed her support for a new arrangement, regarding Sylvia's weekends at school.

"She will need extra curricular activities sooner or later. Won't you consider it?"

"I wouldn't see her very often."

"No one is keeping you from visiting her at the school."

Sylvia's mother was quiet. Sylvia too (thankfully).

"I am paying for it. I don't think the weekend activities cost that much more, and anyway, I'm happy to do it. It'll be good for her."

All three of them turned to watch the TV for several minutes, feigning interest in the advertisements. Then, Sylvia turned to her mother and asked if she could go play. Her mother nodded and Sylvia was off. Gallia apologized and explained what had been going on.

"I'll make some tea."

Sylvia's mother disappeared into the kitchen. It wasn't the response Gallia was looking for, but after some extensive self-analysis throughout the next couple of nights, she eventually concluded that she wouldn't have had any sympathy for herself either.

Gallia felt this way often, especially after a long Q&A inside her head, which was a frequent indulgence. She was engaged in it now, as she reviewed the contents of her remaining calendar days living on Earth. There were only two major events besides her personal farewell party, but they required some preparation as she would be an active attendee of both, expected to provide some kind of leadership or entertainment, instead of just being a courtesy guest.

Two weeks before her move to Mantis Green, she had the Auroral Park dedication on the Auroral Marionette. She was a key participant, but luckily this event would take place in a controlled environment, and due to the high cost of tickets to the outer atmosphere, the crowd would be small. Not much to worry about there.

But nearly seven weeks prior to the park dedication, there was another event she had to attend on Earth, at the baseball stadium no less. Take saliva and air that's been through other people's respiratory and/or digestive systems and add sweat, why not? Athletic venues were some of Gallia's most hated. She was convinced that the odors that can be perceived at said locations carry with them whole ecosystems of toxic organisms, and she always had a quarantine period scheduled for herself and her household after visiting these places.

This time would be no different, but she did have to shorten the length of her quarantine period. To compensate, she had arranged a week-long retreat, where she would spend most of her time with an IV pumping nourishing fluids into her body. Her menu for the week had been exclusively designed by a company selling expensively produced "Cleaner than God" nutrition products. The particular package she had chosen followed a regimen similar to the one prescribed to critically damaged substance-abusers during rehab. An extravagant choice, in my opinion, as this nutrition system was short of a miracle for addicts on the verge of death. However, I suppose in a way, she *was* an addict. And since the treatment was only available to certain elite members of society, the reason for its use was irrelevant anyway.

At some point, Gallia realized, she would have to have people in the house to pack. Surely, Sylvia had already made arrangements.

But why didn't she tell me anything?

Sylvia's phone rang. It was Gallia.

"When are the movers coming?"

"I've arranged for them to come during your quarantine. They should be finished a couple days before you get home. And then I'll have a cleaning crew come and give the place a once-over, just in case."

"How will they know what to take?"

"We'll do some walkthroughs a little closer to the date, to make sure everything is labeled. I started labeling some things already. Do you want me to send you a map of what I have so far?"

"No, that's fine. It's still a ways away, I guess."

"Ok. Well, I can share it with you. That way, you'll get notified any time I make changes and you can add labels too, if that makes it easier."

"That's fine. Thanks Sylvia."

"Good night!"

"Well—"

"Yeah?"

"Will you be here before those two events?"

"Yes, I'm planning on staying over a couple nights before and after each one, to take care of whatever needs to be sent or received and any other things that come up."

"Perfect. Thank you. Have a good night."

"Good night, Gallia."

As she hung up the phone, Sylvia got up for a drink of water. Outside her window, the street was filled with people. Red lights were flashing from around the corner. An accident perhaps, or an altercation at one of the bars down the street. It was past dinner time, a popular hour for freedom gone off the rails. Sylvia made eye contact with a stranger, an older man holding a tiny dog. He reacted to Sylvia as if she'd been spying on him, put his little dog down on the sidewalk and trotted off, turning right at the light and looking back one more time, to glance at her accusingly. He yanked the little dog away, mid-urination, and dragged him off until they were completely out of sight. The flashing lights were gone now and the curious flock of people was starting to scatter. A woman dropped something on the floor and someone picked it up and chased after her with it. They exchanged some courtesies and then went their separate ways.

From a distance, people are so simple. Up close, the complications manifest themselves.

She took another sip of water and sat down on her bed, reading through some nature magazines.

Gallia didn't go to sleep for several hours, walking through the house, thinking about what she would take. She opened up the map that Sylvia had shared with her, on her bedroom tablet, adding and removing labels, adding them back on to some things, removing them again.

Finally, a few minutes before midnight, she called Sylvia again.

"I think I may just furnish everything new."

"What do you mean? Everything?"

"Well, mostly. I just don't know that I should bring all of this up there. Some of these things are very old."

"Ok. That's fine. Were you able to open the map?"

"I was, yes. We'll look at it together in the morning. Can you come over at 6?"

Sylvia looked at her clock. 12:02 am.

"Yeah, sure."

"Perfect. See you then."

"See you in the morning."

Sylvia turned off her phone and went to sleep. Gallia walked around her house in the dark for a couple more hours, before finally taking a nap in the living room. By four o'clock in the morning, she was up and preparing for the first step of her daily health regimen.

Around the same time, Sylvia was onto her own ritual, a cup of tea and an orange in a bowl of yogurt. Her usual choice after a short night. She had woken up suddenly from a nightmare she couldn't remember, but its gloppy feeling stayed with her throughout the morning and part of the afternoon. It was a dark and cloudy Sunday, even after the sun had come up.

Sylvia and Gallia walked through the house for several hours, tagging furniture and making donation piles in each room. Gallia was irritable and anxious, and Sylvia's withdrawn mood was of little comfort. Soon enough, they had come up with a clearer picture of what would stay and what would go.

"It'll be pretty empty down here."

"Well, you can find some new stuff that fits you better, if you want. You'll be able to stay here as often as you like."

Sylvia wouldn't dream of it. The cavernous loneliness of that house was eerie enough with Gallia inside. Who knows how much worse it would be, when paired with complete silence. Or perhaps it was the lady herself who made the space so stiff and barren. It really was a spooky place, although beautiful and all. An immoderate extravagance that devoured you whole. Sylvia had heard Gallia pacing around the halls, sobbing and sighing at night, on several occasions—a sound she knew well (and hated). She felt that she had been trained into a light sleeper throughout the years, in case her help was needed in the middle of the night, but also because Gallia liked to be thought of, if possible, at all times. If every person on Earth had momentarily forgotten about her at the same time, she would have simply vanished from the world instantaneously.

Gallia was also a light sleeper, never wanting to be caught off guard. For her it started with a very real thought: she didn't want to be killed in her sleep, and the only way to rule that out was to sleep lightly, with her eyes partly open, so to speak. For the same reason, she acquired the habit of wandering the halls at night. It's hard to say what she would have done if she'd ever caught someone sneaking around the house.

To think of the smell of blood, to bring to mind the sensation of drowning, to feel a cold blade or a hot stone inside her heart, to dig her nails into the hands pressing down hard on her neck... Gallia fantasized often about scenarios like these. Would she panic or would she fight? For a long time, she was sure one or another would happen, so she should prepare for all. Eventually, after studying her own health obsessively, she determined that she was more likely to die of some breed of respiratory or neurological failure. She was pleased but afraid and accepted the waiting period with disquiet resignation.

BLIND HOLIDAY

Sondras Alluma was an enjoyable little rock. Gallia decided, once she had finished signing all the paperwork for Mantis Green, after the official walkthrough, that she would rather take a short vacation on Sondras Alluma, rather than wait in line for a crowded return flight back to Earth. She had asked Sylvia to accompany her on this holiday. Sylvia welcomed the suggestion and appreciated the invitation. A trip to Sondras Alluma was out of budget for many, still, including Sylvia. It was more a matter of time than money. Traveling there and back (and re-adjusting) was a multi-day affair, even considering the flexible time zone.

Gallia and Sylvia shared a 2-bedroom suite in the main hive. They had immediate access to shopping and dining, and direct access to a grass patch behind the building. Gallia took to drinking her morning tea here. Sylvia held out for an iced coffee fix as often as she could, but sometimes she joined Gallia on the back patio.

"I hope you won't be over-caffeinated."

"I won't."

"You won't get any sleep tonight."

"Well, it's not like the sun plans on setting at a particular hour."

"Fair. Join me a little longer. I want to talk about the rest of the schedule."

Gallia was very anxious about her first week on Mantis Green. After moving in, the environment would have to be recalibrated, to account for her being in it, contributing her own volume, heat, gases, etc. She wasn't thrilled about the idea but understood that we had to do it. And anyway, it wouldn't take more than a week of passive monitoring. The adjustments could all be made remotely.

For now, she tried to enjoy herself around our little hive. The arrival station was next to Sondras Alluma, but there was a large Customs Complex separating the two. Most people could get through the Complex in an hour or so, but there were overnight facilities there, just in case they were temporarily detained. The facilities were privately owned and operated. Most people detained were from other planets trying to get down to the surface. Earth's immigration services had found a way to use our little ring for their purposes after all, but at least we had control over how detainees were treated while they were held there. A large number of them were released into the ring but denied entry to Earth. This resulted in a little bit of overcrowding, but it was great for business, so we tried as best we could to accommodate the high volume of visitors we ended up with.

Most people were just happy to be away from the situations they fled, and a good number of them ended up contributing a lot to the Marionette. We had new restaurants and food carts popping up everywhere, live music scattered throughout the ring, and all kinds of health and beauty services offered all around. A lot of the sanitation and security staff were professionals from other places. The Marionette had only been around for about a year, but it had grown quickly and organically.

I was still living on the surface because I didn't want to jeopardize my citizenship, but also because I had wanted to live on Earth my whole life and it would have been hypocritical to leave it for an artificial orbital metropolis, even if it was my idea to make one in the first place.

"You could live up here, Sylvia."

"I would die from eating these patties every day."

Sylvia and Gallia were enjoying some bean and carrot patties from a cart near the arts district. Gallia had wanted to browse the Galleries and maybe buy some new art for Mantis Green. They'd been perusing the expressions hanging on the walls of half a dozen art galleries, but she hadn't found anything yet.

"A lot of it seems empty, you know?"

"Well, I think a lot of them are still first contracts, so they're probably all Earth artists who paid to be featured, you know?"

"It's a shame."

Of course, there was a lot more art beyond the arts district, especially in the Customs Complex, but Gallia would never venture in there. Sylvia had a small collection of art in her tri-loft back on the surface. Things she had bought from street peddlers in India or on the road in Mexico. Her favorite were some original mosaic trays, hand-made by an old friend of her great-grandmother's in Palermo, Italy. The old lady had collected debris from all over the world for over six decades, and once she couldn't travel anymore, she had started to assemble mosaics from the ruins she had gathered over the years. The results were beautifully textured mosaics of detailed scenes from nature, featuring inter-species cooperations, pioneering bird migrations, new mutations or adaptations to changing environments, etc.

Sylvia's art collection was nowhere near as extensive (and expensive) as Gallia's, but it was certainly more authentic. Gallia required certificates and insurance and all kinds of status proof for everything she bought, so unestablished artists didn't have much of a chance. As a result, she ended up owning a lot of cynical art. Fair.

The vacation had offered some time for Gallia and Sylvia to get bored with each other. They had, for the first time in a long time, let their guard down. Both women lay in bed, naked. Gallia was looking through a furniture catalogue she had picked up. Sylvia was reading through the news. A third of the articles were about the latest nationalist riot back on the surface, this time in Philadelphia. The images showed a bigger crowd than the last few incidents. And the death toll for this one was much higher. The event had been organized by a former governor and pre-approved by the local government, surely as a political favor.

The next day, Sylvia left the room very early and people-watched for a few hours before joining Gallia again. She had been thinking about moving away from Earth. And after considering it, she had decided against it, as she always did. She looked over the platform at the little planet's surface. There was a white swirl over part of the Atlantic: tropical storm Asha, the first of the season, and surely one that would soon become a hurricane, if it wasn't already considered one.

THE TSARINA'S SENDOFF

A flickering engagement. There was little more than that between us, and I doubted that I would receive an invitation to Gallia Sinlava's going away party, even out of courtesy. Still, I wasn't surprised when I did get one. It was a paper invitation package, showcasing her abundance of resources, of course. Inside the little parcel, there were: the invitation in a sheer paper sleeve, the RSVP card and its pre-stamped envelope, a reminder magnet, and a souvenir paper lantern.

Gallia's sendoff party had been planned since her approval of the rock's design. It would take place in the garden of her home on the surface, a few weeks before her move to Mantis Green. I fantasized about her flinging scraps of attention at her guests, all of whom thought themselves important and cherished for having been invited to partake in such a cozy event.

When I arrived, I found a more buoyant scene than I'd imagined. Some of the guests were aware of Gallia's prefer-ence for silent friends, so they gifted her just that. They smiled economically at her, then as she passed, they traded words of judgment. Fair. All these bright and beautiful people. The most wonderful time they could have was the time they spent being truthful with one another, and sharing their coy derision of the host was a shortcut to that. I enjoyed watching the turning points and pitfalls in their conversations. How suddenly they'd be affected and turn inwards.

It was only a matter of time, however, before someone tried to drag me down into one of these pits of my own. I tried so very hard to feel enraged and to build my web of pet peeves and droll jokes. I lost interest in the first conversation almost immediately... and the three or four that followed. I took a break and went to get something to eat. Desperately trying to amuse myself, I spent at least twenty minutes stuffing my face with colorful bite-sized desserts that looked more like plastic chew toys than food. I stood in the corner, like a child, simultaneously ashamed and relieved that no one would approach me, not even a waiter to offer me a napkin or another drink. I was "irked." The closest thing to feeling the way they always did. Annoyed at the smudge in my perfection.

In between the chomp chomp of some mini donuts I was enjoying, I heard a cough. Sylvia was on the other side of the table, choking on something. We made eye contact, so I went over, unenthusiastically, to offer some help.

"Just went down the wrong pipe. [cough] Thank you."

"Here, let's find some water or something. Champagne?"

I offered her the ounce or so of warm champagne I had in my glass. I noticed too late that there was a crumb floating in it. She drank it.

"Thank you," She said.

"You're welcome."

I smiled. She returned it. We stood together in the corner like two shabby utility chairs in a palace. I waited for her to speak and I guess she did the same. We smiled at each other again and then she pretended to see somebody she knew and excused herself. I felt relieved again, but it was sad to watch her walk to an empty table on the other side of the garden and sit down.

I floated from one person to another, mostly people transitioning between cliques. I spoke to an older woman about swimming, which I hadn't practiced in many years; to a gentleman about what his intermittent waves of flu-like symptoms might signify, which I am certain were only allergies triggered by a certain daily activity of his; and to a young girl about some elementary idea she had about self research, which involved manipulating every single person she had any kind of relationship with. I politely declined to comment further and retreated to a table near the caterer.

A waiter came by shortly thereafter—the most responsive the staff had been all night—and informed me that this was just a prep table used by the servers to ready their trays.

"I'll move if you bring me a drink." I said.

"Of course, Sir. What would you like?"

Sir? I rather *liked* to be referred to this way! It didn't happen often, and for the first time ever it occurred to me that it probably should. After all, I had worked my way up some manner of ladder, and I was old enough to expect some veneer of respect from all those who were headed down the same road as me. *Why, yes, my friend!*

"Gin please. Splash of soda. Two limes."

"Rocks?"

"Please. Thank you."

"Be right back, Sir."

Sir.

I stared at the ground until the waiter returned with the drink. More soda than gin. Only one lime.

Sir? Don't bother.

For the rest of the night, I decided I would just get drunk. It wasn't something I did very often, so it wouldn't take much. I would also be sure to drink plenty of water, so the quality of my morning wouldn't be altered. *Here I was, again, thinking too much.*

"You'll never make it," she said.

My brother had not, but I had. My aunt Daliya had told me a story about when she, herself, had died. She was dead for almost fifteen minutes. Her heart had stopped. But my mother, who was thirteen at the time, prayed and beat on her chest until she started breathing again. My mother saved her life. Sometimes I thought, perhaps she had cursed me and my brother when we left her alone. She hated the silence of the house and she didn't like going anywhere by herself. But I'd torn myself to pieces over this time and time again, so forget it.

As people, we owe everything we have from the moment we are born. Sea turtles break out of their eggs in the sand and swim to the ocean all on their own. Their lives are theirs. We sit around in water until we're pushed out. That must have some effect on our perception of the world. We are brought here. We don't break out and go. It's reprehensible, really. I think about people and sea turtles often. Reptiles born from eggs seem the most respectable. They do all the work themselves, and so no one can ever demand anything from them. Predators are a natural danger, and any social politics they encounter are constructed later, as they navigate their survival networks.

The party seemed to shrink in space. The amount of people stayed the same, but each person swelled in volume, taking up more space than before and raising their voices higher, as they grew.

I felt surrounded by loud giants. I kept my distance in an extreme way. For the rest of the night, I didn't say another word. Even when getting another drink. I would just point, smile, nod, wave and sigh privately. It occurred to me that perhaps it would feel more natural to think in images. Stop the translation mill for a while.

I watched a woman laugh. Her teeth looked jagged and sharp, yellowed at the edges, from blood perhaps. Her carefree delight seemed a dangerous call for me to get out. I acknowledged to myself that I was terribly out of place and that sooner or later someone would find me, and they'd escort me out in an unfriendly way. I didn't belong in this party, or on this planet at all, no matter how hard or how long I'd tried and planned to continue trying.

It was time to leave, so I did. For centuries we've tried to rid ourselves of all instincts, now and then returning to a search for the "natural," but eventually fall into our own traps again. But I listened this one time. I was fairly drunk, since I didn't indulge often and had only eaten some sweets. Maybe it was really just low tolerance. Anyway, I'm ashamed to admit how little booze it took to make me feel spaghetti-legged, but that was that. It happened every few years.

My heart muscle was silent. Like my aunt, I had spent a period of time with no life coursing through me, no perception or opinion or choice, and it was very palpable that night. I arrived at my apartment a little after 2:00 AM. The cab driver called me "Sir" but I wasn't impressed this time. He didn't say it *to* me. He said it *about* me. Felt more like an accusation than flattery.

I'd picked some tomatoes off my vine and left them on the kitchen counter that afternoon. I washed and cut a few, and baked them with some salt and cumin, for a snack. While I ate, I watched my fish in their tank, floating in place rather than swimming around. They weren't especially unique in their personalities or striking in their looks. They were simple, shiny, silver-scaled fish. Long, thin, with static-looking eyes. Still, I felt that they knew me in a more truthful way than anyone else did—well, anyone except Jones, my dog. He was a goofy black lab who slept a lot and chewed up all his tennis balls into mulch.

I dozed off several times while watching TV next to Jones. My instinct was saying to take advantage of the dark and rest, but I refused. I thought I owned my own brain and thus, I should be the one to choose when we rest and when we go on. I fell asleep at some point, without brushing my teeth or taking off my clothes. When I woke up, there was a report on the TV about a fire a couple miles down the road. It had started "a little after 2:00 AM and had only recently stopped burning." It was 6:42 AM. I had the fishbowl feeling about my head, and since it was Sunday, I decided that it would be best for me to throw up, take a shower and go back to sleep. Of course after I had showered, I couldn't come up with a good trick to make myself sleep, so I stayed up and watched the rain instead. Interesting thing that is, when water stokes a fire.

ALONE AT NIGHT

Gallia was lying awake in bed. She couldn't get herself tired enough to keep her eyes closed and her breathing steady. There seemed to be subtle shifts in the ceiling's texture, like its surface would get goosebumps every few minutes. A glittering quality would come over it while Gallia stared.

Tricks that my eyes play.

Suddenly, she heard a loud screeching sound, like a car on a driveway. Phantom sounds.

There are no cars outside, I know it.

But I heard one.

She got up and walked to the window, which lit up in an orange flash. The sound of a small explosion. Once the cloud of smoke dissipated, Gallia spotted a blue bicycle and a plain-looking man standing next to it. He pointed up to his chin and all color drained from his face. Gallia looked up above his head and saw a massive tidal wave. She looked at the man again, who made eye contact with her, and then the water hit, first white and blue, then a greenish yellow. She looked to where the water came from and saw nothing but an ordinary street, wet, bathed in glistening yellow light.

She felt her grip on the floor soften, and as she looked down at her naked feet, her clean cork floor had become soggy and spongy. She walked past the kitchen, where Giancarlo was perched on the faucet, silhouetted and very still. She could just barely see him breathe.

She reached the hallway. To her left, there was only gray; a thick murky air. And she saw her mother's dead green corpse approaching her, asking her,

"Please? Please?"

The spongy ground turned to mud as it began to rain, and in the wet darkness, Gallia found a staircase. She walked up the muddy steps, which were stickier than the ground before, the same thick clay from her other dreams. She reached the top of the stairs and found a slide, saw no other way out than to slide down it. As she did, a cloudy plastic closed in on her and she was stuck in this diagonal tube. Shadows watched her from outside, but she couldn't make out their faces. There was a small opening at the bottom of the tube. A sudden panic struck her. She felt it in her chest and in her lower back. A very real thought:

I'm running out of air.

The opening at her feet was narrow and she had no mobility inside the tube. She would die trapped in this thing.

As she began to gasp in despair, she awoke to find herself in bed, in her spacious room, in the middle of her first artificial storm on Mantis Green.

The storm system finally works.

But the rain and thunder were assaulting her senses. Every spatter felt like needles in her ears. And the thunder seemed to clap directly on her chest, strong, violent. She ran out into the hall, where the controls were, to try and turn it off or dial it down. She had no idea how to work the panel, so she yelled out,

"Stop the storm!"

And for a moment it appeared to have worked, until another thunder clap hit, hard, merciless. Gallia collapsed to her knees and rested her head on the floor. She heard a different kind of pitter-patter. Giancarlo walking up to her face. She held him close. The two spent the rest of the night in the media room, watching movies, Giancarlo napping every few minutes, waking only to reposition himself or to look around, questioning the sounds of the storm, alert, just in case.

Gallia didn't rest, but she studied the storm and found its patterns. In the morning, she would contact the team at Rotari to have the system fixed right away.

Fixed. When will it all be fixed?

SYLVIA'S DREAM

When she got home, Sylvia stopped at the owl cage in the lobby of her building. For a prolonged second, the owls were synchronized with each other, staring at her. They blinked at the same time and their pupils dilated together.

That night, Sylvia had a dream that she was a child on a school bus, going through an empty road along the edge of a forest, where no light could penetrate the heavy foliage. Through the windows, she could see owls staring at her and the others. Why? And why is it that nothing feels safe but everything feels stable enough? Like the owls would like to attack, but won't.

Sylvia awoke from this dream at 3:33 AM, in her tri-loft, which was a small apartment partition located on the top floor of a building belonging to the Sinlavas. It wasn't very wide or long, and the walls were very thin, but she had everything she needed, and access to much more at Gallia's house, where she was welcome to stay as often as she liked, which was seldom.

Most tri-lofts were cramped "space-saving" affordable housing. They usually included only a sleeping bunk that was elevated over a desk, a toilet and a sink. Like a private room on a train. Sylvia's was a corner unit, which allowed her a few extra feet of space, so she could also fit a small fridge and a hot plate near the window. The main perk of living in a tri-loft was a guaranteed central location. Every time Sylvia woke from a dream at three in the morning, she was grateful for that very thing.

She grabbed her towel and went down the hall to the showers, where she rinsed off quickly within the allotted time. She paid her bill and returned to her room to get dressed. The sky was that strange reddish gray color she loved so much. The clouds looked heavy. She had wished for hot rain earlier, her favorite weather, and it looked like she would get it.

Sylvia gathered her things and went downstairs. As she approached the lobby, she readied herself to merge into the flowing crowd. While joining the condensed pedestrian track, she thought about breakfast. Is it too early? She saw the line outside the donut shop and it didn't seem too long, but come to think of it, she wasn't very hungry yet. She merged more to the left, preparing to exit into the coffee bar.

She spotted the short purple-and-gray building and prepared to break away from the crowd. As she approached the first door, she was startled by her phone ringing. It was

Gallia. When she looked up from her phone, she saw that she had just missed the door. She answered the call while scanning around for a way back, preparing to circumvent a heavy trio of tourists at the next turnaround. It wasn't a graceful maneuver. She had run right into the sweaty belly of the man closest to the exit and had ended up on her knees, crawling off the track into a doorway. The trio yelled things at her that she couldn't understand.

"Hello?" A little voice projected at her from somewhere she couldn't immediately place. Then, she lifted the phone to her ear.

"Gallia. I'm so sorry. I just missed my door. Can I call you in a few minutes?"

"Of course."

The moment she entered the building, there was a graceful silence and a freshness that filled the air. What a relief!

To her surprise, there was an underway entrance to the cafe right in the lobby of this building. She descended into it and merged right into the counter line. She thought of calling Gallia while waiting for her turn, but chose to savor the moment instead. The cafe had been there for a long time. That was obvious from the contrast with the look of the newer underpass that connected it to the lobby. The molding where the two structures met was completely different from one side to the other. The cafe side was dark brown, almost black, desiccated and crumbling. The underpass side was off-white, plump and flexible. As she left the newer space behind, she was struck by the legacy of the many smells that had filled the cafe over the years. All that roasting and toasting and baking and brewing had seasoned these walls with a complex flavor. That flavor promise brought her back here over and over again, although she always left a little disappointed that she could never choose the one thing that tasted the way the place smelled. When it was her turn, Sylvia placed an order for a large coffee and a chocolate croissant. Both came out quickly and steaming. She was pleased. Once she had eaten her breakfast, she wiped her hands clean and called Gallia back.

"Hi."

"I think I'm gonna need someone to show me again how to change the settings on the storm panel."

"Oh ok. I'll be up in a couple days. I think I remember."

"Well, bring someone from Rotari, too. There's probably just something wrong with the actual system. I don't think it's working the way it's supposed to."

"Oh I see. Well, I'll give them a call when they open in a few hours."

"Yeah… What are you doing up so early?"

"Couldn't sleep. Neighbors got home late, made a lot of noise."

"Sylvia, you can stay at the house. It's just sitting there empty."

"I know. I just, you know, I feel more comfortable at the loft."

"Ok. Well, maybe just stop by a couple times a week to check on everything. Get some good rest. The deliveries are still on, I thought. Are you still working from there?"

"Yeah, I'm actually headed there now."

"Perfect. Well, let me know what they say about coming up."

"Ok. Are you awake at an odd hour of the night or is this day time for you?"

"I can't really tell, but I feel pretty good, so whatever it is, it's just fine."

"Sounds great. How's Giancarlo?"

"He's doing ok. I don't know if I'm feeding him too much, but he does seem to enjoy the sun, so that's neat."

"Cool."

"Yeah we've been getting acquainted. He's fluffy now, so he looks more like a real bird."

"That's pretty fast."

"Yeah..."

Gallia wasn't sure what she was feeling, but it wasn't good.

"I, um... Ok, well, I'll talk to you later."

"Bye Gallia. Enjoy your day."

"Thank you. You too."

Sylvia hung up and sat smelling and drinking her coffee for another twenty minutes before merging back into the people track.

PREPARING FOR THE PAIRLY GALA

A heated debate was bubbling inside a conference room at The Stellarium—a football stadium, something about plantain and carrot hash and toasted algae to start. The Pairly Gala took place every year in the fall, and always with a fresh design. Since its conception, the event was meant to highlight and celebrate timeless vision and innovation. This would be its seventeenth year and Gallia would be presenting an award to a pair of seasoned inventors for their development of mobile marine farms. Their plan rolled production and distribution into one, streamlining an old idea into an attractive line of conveniences. Their tools had taken off immediately and several companies around the world had already adopted the process for their own needs. The new perspective was beneficial to the pharmaceutical and cosmetic branches of agriculture, but it was the food industry that had relied on it most, in order to revive its culture and redefine its standards. Gallia herself never purchased marine produce, as she preferred the earthier flavor profile of sun-bathed soil-grown fruits and vegetables, but she recognized and publicly praised the impact of the practice on the rest of the world.

Food was a hot topic at the event, since everyone was guaranteed to be thinking and rethinking their choices and tastes that night. Thus, the conference room was packed with a team of chefs, who all seemed displeased with each other, nursing their egos, adamant about their brilliant ideas and resisting compromise. D'Alsace, the youngest, felt a little out of place, so he chose to mediate and write everything out on the board for the others to argue about.

"Polenta's a mistake."

"This again…"

"It's overused."

"I agree, actually."

"Fine. It's out. What about the hash?"

No issues there. Each one of them thought it was their idea first. For what it's worth, it was D'Alsace who had come up with it first. They'd also keep the Brandied Coconut soufflé he had pitched, but insisted on serving it in little chocolate boats.

"That'll be fine."

When the meeting adjourned, Caspar Fanti approached D'Alsace and offered him a job. D'Alsace refused.

"I'm moving actually."

"Oh. Where to?"

"I've taken a position at the main station on the Marionette and there's an available apartment on Sondras Alluma that I've qualified for."

"Oh. Well, congratulations!"

"Thank you."

"You'll do very well there."

D'Alsace presented a polite smile.

"Tough crowd but they're too hungry to be picky by the time they get there."

"You're right. Thank you, Caspar. It's been a pleasure."

They shook hands warmly. A sendoff to each other and a souvenir for themselves.

"See you tomorrow!"

"See you!"

As they parted ways, the conference room was left with no other contents than the hot air of the discussion that had just taken place. It had lasted several hours, as the team sampled the carefully designed morsels, refining and consolidating the menu for the event. The halls were still cluttered with bodies carrying boxes of decorations and party favors, banners, extra chairs, seat cushions, linens, candles and other tableware.

Rehearsal had gone well. All the food was appropriate and delicious, the seating well-planned, the pauses in the ceremony just long enough to allow for new strike-ups between collaborators. D'Alsace was pleased but a little sad. He would miss this type of event up in that "tourist trap" on the Marionette. He was a little drunk, so he entertained the thought of backing out of the offer in the morning. A daydream.

I'll call them up, thank them graciously for the opportunity, then politely decline. Apologize—

No, it's too late, too much has been done in preparation. And anyway, the opening is in less than a month. I can't leave now and tarnish my career like that.

No, I chose this and I have to do it. Who knows, maybe I'll even love it. Maybe it's not so bad out there.

D'Alsace watched a star flicker in the sky, through some dark red clouds. He wondered what it would look like from the Marionette. Certainly not the same, no clouds at least, *but the star maybe...*

It's possible that up there is not so different from down here, after all. As they say, that orbit is just the brim of the hat.

Admitting that he was probably just enamored with the glamorous feast he had been working on that evening, he sped up his walk to the dressing rooms, changed his clothes and headed home to sleep his feelings off.

The streets were hot and bright, and humid, too. Or was he still sweating from the excitement? No, it seemed as though the breath of every person had floated up and congealed into a cloud at eye-level. The smell of it especially made

101

him think of this. It was fresh in temperature but not otherwise. There were faint aromas of different breeds of breath: acidic, stale, milky, dry, juicy, smokey, sticky with coffee, etc. He wondered if maybe it was all in his head. No way to prove it one way or the other, so he continued to find all the little notes of the scent, its textures, as many as he could, the whole way home.

D'Alsace didn't live far from the Stellarium, which was like a modern coliseum, visible for miles, despite its distance from the rest of the city's main spots. The Stellarium was still thought of as a new structure, even though it had stood for at least 15 years. Long-time locals and natives enjoyed mocking and resisting new cultural icons, and this was no exception. However, since the Marionette had gone up, plenty of scoffers had shifted their focus there instead. That was when the directors of the Pairly Gala decided to set the affair at the Stellarium. In previous years, they had held the event at other more established locations: Grand Central Station, La Maison de Victor Hugo, Agra Fort, Easter Island, etc. All had proven problematic for one reason or another. If only FC Stadium had installed the room converters they requested, there would have been no reason to ever change venues, but that love affair had soured in an ugly fight over the price of customization.

Nearing his front door, D'Alsace actually felt like walking further. He had started to enjoy the hot humid air, smelling of the many faces that had swum in it throughout the day. What was it about this air tonight? The heat was a major part of it. Never had he enjoyed such a thing as hot air, especially after cooking all day. Knowing perhaps that he would be without it for years, his mind had surely tried to appreciate these last few encounters with Earth's layered breeze.

If I set foot up there, I don't know that I'll ever know how to come back. I don't know that I'll want to. It's probably just the same but less crowded. And that might make a difference. Saturation point and all that.

He looked up at the sky, expecting a blanket of dark clouds. Instead he managed to see a star or two. Maybe the same one from before, he thought. Squinting a certain way, he could see more, but it was a hard gesture to maintain. And besides, his father always told him not to do "anything funny" with his face.

"It'll get stuck that way, when the wind hits it, and you'll be embarrassed for life."

His father died on a windy day, when he was eight, and D'Alsace didn't cry for that very reason.

THE AURORAL MARIONETTE

I had taken the trip many times, while the Marionette was being built. On the day we went up for the inspection, I was a little sick. My hearing was muffled and I couldn't smell much, but I could still tell the moment we exited Earth's atmosphere. And I liked it very much.

I want to say it felt liberating, but it wasn't that dramatic. It was a domestic kind of comfort. The orbital habitat was simple. On the surface, I felt like a flailing mime sometimes, mirroring established gestures but failing to communicate in the same terms. Here, there was less repetition (more chances to listen).

The inspectors and I arrived at the Stratos Station in roughly seven and a half hours. As soon as we stepped off the capsule, I remembered why I'd wanted to move to Earth, but also why I missed not having to wear shoes outside, as it was in Yarey—my much smaller, less popular home planet.

We had already submitted hundreds of items of audit evidence for the Marionette and its different parts, so this was just a final walkthrough for them, before they all signed their inspection reports. If they had found any weaknesses at this point, Rotari would have certainly rebuked it. They wanted to open the doors to the public in less than three months, and anyway, the Auroral Park dedication had already been scheduled, slogan and all:

Believe in the hype.

We walked through the docking station, which was more or less what they had expected: a bare-bones ship terminal with a clean aesthetic. As we entered the tunnel, the light became warmer and denser. We walked down slowly, enjoying the art projected along the way, silhouettes dancing then noticing the passersby, playfully pointing and waving hello before returning to their dance. Acrobats whistling from above. It was a temporary exhibit by a new artist from the Independent Caribbean Republic of Margarita named "MN."

It was her name that had captivated me. During her virtual presentation, she had been thorough and unemotional when pitching her art, apparently to compensate for a nervous mood. It was a big opportunity and she hadn't done many shows. At the end of her pitch, I asked about her name. She explained that she had chosen this name superstitiously right before her first show.

"It's a sound that must be hummed." She said. And then she closed her eyes and tilted her face up at a playful angle, as if her chin were being pulled up by a string to the right corner of the room. Then she hummed. *Mnnnnn.* Part of her head went off-screen. When she returned to a neutral position and opened her eyes, her face had changed. She was very still and there was no discernible effort in her smile, which was open mouthed, showing her two big glistening rows of teeth. It was one of the most natural things I had seen since I could remember. She was a heavy-set woman in her late 50s, a former dancer and teacher, and had that manner of being that feels like medicine. I thought about her for weeks. How she had transformed before our eyes from jittery applicant to jubilant philosopher. She'd been way ahead of us all along. I lamented knowing I'd never be like her. But I wanted her nearby or involved with my life somehow. That was her power.

When Rotari approved her piece, I went home and danced by myself in her honor, and for the first time in my adult life, I sang. I danced to what I sang. And I smiled the way I thought she had smiled. I went to admire my enlightenment in the mirror. All I saw was a grotesque bozo baring his teeth like a sneezing horse. I was embarrassed but I chose not to dwell on it. That night, I think I picked some basil from my wall garden for a pizza—I was no good at making things with flour, so I made my usual shaved taro root, tomato, basil, and cotija pie.

I recalled that flavor as we walked through Mn's piece in the station tunnel, which delivered us—with cheers and good wishes from the dancers—to the main body of the station. It hit us all at once. The bright warm lights, the expensive organic architecture, quik-compost planters throughout, sandy walkways, etc. We had done everything to ensure a Platinum eco-score, and seeing the inspectors' faces, I knew we would get it.

The "sky" in the station was open space. At eye level, a view of Earth. The "time zone" on the station was fluid, but we liked to keep some semblance of night and day, for wellness' sake, so the ring moved around Earth, finding day or night according to our mother's natural timepiece. There is no undoing the evolution of the Earthling body clock, just as there was no undoing my own. I could never sleep regular Earth hours. The Marionette was no different.

We took the inspectors through the facilities, showed them the two main Earth observation decks and the four on the space side. According to them, we probably wouldn't need all four in a few months. A cautious young inspector took the opportunity to assert himself, commenting outside of the natural timing of the conversation,

"People have lost interest in that kinda thing."

He chuckled by himself as the rest of us moved on. I glanced at him and he averted his eyes, pretending to be engrossed in something he'd noticed. I looked away.

People hadn't really lost interest, but the new wave of nationalism that had arisen around the world was challenging the established interest in exploring what was out beyond our atmosphere. It was making that kind of curiosity more taboo than it had been in a long time. It had happened before, of course, especially when all space exploration had halted completely a few decades ago. But it hadn't been a measure of personal identity before. It was mostly due to it being inaccessible, unless you already had ties to another planet. The prospect of economic growth by way of space reconnaissance and exploitation had ended the official prohibition, and a few projects and missions had flourished despite initial skepticism. However, now that countries around the world were turning into themselves and shutting each other out, the atmospheric border was often ignored altogether. I'll refrain from crossing too far into this territory, for I am unsure of its usefulness.

The point is that anti-expansion sentiments had caused many problems for companies like Rotari, who were universal by design. From their very foundation, they intended to resolve unprecedented global—and in some cases, super-global—problems related to population and climate instability. Their raison d'être was to optimize Earth's use of the infinity outside. There was nothing crusader-like about their work. It was all statistics and logical responses.

It was the same way for me and people like me, lately. Friendships had become transactional; business relationships suspicious. All we had was our work. If only I had known... that a couple decades after leaving my own planet's militant isolationist situation, I would be escorted away from the surface of Earth because of a similar emerging ideology... but I may still have gone through with it. I may have still left. And perhaps years from now, it will all have been worth it. For now, I could do little more than observe and oppose the fracturing of the face of my dearest Earth, the literal and vicious finger-pointing and corrupted veil over much of the leadership that plagued that perfect little planet I had watched and loved my entire life.

I didn't doubt that eventually the planet as a whole would regain interest in what isn't pulled in by their gravity, and if the Marionette helped to remind them of this option from time to time, then I would proudly stand by what we had to offer out here.

I explained to the inspectors that, in addition to the station's rotation allowing for different Earth and space spots to be explored throughout the day and night, none of the observatories were fixed and could be easily moved. They were sufficiently impressed but suggested that we might want to advertise their mobility rather than promote them as fixed viewfinders.

"We'll bring it up to our team." We didn't discuss this further, and since it had nothing to do with our objectives or controls, it didn't show up on the report either. Of course, Marketing ended up advertising versatility anyway.

"Most people just want to try to find their hometown."

That was true. Once the station opened, most tourists came all the way up here and then wanted to look back down to where they had just come from. A few—usually science enthusiasts or spiritual types—went to the outward perspective first, and then found their way back to the surface later.

I didn't want to judge them too harshly. It was a curious thing to see home from far away. Sometimes, I was disappointed, though. No one ever looked for my planet. Not many people knew it existed. They unintentionally spotted it often, though. It was a tiny greenish-brown spot in the distance to the right of Mars, when viewed from here. Nothing like the damp yellow glow of its inside, as I remembered it. Anyway, nobody ever asked about it, except for a couple people, who only wanted to know what it was called.

We walked the inspectors to the operations hall. It was a large room partitioned into functional spaces. Everything was accounted for: security, environment, metrics and statistics, weather, utilities, services, research, transportation, corporate, hospitality, human resources, compliance, sales and leasing, marketing and promotions, technology and data, client services, diligence, entertainment, legal, community services, infrastructure, etc. They had already tested each department individually, probing here and there for weaknesses. They found none, of course, and only made suggestions when they found redundancies.

We exited the operations hall, and I led the inspectors to the next rock, Sondras Alluma. It was warm throughout but empty. It smelled of caulking and cement, paint and fertilizer. The pallets of St. Augustine grass were clearly marked by a grid. Uniformed personnel were sparse but busy.

I invited the inspectors to enjoy some coffee and pastries at the Bing cafe, where the newly arrived chef D'Alsace had prepared a tasting for the occasion.

The Bing cafe—and the whole district of Sondras Alluma—was managed by Mr. Clarence Sobierv-Bing, who was a retired principal from IDSA-TPL (The Institute for Discovery and Social Accommodation — Trans-Planetary Life division). Like Gallia, he had spent much of his time studying, deconstructing and rehabilitating the human condition, both on Earth and outside of it. He had retired seven years ago, following the death of his husband, Art Klements-Bing. When he heard of our plans for the Marionette, he wrote a proposal to Rotari right away, offering his advice and services, in exchange for a permanent home on the ring. Given his experience and reputation, Rotari gladly accepted. Few people can secure a retirement plan this satisfying. But then again, few people were as dedicated, good-natured and jovial as Bing. We were lucky to have him on the Marionette.

Farah Ysvette Mourad Vera

DISAVOWING SHADOWS

As the situation grew complicated, I found myself in a repressed state. It wasn't until I acknowledged that I was, voluntarily, without the basic privilege that I began to feel the urge to honor my opinions.

The walls have ears.

I remembered the feeling well. Neighbors and friends and family kept a protective (and suspicious) watch over each other.

Don't go too far.

Don't say too much.

Don't think out loud.

I had been keeping to myself, adjusting and spinning my expression to fit the model of propriety on this planet. I wasn't any different from the people back on my home planet, squeezed into fear and complacency by poor leaders. But displacement reveals that comfort is an illusion, so it's just expression that we struggle for.

I packed my mother's skull and headed for the furnace

113

at the sanitation structure on Sondras Alluma. I asked the workmen to burn it up for me and place the ashes in a jar. They asked for her paperwork and had me fill out and sign some forms. If I were an inspector, I would have asked how exactly they were sure that the skull I had in my hand was the skull I said it was. But I was tired. And it *was* my mother's skull. So I didn't dwell on it and just sat in the hallway waiting for my ashes.

When they handed me the small container, I froze in place. I saw myself alone in a gray hallway on a ring built around the Earth—my design—with the partial remains of my mother in a small receptacle, and all I could think to do was apologize.

I am sorry. This is how it is out here. It's not the same as home. I'm sorry.

I remembered her. I remembered my brother. When we had gone to see the historic ships on a nearby beach, during the carnival holidays, early in the year. We had been completely covered in flour and confetti by the end of the day. My best friend was working the haunted house. I had lost my brother in there for fifteen minutes. I thought some awful thing had happened. My friends thought a real ghost had snuck in, or a demon perhaps. I was worried about a murderer, or a government guerrilla agent. They had been coming by the house more and more, since my father had defied one of their generals in public, refusing to pledge his allegiance to their newly established regime.

My brother was fine. He hid around a corner, waiting for a friend, so he could pop out and scare him. I was upset when he emerged, so I didn't react appropriately when he told me all about it. I regret that. All my life I took things very seriously. What was generally accepted as innocent jest was usually masking something else. Many times, that *was* the case, but other times it wasn't. Still, I didn't dare take a chance.

When Mr. Caretta called asking if he and my aunt could join me on the Marionette, I welcomed the opportunity to set things right with my brother and mother and put them to rest.

You'll never make it.

My aunt echoed the sentiment. Pessimistic blood running through the family, maybe.

"I'll never make it, Ascilogo. Just take me up the hill to Miss Karare." I heard my aunt say faintly. I assumed Miss Karare was one of the many healers that had cropped up around the city. Many of the hospitals had closed because of lack of resources. Even the ones that remained open had high mortality rates. Medicine was hard to come by, and those rushed into hospitals were usually in grave condition already, presumably having already tried a nearby healer, who had given up. My family had been using alternative healing for some time, anyway. Fevers, small scrapes and fractures, kidney stones; all these things could be given the *corpo cura*, as my father used to say. The body will heal itself, with a little help. The hospital was for bullet wounds, pierced organs and serious infections. Lately, however, many of those who arrived at the hospital just didn't make it out. Lack of maintenance or medicine, and poor staffing, left people waiting too long. Many bled out. Others died from their infections. And anyway, it was cheaper to die, since the state provided burial subsidies for all citizens, one of our proud luxuries as a society. Street healers had responded to the healthcare crisis with their talents and good will. They were widespread and significantly cheaper than standard medicine. But many healers were scammers, of course. And maybe that's why Ascilogo was hesitant to take my aunt to Miss Karare.

"Be quiet." He told her.

"What happened?" Even knowing that the answer would be complicated and unpleasant, I felt obligated to ask.

"She was stabbed on the train home. She's okay though. It doesn't matter. It happens everywhere. Listen, son. We're old. We don't have many people left. We need to leave."

He paused and I heard my aunt scoff in the background. I was too afraid to hear my voice fill the silence. He continued,

"We don't have to stay with you, but we need a place

to rest and plan what we'll do before we hit the surface."

The surface... I didn't feel comfortable directing them anywhere down there. It wasn't my place anymore. It was a miracle that corporate legislation was still so undefined for the ring that they couldn't legally kick me off the orbit.

I didn't think they would make it. They would either change their minds or be captured. Anyway, I promised to help them out.

D'Alsace had arrived on Earth just five years ago, before the new nationalism got its full voice. He knew more than me about the current immigration system, so I intended to ask him for help getting Caretta and my aunt to the surface. I promised to help them get to the Marionette, where I knew I could secure them temporary orbital papers, to start.

"You're on vacation, ok? Otherwise, you won't get in."

"Thank you, son. This is something else! Thank you."

"Of course. Just remember not to bring any produce."

Ascilogo laughed heartily.

"I remember that much."

I smiled at the phone, like an idiot, and pictured my aunt having to give up her herbs at customs. She carried them everywhere in a little jar, some dried, some fresh. Mint to chew on, for her breath, basil for digestion, tila flower for anxiety. All my life I've known my aunt as that tall dark woman chewing leaves in the corner, watching everyone go about their business, suspicious but amicable, and always willing to help. She hated depending on others, though. Caretta knew that, but he didn't seem to care.

"Ok. See you soon, Mr. Caretta. Give Daliya my love."

Give my love? Was that appropriate? I wasn't sure how to handle my messages to my only living relative, having been away for so long.

I heard him tell her that I asked for her blessing.

Thank you for translating.

Asking for a blessing was a custom I'd forgotten all about. Back home, you ask for blessings instead of saying hello and goodbye. It's also a way to confirm that a conflict has been resolved. Growing up, I'd been in that situation many times. I'd argue with my mother and she'd stop talking to me. I'd ask for my blessing and she'd return a grunt. When the tension had subsided, she would finally answer,

"Bless you," looking at me like she hoped I'd learned my lesson and would never do that thing again.

I'd kiss her and walk away, grateful for her forgiveness, but also hoping that she knew I expected her to accept part of the blame.

The back and forth tugging of parent-child politics were behind me forever now, but I'd never outgrow the heartache. Though I'd resisted the rush for many years—since I'd arrived on Earth—I felt rising anger now. I knew it would end only after it ran its course. And I knew that its course would carve a canyon through the middle of me.

Still, it felt right to be angry. That I had been blamed for something I had nothing to do with. Somebody else's irresponsible actions, her fear and delusion. That I had been a removable problem, despite my sincere efforts to build on top of the progress of those before me. To contribute to, and sincerely uphold, the little planet's values, which I held so dear. That I had paid more tribute to their legacy than many of their own. And yet, here I was. Close enough to see the difference between land and ocean on Earth, but too far to inhale its air or let myself fall for miles through its gravity.

I was angry at Earth. I was also angry at my home planet.

How dare they.

Born and growing up in Yarey, we were bombed and betrayed, made to feel like outsiders and conspirators. When I left, I was a traitor. When I returned, I was inadequate, an outsider in my own land. Rude and inappropriate. Unwanted. So I left again. I came back to Earth's orbit where I could at least lean on a lack of precedent, an absence of a historical establishment.

Here, though, Earth stares at me while I greet the pieces of my childhood home that have had to flake off.

It was in this broken state that I always wished I'd been

born a turtle or a pigeon. A functional animal. Eat, sleep, survive, and die. I was doing that anyway, but it didn't register as natural. I felt like the most unnatural being to live in either of these places.

MILIAN'S QUESTIONING

Milian Sieglund, an extraordinarily tall man, stood before a group of about 2,000 people, all extraordinarily tall as well. As he felt the thousands of eyes landing on him, his skin became gray. His eyes glossed over, overwhelmed. *Rising anger.*

"My name is Milian Sieglund, independent contractor. I have just presented to the committee some key records and other pieces of evidence that provide an insight regarding the events that have taken place on Mantis Green. The evidence suggests that the untimely passing of the tenant developed as a result of the tenant's own instability and irresponsible dismissal of maintenance, repair and homestead services. I invite you to peruse and analyze these materials now placed in public records."

The audience began to rumble. *Skepticism. Flash judgment. Anger.* And they hadn't even looked at the evidence yet. Opening the documents to the public was my last chance to

121

affirm my innocence and force the law to recognize the tenant's role and impact on the *event*. This room may have been filled with neo-puritans and anti-multiculturalists, but everyone else outside was welcome to chime in on the verdict. Of course, the public vote usually didn't sway the final decision of the suited up panel that sat on my left through the whole trial. And to be on the panel, you had to fit certain characteristics which were meant to dissolve bias, but actually ended up affirming a specific point of view that was aligned with the small group running the business of justice. This business tended to favor popular politics. It had always been that way. In fact, it was that way everywhere I'd been. That's why my two uncles had been convicted, tortured and executed back in Yarey, for opposing the newly established authoritarian government. The same government was still in power now. Democracy had died back home a long time ago. And with it had perished unbiased justice. Earth seemed to be heading the same way, and I didn't realize it until I saw those faces, all from a very specific demographic, regarding me with one thought at the forefront of their argument:

You never belonged here in the first place. We have a chance to get you out, and so we will.

"That's as much information as I am permitted to share with you at this time. Please take a moment to review the evidence with a clear and humble mind. That's my last plea."

I hated performing in this charade, but I was too exhausted to decline the opportunity to do so. A group of media makers gathered at the entrance, yelling over each other. Cameras colliding, spit flying and landing on the reporters' cheeks. It would have been a real nightmare for Gallia. I liked it, though. They were after something and some of them would find it. Whether the rest listened or not had likely already been decided, even before they spoke.

Rotari had already drawn up termination papers, and my citizenship status would have to be reviewed as soon as they were signed. Naturalization had become an unprotected status a few years back, with the most recent wave of so-called patriotism effectively nullifying its key benefit. Being a naturalized citizen of Earth was not at all the same as being Earth-born. No guarantees. *We* were beggars. *They* were owners.

Rotari felt a little bit of the pressure, too. They had grown exponentially since the next set of plans for the Auroral Marionette had been unveiled, highlighting their powerful place in the new frontier. But when the initial curiosity about the orbit's new potential had been eclipsed by the old "troubles at home," the Earth's safety-hungry xenophobia reignited. Everyone seemed to renew their subscription to the same old manifesto that had stalled society's progress time and time again.

We have to sort out our issues here at home first. Before we

123

venture out into space again, we have to be sure that we will not be undermined or attacked by any of those people out there, some of which are desperate for resources or running away from a dangerous past, bringing their trouble right here to our own backyard. We must protect ourselves against them. And so on...

Then, they'd split back up into their own small tribes and undermine each other. Social issues. Plausible conspiracies. Then an economic collapse. Persecution. Suicides. Then someone's fresh idea about exploring what else is out there... Same always. Same everywhere.

For the time being, Rotari had promised to hire local people to fill 75% of all positions, to rekindle interest in their projects by way of patriotism. As of the day I was sued and dismissed, they had fulfilled only a third of that goal.

I defended myself as vigorously as I could. I can take solace in that. The trial was a circus act. I was the sad clown that got dragged away by the happy ones with weapons. I'm just one strange man from a poor planet. Can they be blamed for being suspicious?

I hoped Rotari would at least speak on my behalf, even if they were letting me go. But they didn't want to stir things up.

"I'm so sorry this happened, Milian."

Knowing that I'd soon be gone for good, Anaiida had come to visit me. She'd ignored my calls for weeks. I insisted on telling myself that she had been legally required to ignore me until the decision was announced. It was probably true, but I never confirmed it.

"Can't you talk to someone? You saw the files. She threatened everybody when we tried to—"

"I'm sorry. I wasn't there."

"But you know—"

"There's nothing we can do, Milian. I'm sorry. I think you'll find something else. You're talented. Think of it as a new opportunity."

Why do people always say things like that, when you're knee-deep in quicksand?

After that conversation with Anaiida, I knew there was nothing anyone could do. Anyway, I shouldn't have put her in that position by asking for her support. It was unfair, I suppose. She had to think of her reputation. Even though she was technically born an Earthling, her heritage was almost as foreign as mine, so she could get swept over to the side with the rest of us. Easily.

There were stories cropping up all the time now about Earth-born people who had been detained indefinitely because they were unable to prove their status as legal born-citizens. Many of them, especially in the colonies, couldn't speak any Earth languages and didn't *look* like Earthlings. They were locked up for months and even years, while authorities *figured things out.* Meanwhile, the detainment facilities collected their population bonus and their suppliers made a fortune from the extra shipments. Incarceration may have become Earth's best business, after all. And it also sent a message of false security to the sunscreen-obsessed inhabitants of the little planet:

Look at all the criminals we're protecting you from!

At the end of my trial, I was ordered to leave Earth within 60 days, barred from the surface for a period of five years, at the end of which, I could apply for reentry as a temporary visitor. That application could also be denied, based on my records. I could still return to the Auroral Marionette to fulfill the rest of my contractual obligations, and I planned to fight to retain my access. My authorship had implied rights and technically the Marionette still fell outside the general scope of Earth law, so I planned to employ those arguments for as long as I could.

Unfortunately, my citizenship was rescinded for life. A citizen of Earth is a privileged person who has demonstrated remarkable loyalty. Someone who upholds and respects the values of the community on this planet and seeks to abide by its laws and customs at all times. In the eyes of the law, my citizenship was little more than a club membership. And I was no longer a welcomed guest.

Maybe I could have convinced them to allow me to re-apply after my exile period. But my life on Earth had become a collage of imitations. Always trying to blend in, forget about identity, fulfill my impulses in private. I ate food I didn't like. I went places I didn't enjoy. I didn't experience friendship, as they'd described it. I wore their constricting clothes and toned down my make up. I muted my color and softened my flavor to suit their palate. And when they asked to see what else there was beyond their reality, I showed them a glimpse. As long as I could return back to *normal*, after the show, they enjoyed themselves.

I had some friends over for dinner a few months before the Marionette opened to the public. I made a dish my mother used to make, but I did it with an Italian twist, because I was afraid they wouldn't like it. I played them some music from back home, songs that made people there joyful or melancholy. With Earth people in the room, though, the music seemed ridiculous. It sounded silly and shrill. Stupidly wholehearted. I was embarrassed. They laughed it off, so I was glad that at least they hadn't found it offensive.

A few weeks later, I overheard two of them bragging about the experience to someone else. They seemed so proud to have such "diversity" in their lives. They *really* understood other cultures and were eager to spread their knowledge. At my apartment, they had mocked my music, but now they called it "unique" and "fresh." They wrote me a little sorry letter when the verdict was announced:

127

MANTIS GREEN

Wish there was something we could do.
So sorry and good luck!
Love,
Ray & Linda

More of the same. All problems and no solutions. Same as Gallia.

If it's wrong, why won't you let us fix it? Or is it not really wrong? Maybe this is what you want.

Doesn't matter now. Once she had moved in, there was nothing we could do. This woman's only salvation was on that rock. She assured me there was *so* little time for her to enjoy her "last years." She wasn't even sixty and was already prepared to receive death with open arms.

Milian and Sylvia had discussed Gallia's preoccupation with the fleeting quality of time. One evening, they sat going over the next set of enhancements at Gallia's house. Gallia was in Canaima Park in South America, purchasing some artwork and furnishings for the rock. She liked to buy Amazonian knick knacks and instruments. On the last trip, she had spent a day watching the waterfalls,

Their power, their freedom, their endless energy.
How can something so precious just be allowed to flow like

this, with no limits at all?

But at the bottom of the tallest one, the water was nothing but mist.

It does run out. It does become thin and light. The sky gets dark as it gets late, but the moon is maybe brighter than the sun. The water and the plants are tinged blue and green. My face smoother than it was in the heat of the day. Well, except for the cluster of mosquito bites underneath my earlobe.

Gallia's return would be marked by the usual preparations: a visit from the cleaning crew to sterilize the place, the rearrangement of the furniture by a mystic interior designer, whose goal was to align the house's demeanor with Gallia's expected mood, and a tormenting couple of days of contradictory requests filtering from Gallia to Sylvia by all possible communication media, including what food to buy, what towels to put out, what candles to burn, etc. For now, those days were still a ways away.

Sylvia and Milian sat together at the table, enjoying a delivered meal, while they flipped through the change proposals together.

"She was always like that."

"How long have you known her?"

"Well, I was born in this house, actually."

Sylvia enjoyed talking about this. It made her feel entitled to the full extent of her life. She didn't enjoy the same every-day conviction and freedom as her peers, but she did have this qualification to whip out at them, if they caused her any loss in self-assurance. It was her branded disadvantage, her inherited circumstances and her all-purpose excuse, should she ever need one. How come you never have any money? Don't you want to buy a house someday? Have a family? Why didn't you take the internship at the UN, when you had the chance? *Well…*

"My family worked for the Sinlavas. I owe her a great deal. We didn't have much of our own, but working for them, we were able to live a better life."

"Did you ever think about leaving?"

"I did. I wouldn't have made it. My mother always warned me that the day would come when I would feel that urge. But she told me to resist it. 'You'll never make it.'"

She impersonated her mother saying the usual nagging phrase, and noticed immediately that it caused Milian some discomfort, which he swallowed back down with a sip of beer. The two retreated to their plates for a little while.

"This place is great."

"What is it?"

"Lloyd Donato's. They haven't been around that long, but they're pretty consistent."

"I like it."

"I think she's just afraid of death."

"Gallia, you mean?"

"Yeah. I feel like, for some time, she didn't think about it at all. Then, when my mother died, she thought about it all the time. She'd wake up screaming in the middle of the night —she still does, but not like that. Back when it first started happenning, she used to do it almost every night."

"How old were you?"

"That's the problem, isn't it?"

"What?"

"Would my age at the time have made it any easier for anyone?"

"I suppose so. If you were little, she would have had to take care of you."

"I was. And she did. But she didn't have to. I guess that's kind of what she's looking for now. She doesn't want to see that again. And when it happens to you, you're not all that aware of it anyway—not the way you would be if you were just the one watching it happen to someone else."

"It's a different experience, I guess."

"She wants to be alone. I'm not gonna stop her."

"Are you upset that she's moving up there by herself?"

"It'll be very good for me. But I can't help how I feel right now."

"Which is..."

"I can't tell. I feel betrayed and jealous and relieved, all at the same time."

"Do you love her?"

"It's not about that."

"I know. I just want to know."

"In a way."

The response took him by surprise. Milian wasn't sure what to say. He knew that she wasn't really paying attention to his papers. He also knew that she had no intention of listening to him for any reason. She just wanted someone to listen to her. But he wasn't in the habit of giving that to anyone.

"Speaking of time, I have to send our notes to the team tonight, so did you have anything else to add to these?"

Sylvia was hurt, but it was a bruise she knew how to hide until it healed on its own. They finished their review of the proposals quickly and efficiently. She didn't have much to add. It wasn't her place. It wasn't her life.

Whatever she wants to do, she can go ahead and do it. I don't have to devote all of my time to this. I have to think of planning my own life.

What will I do? What will happen?

OTHER PLANS

For a while, I wanted to be a dentist. It seemed like a peaceful enough job with a real purpose. I gave up on it, though, when I thought about the smells I'd encounter. When I was little, I hated family gatherings because there were two old ladies who always showed up and went straight for my face with their wet painted lips. One of them had a habit of drinking coffee on the way to our house and she (unfortunately) also liked to talk a lot, so the syrupy sourness of her breath hung in the air for hours, even after she had gone. The skin on my cheek retained the caramelly stink for a while, too, although I usually snuck away to wash up in the bathroom upstairs as soon as I could.

Marielte was her name. A vibrant old lady with terrible breath. What a pity. Her remains were on the same floor as my mother's. I thought about bringing her flowers, but it occurred to me that I didn't know if she was actually related to the family or if she was just a friend. Bringing flowers to someone else's family member could backfire, as lately it'd been used to

133

signal a threat or a warning by local criminal gangs. Anyway, I thought perhaps I could just stop by, say something, as silly as it seems. I've often found it easy and logical to speak to the dead. I suppose it's hereditary, in a way.

My grandmother was the undertaker's apprentice, mostly handling the make up, clothes, etc. A couple times, she told me, she got to do some embalming. She didn't enjoy it as much. What she really loved was, "painting youth and peace back onto their stiff faces."

"Hardly any wrinkles." She'd say. A job well done.

"It's like he's only sleeping."

She wasn't a humorous woman, but she was funny like that. And she had an infatuation with "little angels," which is what she called the bodies of deceased children that arrived at her table every once in a while.

"I prepared a little angel today. He looked wonderful." She'd smile and look at the sky, hand dramatically placed on her heart. Then, she'd sink down between her knees and cry. After a couple of minutes, she'd look up again and kiss the tip of her finger while closing her eyes. Then she'd get up and go clean something. Quietly.

Before bed, my grandmother had a ritual. Fetch two glasses of water from the kitchen. Drink one and place the other under the bed, directly beneath her head. For as long as we—her children and grandchildren—knew her, she had claimed that she needed the glass of water under the bed because otherwise the ghosts wouldn't let her sleep. As a child, I took this at face value. My mother, perhaps, knew what she really meant. Perhaps not. I never asked.

All I know is that as long as I knew her, my grandmother said she convened with ghosts. They relied on her daily assistance. Every night and every morning, she would light a candle for each of them and dedicate them prayers. She'd do longer prayers on Saturdays and Sundays, when she knew she could devote more time to a specific person, usually one of her parents or a beloved uncle—and sometimes, I think, her husband, although she never spoke of him to us.

Come to think of it, I knew very little about my grandfather, other than that he had been a boxer and a drunk. I heard stories of him waking the family up in the middle of the night to go fishing, and stories of him crafting flowers out of candy wrappers for his two older daughters. My mother had no remembrance of flowers, but she did go fishing at two in the morning a few times.

"It was oddly fruitful, actually." She used to tell me.

Apparently because of the thickness of the fog at that hour, the fish were basically blind and couldn't tell that their morsels were hiding shiny little hooks. Some people say fish can't tell the difference, but my mother disagreed. She always believed that fish needed sunlight just as much as the rest of us. And she was convinced that they always caught more fish in the dark. I'm not sure how often they went fishing during the day, if at all. I never asked.

I wondered what Caretta and my aunt would bring. Did they have strange rituals to share with me? Or would they do as I did, and try to adjust, desperately and willing to dilute themselves into an identity oblivion?

My displacement was supreme. I was isolated from myself and had not retained enough samples from my life. The swinging kid shopping with his mom, the aspiring architect, the studious introvert, the disastrous charmer of a friend, the stylish consultant, the quiet fixer. Whatever I had been, at any point, had been irrelevant. A bygone expression.

Home can be lost. You can lose the connection. The thing that makes you beat as you. The substance in the tube. That happened to me. This is a story of loss. No matter what I tell you from here on out, know that much. This is a story of loss. I attempted in every way I could to leave behind my part and to avoid perverting my future with nostalgia. I ended my relationship with my origin. And here I stand, faceless, forming words to fake my way out of it. Don't let me tell you, going forward, that I'm fine. I'm a slave to my vanity just like everyone else. I'm frivolous. And I'm dead.

A SYMMETRICAL

When Gallia first moved to Mantis Green, she still had a lot of tests to undertake and paperwork to complete. We had tried to make it as painless as possible, but without an official program for private civilian real estate in orbit, we just had to comply with the recommendations of Rotari's commercial committee, and as usual, we were in a rush to get it done and move on to the next part of our work.

I got a call from Sylvia one afternoon. She was distraught. I could hardly get her to tell me what was going on, but I pieced together from her fragmented muttering that the Tsarina was undergoing a crisis.

"Can you press them to go through the evidence faster?"

"I'll do what I can."

"Thank you. They called her a few hours ago with a new list of requests, which we should have no problem fulfilling in the next couple days, but then they said they were planning to review them in two weeks, when their head of controls

returned from vacation. I asked if maybe someone else could approve them on his behalf, considering the time constraints—
"

"Yeah, that really shouldn't be a problem for them. Let me call them."

I don't know how or when I became an unofficial assistant to the Sinlava estate, but it was exciting to be involved in such conversations, even if I wasn't qualified, or being paid, to do so. I called my PM at Rotari and explained that Gallia was eager to finish the paperwork as early as possible. They already had a solution.

"Gary will review everything. I'll send you his information and put you guys in touch."

"Thanks, Anaiida."

"Of course. Take care."

"You too."

Sylvia and Gallia were a week late with the paperwork. It seems Gallia had developed a severe headache that decommissioned her completely for a few days, but that's not what we told Rotari. Gallia wanted to avoid further scrutiny regarding her ability to live healthfully on Mantis Green. A chronic migraine condition wasn't likely to ground her, but it would have to be well documented and properly tracked on the rock. At the very least, it would have caused a significant delay.

Gallia had never received a formal medical diagnosis

for her migraines, since she had identified and treated the condition herself, so she bypassed the topic altogether. Sylvia and I supported her decision.

On the weeks leading up to her move to Mantis Green, Gallia had decided to rewrite some of her articles and books, to match her current perspective. One of them was about the human obsession with symmetry. It opened with this:

Cultures have valued symmetry for a very long time, but we've seen in recent years that the concept, although aesthetically excellent, is little more than a daydream. The human body is any-thing but symmetrical and yet, we continue to emphasize the impor-tance of balance and balanced strength and flexibility, in sports and exercise. In medicine, however, a shift in practices has slowly favored an off-center balance. The right side may need more of this and less of that.

I hesitate to guess what the rewrite would have stated, but perhaps she found herself to be heartless or equally tremu-lous on both sides, and suggested that maybe the mere goal of balancing both sides was a part of survival, in itself. Rather than nursing and contributing to off-kilter tendencies, we tried to counteract them, so as to "set things straight." Or perhaps it's the inevitable road to thermodynamic equilibrium, or death. Maybe we know that living is an abomination of nature, a bizarre state where spooky things happen, so we take matters into our hands and try to force balance on everything until we're at perfect equilibrium and no longer in a weird state of being alive.

Luckily, she didn't get to officially make any of these changes to any of her books. She may have eventually decided against it, if she had continued to live. I don't know. All I know is that I enjoyed reading the original book. I picked it up and read it while we were building Mantis Green, to get a better idea of who this vigilant misanthrope was.

After living on Earth a few years, I learned to distrust doctors and pills. I mostly stuck with what they called "holistic medicine," which ended up being very similar to regular medicine from home. While reading Gallia's book, I realized that all of the healing approaches I had experienced in acupuncture and physical therapy were imbalanced on purpose. They tended to follow the body's design, which only *seems* symmetrical, in appearance, but not in function. I was engrossed in this book until the very end, and I respected her for helping me see things in that way. I tried speaking to her about what the book had done for me, but by then, her perspective had already changed.

Her other books weren't nearly as interesting. Mostly just factual reports on weather, agricultural practices and health. They were well written but dry and unsmiling. Those, I suppose, could have used a shift in vantage point.

A CURIOUS DEVELOPMENT

A curious development occurred while I was sitting around my childhood home back in Yarey: I was offered a chance to return to work on the Marionette.

I don't know exactly what gave her the idea, but Sylvia Dynes called me up. She said that she wanted to help me return to work on the Marionette. She had spoken to the estate lawyers and could secure an orbital permit for me, without surface privileges, of course.

"Of course."

"What do you think?"

I silently conferred with my mother's skull, which was perched on my bookcase, while I lay on the floor. Her voice was clear and urgent—Sylvia's, that is.

I decided to take this chance at reconstruction. I looked around and saw a box of palmiers and my unzipped suitcase by the door, with my clothes bunched up on top. My father's plants were all leaning toward the windows, with the fog pressing hard against the pane on the other side. The entirety of the second floor was painted evenly with darkness. How alone we were. Sylvia and I, together in hell, doing everything we could to escape to purgatory.

I accepted. Within a few hours, I was writing my statement, as directed by Sylvia's lawyers. In the book of my experience, everything I had been through here and on Earth would just be a set of layovers in my airport life.

Since I'd been back in my home town on Yarey, I'd developed a habit. Whenever I couldn't sleep (which was almost every night now), I liked to spend some time perusing through the DotCom Digital Museum. It was a massive domain, containing archives of webpages and digital artifacts. Last year, they'd made a special announcement: the first full set of records had been compiled. This meant that evidence of every single thing, every page, every object, every line of code that was out there every day, for one year, had been stored in the Museum's archive. Whether they could maintain that rate or capture each year forth remained to be determined. Of course, they didn't keep the full set of records available for browsing. Most of them were stored locally in one of their data centers. Any public record for that year could be recalled by special order, for a fee. That's how they made money. Like everything else, the museum catered to society's doughy sense of nostalgia. It sat well with them to pay a fee and time travel. Always to the past. Like paying a fee, a salacious visit to what's passed never yields a neutral difference. It invites comparison, plus or minus. It's either better or worse. Upon return to the present, they often had more disappointment, and always less money. I wasn't so hot on looking back, but what I really loved was a section called, "Philosophy of the Digital Continent."

In there were hundreds of articles, galleries and videos about digital topics like *The Nature of Social Media*, *Why Hackers Hack (And Other Social Engineering Fables)*, *Blogger Types*, *The Relativity of "Real Time" in the Digital Sense*, *The HiFi/LoFi Self(ie)*, *Advertising for Jane and John*, and *.Net Violence*.

My favorite one to visit lately had been Blogger Types. It was a collection of simulated blogs, each describing one of a few types of blogs that all blogs everywhere could be bucketed into. This seemed to me like a digital expression of anthropology. We become the same few things no matter what format we try to filter ourselves through.

The night before I was supposed to leave for the Marionette, I read a blog type called "Just Giustina," which was about a person with a large family who wanted to share their knowledge of how to manage a busy life. They respected nature and obeyed the law and embraced change and loved life. They also adhered strictly to a specific religion, and followed its guidelines like they were orders (even when misinterpreted). Conflict and hypocrisy were byproducts of their way of

144

life, but they made up for these shortcomings with folksy charm. This particular blog type had a special feature attached: social media presence, which included a massive photo gallery featuring hundreds of family pictures and expertly photographed food. The quotations database compiled public comments from the blogger on social media, be it other blogs and websites or social-only platforms. This blogger had questionable ethics and was ignorant but vocal in politics. As an animal lover, however, they delighted in sharing endearing images and videos of wildlife originally generated by animal rights and environmental wellness advocates. But their photo history revealed a carnivore and hunting enthusiast. And a US nationalist (with a foreign name).

It was a digital museum of stereotypes and I loved it because it was uniquely "Earth." Sure, we had similar (or exact) types on Yarey, and everywhere else, too. But Earth stereotypes were always so confident. The closer you got to the type's bullseye, the more it made them feel jealous and inadequate to be anything else. Most of us fall in between, of course. I believe that most discontent emerges from being stuck in the middle. You either begrudgingly join or walk away scorned. Join and then walk, or walk and then join. Then frustration sets in. It turns into pain. The wound heals with time, but the scar remains.

We lead a curious pilgrimage.

READYING GALLIA

It was still light outside, but if we had been judging by the brightness of Gallia's waiting room, we could have assumed it was night. Night would have marked the start of the Gala, and most likely this would have meant that Gallia was en route, adorned with fashion items that relied on her parading *bod* for advertising. Displaying a perfectly crafted half-smile on her face, she would be fuming internally about the seating arrangement or questioning the wholesomeness of the hors d'oeuvres, choosing her thing to pick at in front of the other guests to entertain her table, deciding on appropriate anecdotes and topics relevant to those sharing her table, pre-pitying their ignorance of this or that thing, which she would have to discuss later with "better" people.

Well, maybe I judged her too harshly by assuming she was that much of a cliche (which she most certainly was). Still, I felt guilty, knowing very well that she could not defend herself now against my derision. But I think it's always been my fate to feel this way: ashamed of my rage and enraged by my shame.

Anyway, had it been night, that's what would have been happening. The point I was so clumsily trying to make was that it was early on in the day, but Gallia's house was dark. She should have been home, readying for the party, but instead she had come to see me again. She had come up with an enhancement to our design and wanted to deliver it personally.

Funny that, at places like Rotari, we have separate people in charge of gathering content, designing the presentation of said content, and actually presenting it. She had done it all herself that morning and was clicking through her slides in my office now. The whole thing took no more than twenty minutes. She wanted a deep grotto with a reading room in it, a miniature forest along the courtyard loop, and an artificial storm system. We had initially suggested a small rain generator for the garden, as part of the regular irrigation system, but she wanted lightning and thunder and wind and all that. She acknowledged, and was prepared to accept, our limitations, but she hoped we'd *at least try*. I reassured her and promised her we'd be in touch soon, and she was off.

I went home and read some "Dog Poems" to Jones. "Dog Poems" was a book I'd bought when I moved into my first Earth apartment. It was a dumb book that had spent too much time soaking up steam in my bathroom's magazine rack.

Jones had eaten half of it. We used the half that was left for playtime. Most of the poems in that half were basically Taoist teachings through the dog lens. There weren't a lot of funny ones. I wondered if such a thing could be funny anyway. I never know with some humor on Earth. It might be the funniest thing in the world to an Earthling, but it might drive me to tears.

Back at the stadium, the field had been covered up with a temporary wooden floor for the event. It looked nothing like a stadium, actually, more like an inverted wedding cake. All the seating sections had been converted into nine concentric rings of tables, using platforms and lots of the same wooden floorboards. Paper star lanterns of various sizes and shades of off-white, light blue and pale pink cascaded down the levels, across the field and back up the other side in alternating patterns. Constellation lighting, they called it. It was impractical but beautiful. In between every few tables, they had set up snake plants and bromeliads. At the center of each table was an arrangement of fresh herbs and spices, surrounded by pristine wine and water glasses, sparkling crystal dishes and glittering silverware, all atop shimmering champagne-colored tablecloths. It was like an iridescent oyster world. Staff members marched up, down, and in between the different levels, securing plants and chairs, checking the sturdiness of the platforms and floor boards, etc. They wore Hawaiian shirts with patterns containing yellow, orange and green, and dark green slacks. A palatial bar had been set up inside a set of boxes in the center of the lowest platform.

Just before the sun started to set, the stadium was deserted. All of the system tests had been performed that morning, the final touches had been added, the finger foods were ready to be served... And Gallia was now home, preparing. Sylvia, who had inherited the position assisting the Sinlavas (or what remained of them... which is to say, Gallia) sat straddling Gallia, massaging her neck. Gallia had buried her face in the space between her crossed arms on top of her glass table, watching the shrinking oval of foggy moisture that her breath painted on its surface, trying to calm down.

Clarity. Bring me.

"Do you want another drink?"

Gallia thought it over, blowing once more onto the glass with her hot breath. She raised her face from the safety of the arm pocket, looking down at the frosty little dot.

"Yep. I'll try another. Thanks, Sylvia."

"Same?"

"Uh... well—"

She started to feel brave but when she glanced down and saw her reflection, she sank back down.

"Same."

MANTIS GREEN

Sylvia walked over to the bar behind an artificial waterfall in Gallia's living room. She chipped some ice off a big block that was kept in a special freezer drawer and put it in a glass. Over it, she poured some Cuban rum and then squeezed a couple lime wedges into it. To finish it off, she garnished it with one star anise and brought it to Gallia with a burgundy cocktail napkin.

"I went to see the architect."

"Oh yeah? How was that?"

"I think he's gonna make it happen. We'll see. You never know what they mean and what they don't, but I think he will."

Gallia took the drink and sucked down half of it, gagging a little before swallowing in one gulp. Sylvia picked up a bottle of pale blue liquid and poured some on a cloth, which she then applied to Gallia's temples. Gallia welcomed the refreshing sensation of the tincture, a Caribbean product her family had imported into the US for nearly two centuries. Sylvia pressed on both temples and guided Gallia into a deep breath in and then one out, again in and then out, breathe in... and breathe out. Gallia closed her eyes and did a few more on her own, until she was visibly more calm, her eyes and forehead un-crinkled, her lips loose, her shoulders down.

The headache remained, however. That hardly ever went away. But Gallia knew how to live with its hot sting exhausting her. On good days, she managed to forget about it and accepted it as *just the way a head feels*. The weight of it because of its shape or because of its contents or whatever else. She vowed to keep as calm as possible and trust that relaxation would transform the pain into mere processing noise. Taming the idea of migraines this way seemed to stop them from overtaking her emotionally. She could calmly tell herself that the headache was logical and healthy, and then she could move on with her day.

The party would last a while.

Sylvia would surely be asleep by the time I got home. Unless, of course, I asked her to wait up for me. It wouldn't be fair, but maybe she wouldn't mind. Maybe she would suggest it herself. That would be likely to happen on a night like this, with me so distraught and her so concerned.

"What time do you think you'll be back?" Sylvia *finally* asked.

"[Sigh] I was gonna ask you the same thing."

"I'll be here."

"Oh. Yes. I mean I'm not sure how long I'm expected to stay."

"I think twelve thirty is probably a safe bet. They'll understand. I don't know that they'll even question it."

"You're right."

Sylvia smiled at Gallia, as Gallia finished her drink.

"You look great. And you'll be great."

Gallia didn't respond. She was phrasing and rephrasing the question in her head, not listening to Sylvia at all.

"Will you wait for me?"

Sylvia knew it was coming. She didn't like it, but she felt she had no choice but to accept it and play her part in it. And anyway, once Gallia moved to Mantis Green, this would no longer be an issue. What's one more time? But it didn't quite comfort her to think this. It didn't comfort Gallia either, to know this was how Sylvia felt, even if she had never said so in words. They had been thrown together long enough to grow accustomed to these discomforts. And they both clung to their shared experience.

"Of course…"

Gallia hated herself for doing this again, but she was relieved. Sylvia was unassuming and personal. And she could trust her. It was guaranteed that Gallia would return emotionally and intellectually wrecked and in need of release and comfort. She found it only in Sylvia, who really did have little choice in the matter, if she wished to continue to enjoy a life of perks and privilege. And she did. She also enjoyed being needed, something she'd never found (or looked for) outside of Gallia's house. Sylvia held Gallia's face and kissed her. Putting the glass down on the table, Gallia got up. She looked at Sylvia in a way Sylvia expected.

The evening began as it should, with a trickle of low-profile early birds followed by the sensational mess of the late-and-great crowd. Gallia was in the latter group, although not by choice. She had spent some more time on the floor at her home with Sylvia and had suddenly decided that it wouldn't be worth it to attend the event. Then, as customary, Gallia and Sylvia engaged in an explosive little fight.

"I am going to go insane! You were the one who said you should go. It doesn't matter at all to me whether or not you do! I don't care!"

"I said that because I knew you would get all over me about it, if I didn't!"

"Why would—"

Gallia took a step back, as if surprised by hurt.

"You love it. You love to see me like this!"

"I'm not doing this with you."

Sylvia walked out of the room and grabbed herself a beer. Gallia followed, looking at her with eyes full of water. When Sylvia looked back at her, she too crumbled. Sylvia and Gallia sat behind the waterfall, on the floor, sobbing for several minutes. Then Gallia got up. Sylvia followed immediately, afraid of what she might throw at her next.

"I'm just getting a beer."

"I'll grab it for you—"

"I can get it." Gallia snapped back, clipping Sylvia's words.

Sylvia backed off, remembering stories about her own father, coddling Constanza Sinlava, Gallia's mother. They'd spend hours yelling and crying and lying on the floor, drinking. It seemed that many (if not all) family habits were hard-wired.

Gallia seemed busy—pacing around, beer in hand, working through her confusion—so Sylvia took the opportunity to daydream. She would go home, buy a ticket to the Everglades and get lost there. What would she bring? Anything? Everything she had she had earned by working for this family her entire life, living under their canopy, adjusting her lifestyle to their whims and fancies, attending more champagne brunches than she would have ever cared to attend... which she never would have had access to, if not for this family.

Gratitude, she thought.

That's the reason. I never would have graduated. I never would have made it out of the lower brackets. I never would have traveled or known another language. I never would have pushed myself to be better. I never would have gone to space. When I was small, I would have liked to work in space, even if it was just in shipping. Now I'm here, coordinating the construction of a luxury satellite for this woman. This woman who hates beer but she'll drink it with me. Keeps it fully stocked. Beer from all different places, specialty brews, rare infusions. Gratitude. It must be the currency or else we're all wrong about our compromises.

When Gallia sat back down, with the drink in her hand, Sylvia asked to see the bottle's label. It was a porter. One of the only beers that Gallia truly enjoyed.

"Where's it from?"

"Chile."

"I didn't realize you had any of that."

"Just arrived this morning. You can have the rest of them, I just wanted to try it. It was a gift actually."

"Oh great, who sent it to you?"

"A gift for you. [Pause] From me."

"Oh... Thanks."

"Thanks, Sylvia." She spoke in subdued song, as if drugged or tired.

Gallia drank the whole beer in two gulps, set the bottle aside and got up.

"I hope you like it. It's apparently got some chocolate in it, but it's actually kind of tart."

Sylvia took the empty bottle to the recycling bin. She watched Gallia walk away with hollow purpose, a sign that the panic had passed. She had finally disengaged. For the rest of the night, Gallia didn't make eye contact or say anything personal. She got ready efficiently and without much fuss, remembering all the jewelry and other accessories and putting everything she needed in a straw satchel she had pulled down from the glass case, in her dressing room, where she kept her family's unique pieces on display.

Finally, with only 15 minutes to spare before the start of the party, she posed in front of the mirror for herself and then turned around, maintaining the pose for Sylvia, whose presence she felt, urging her to depart.

"Fantastic!"

"Thank you." She said dryly.

And then she was off. Sylvia laid down on the floor behind the waterfall for a well-deserved nap. An hour and a half later, she got up to try the porter from Chile. She drank it in the dark library, watching gusts of wind lift and swirl fallen leaves outside the window, as the incoming storm clouds rolled in, red and gray, eating up the stars.

On the way to the party, Gallia's driver encountered a road closure. Cars were directed to go through the neighborhood roads instead of the main throughway. Gallia recognized the area. There was a small bookstore nearby that she liked to frequent years before. The owner only stocked it with vintage books, nothing newer than 100 years old. She loved the way the books smelled and the way the shadows would bend inside the place, while people moved through the aisles, browsing not so much the titles but the feel of the aisles themselves.

The science section was filled with small thin books. Table books were big and colorful. Novels were boxy and drab.

In the poetry room, there was paper everywhere. Many of the books had been torn. Gallia had once asked the owner if they arrived like that.

"They get here whole, then folks rip the pages out. Who am I to say... If they feel that strongly about a poem, it's theirs."

When they passed the bookstore, she saw that it was still open, so she decided to stop and go inside for a moment. The owner was on a ladder rearranging some books on the shelf. The flavor of the place had not changed. Gallia watched the old man, as he scanned the shelves, reading titles out loud to himself. He was looking for a place to squeeze in a small green book he was holding, measuring its height against the rest of the volumes on each shelf. The rows were supposedly organized by publisher and year published. In the end, he slid the book between two others that were close enough in height and color, but several years off, and from a different publisher.

Gallia saw the shadows bending along the walls, the ceiling, the corners. There were at least seven other people meandering through the aisles. There were always at least this many but not many more. And they were always silent. In the poetry room, a man stood wearing a raincoat with the hood up. He read from a torn book, shaking his head. Shifting his weight, he would chance a glance over his shoulder, every few seconds. Whenever he did this, Gallia shifted too, hiding her curiosity. A dance (or something like it).

The man tore some pages out of the book and quickly walked out, hiding what he could, of his face.

"Hey! You need to pay for that!" The old man yelled.

Gallia walked over to him and asked if he wanted help contacting the police.

"No, if he wants it that badly, who am I to say."

And he went right back to rearranging the books on his shelves, putting them in the new order he'd discovered, by height and color first.

Gallia thought about stealing a poem. She stood in the doorway, trying to come up with a good one to search for. The old man watched her, eyebrows raised, no smile. Gallia let her eyes drop to the floor and adjusted her coat's collar. She exited the shop and resumed her trip to the party through the neighborhood roads.

When Gallia arrived, a group of loud media makers hurried toward her, asking an uneven array of stupid and smart questions. She answered whatever she could, then continued on.

"What are the structures on Mantis Green like?"

The last thing she heard before the doors closed behind

her, as she reached the check-in tables.

The structures…

Assuming that Gallia would later change her mind, several of the structures on Mantis Green had flexible parts. The cave could expand or contract with the simple touch of a button. The ceilings inside the house were designed tall but could be lowered at will. Then there was the garden. Only the top layer was visible; the other two were subterranean. They were accessible from the basement, and through an external elevator in the courtyard. We mimicked daytime and night-time underground, in the same way as on the dark side of the rock. It all came from the same flexi-panel domes that were attached to the bubble.

Most of the machinery on the rock was hidden in cork capsules. As a result, the landscape had a fantasy about it, a soft dreaminess that surely would have been appreciated by a character more alive than Gallia. I can only hope that the owl looked up once or twice and thought something of it.

A PROPER INTRODUCTION

Since I was a child, I've had a habit of removing myself completely. As a kid, I did it by way of imaginary life, and eventually I learned to do it literally.

I had come to live on Earth at the age of 17. My younger brother and I had sailed off from a nearby—and insignificant—planet full of highly skilled but disastrously passionate creatures. Upon landing on Earth, I stepped out of the ship onto a marshy stretch of land in Florida, with my brother's body in my arms. We had taken a wrong turn. I was trying to avoid a cloud of debris in the distance. I swung too far and delayed us more than a week. We didn't have enough supplies to last us the extended journey. My brother had stocked the ship himself. He took his own life and left me a note advising me to do the same, telling me it would be better than waiting to run out of air or water first. He was 14.

I had no chance to dissuade him. Once someone decides to die, if they mean it, they will be as efficient as possible and do it quickly and quietly. My brother killed himself in our ship, while I slept, six days prior to landing. He had left the note on top of his ice-cold chest, along with a small container of poison, half emptied. I should have packed emergency supplies. I should have pretended we weren't off-course. I could have suggested that we make a turn for a closer planet, just to pick up food and water. None of it would have worked. We both knew that. And if it hadn't been for my little brother taking his life, I would have never landed alive, for better or worse. It may have been nothing more than the firm and stable assertion of Earth's gravity, but I felt a great heavy shadow leaning its weight on me freely, like I deserved it. My mother had foreseen it.

She sang a song in front of a gathering for the holidays. Right before she stepped off the plaza stage, a man had come running from the other side of the street and up the saggy little steps. He ran right into her and stained her dress with his blood, where her heart was. She looked right at me and came running toward me and my brother, yelling,

"No, don't go! Don't go!"

She grabbed us firmly, pressing down on our shoulders with her fingers, as if to plant us into the ground.

"You'll never make it!"

She said it again and again, as she held me and my brother close. Her breath smelled hungry and tired. Then suddenly she stopped, she looked at us both, her expression hardened.

"You'll never make it,"

She said it one more time before walking away. My brother cried all the way home, then got angry, locked himself up in his room. Early the next day, a couple hours before sunrise, he came in and woke me up.

"Let's go. I'll be outside."

He whispered quickly, hissing almost, as he zipped up his bag and headed for the front door. I scrambled to gather my things and followed. My brother was desperate to leave Yarey. He had never felt at home there. And neither had I.

Living on Earth had been a dream of mine since before I can remember. I could see the Earth's glowing rim from my window for most of the year, except when the fog stayed thick throughout the day. I played out stories in my head of things I was witnessing, even though I couldn't make out any details. All the volatile conversations and fights and lawsuits, people arguing over parking spaces. I wanted the comfort and the confidence, the surplus. It's hard to say anymore who is "more advanced," although that's been a common infatuation of all involved for millennia.

We had almost moved once before, the whole family. I was in the single digits, my brother barely old enough to walk, my mother too old to feel *young* and my father too desperate to know he was being swindled. He signed us all up for an expensive expedition, privately owned and independently run by a group of recent graduates from some place famous. We made plans for where to go once we were there, what foods we would eat, what things we would buy and where. My father and mother about what jobs they would get. But my mother was suspicious and limited her participation to yesses, maybes and okays.

"Maybe it will work out, yes."

She grabbed and squeezed his hand while saying it. He was satisfied. I knew better. My mother looked up at me as she walked away and I knew we would not leave when the time came. She had a curious way of knowing things before they revealed themselves. Her intuition was so on point sometimes, that as a child, I had feared she was a witch and could see everything, always. My mother trusted nothing and no one, aside from her connection to nature, which was the main thing tying her to my father. They were opposites built on the same natural foundation. They connected with each other when they connected with everything else. My father often expressed his loneliness directly (and exclusively) to the plants he cared for so diligently. My mother admired him from afar. How he would give and receive so purely with the plants—and through that, with her.

Plans for the move continued, despite my mother's

skepticism. My father started selling some of our furniture, and even his car. On a cold day, a few months after planning began, my father cried. He cried for days, going on and on, something about a *deferment clause, had I known then what I know now*, etc.

His funeral was simple but well-attended, lightly catered but with an open bar. This we all believed: there's no use in dwelling in sober sorrow, too overwhelming and of no practical use. Physical pain, dehydration, exhaustion and headaches could work wonders when digesting grief.

My mother and her sister had delighted everyone with a twenty minute duet. Together, they had an impressive range and could melt the shared tension we were all feeling with their clean jousting harmonies.

I recorded them a few times, and would listen to the recordings at critical moments, when I felt overwhelmed. The funeral was the first one I recorded. I wasn't sure why, but I knew I wanted to hold onto those sounds for a while. Of course, I have always regretted having missed the first couple minutes, which were the reason I felt compelled to record in the first place. They had sung so perfectly, their voices acrobats improvising impeccably in a rubber jungle, colors that blend and separate in mid-air, lights dancing through prisms, and at no point was there a sense of struggle—or even effort—that would give it away that this sound was coming from two people's throats. Maybe it was not. I've often thought that maybe I hallucinated it all. It was my first time drinking heavily, so it could have been. Whatever it was, it registered as real and I have since believed it as such.

After the funeral, we all assembled outside for a procession. My aunt held my hand tightly and smiled at me tragically whenever I looked up at her. Her eyes were glassy and red. She apologized to me over and over and watched me for long stretches without blinking. Her eyes were amber yellow, almost green, and beautiful, even when swollen and irritated.

I hoped we would go home soon, but first we had to stop at the homes of several people, to accept gifts and food from them. We placed all the offerings in my brother's carriage, and my mom and aunt took turns carrying him. I don't think I have ever felt so alone and invisible in my life as I did that day. I felt like I was a part of what was going on, but I didn't get the sense that any of it was intended for my benefit. I feel selfish to this day for thinking that, but maybe it's not so far fetched that I wanted some focused sympathy for having lost a parent. In the end, I guess, everyone does, and why should I receive more sympathy than others?

For many years after that, until recently, I lived a more subdued experience in terms of my personal interactions—although it's hard to say when this started. I spent a lot of money once I got to Earth, making it a habit to indulge every whim

—just like everyone else, it seemed. But there's no comprehensive vantage point into any human's life that lets you see the whole, so I never knew if I was more or less indulgent than others, only that I was determined to try as hard as I could to emulate the happiness they distilled from their lifestyles, in the company of "friends," indulging in expensive treats, edible and otherwise, reading literature, going to museums and celebrating rites of passage. These things were not for me, but I was there, and so I took them. They never seemed to mean as much to me as they did to them, but I committed myself to playing the part, convinced that they were playing with me.

When I found myself the fool, at last, I had nothing to validate. I found myself with no choice but to follow the order established by that which I loved most: the lackadaisical social structure of this shiny blue marble, Earth. And I was grateful, from time to time, that instead of walking from place to place in a procession every time somebody died, I could go home alone and feel my sorrow, sober or not, real or fake, sincere and late. I was never one to celebrate or mourn, but I liked having the choice and the right. Being unfit is an option, not an abomination.

I mourned silently as I waited for the ship that would transport me off the surface of the Earth. I thought about my fish and Jones. I thought about my mother and aunt singing. I recalled what Covas had told me about his parents. They had been ideal Earth people: sunny dispositions, grateful attitudes, indulgent but unattached and singularly present. They had died in poverty but nonetheless happy. In their last few years, they had decided to join a walking pilgrimage. Sofia, the youngest, had died first. Atha had her remains composted and mixed into the soil of a field, at the base of a small tree, near the site of their last breakfast together. Seven months later, Atha also died. Her companions on the pilgrimage had her remains composted also. Then they walked her all the way back to Sofia and mixed her in, nearby, at the base of another small tree. Both trees thrived, despite droughts and floods and weeds. Covas showed me a million pictures of them during each season, at all hours. He derived great comfort from seeing his silent parents standing up, perennially green and bending slightly toward the sun.

"What is your biggest regret?" I asked him.

"They asked me to come along and I didn't."

While we spoke, Covas played with a leaf pendant he was wearing.

"I told them they wouldn't make it to the beach. It was a walk coast to coast."

"What'd they say to that?"

"They asked what I was planning to do with my time while they were gone and I told them I was going to school

167

and working."

"And that's when they regretted having you?"

He laughed and I wondered if my parents ever felt that way.

"They were actually really proud!"

"I don't believe it!"

"Yeah, they were. They were! They said I should do it all until there's nothing more to do. Lundlege Law."

"Were you proud of them?"

"Of course! They really soaked it all up. I wish I had it in me, like that, you know?"

"Well, we all go our own way."

"What about you? What were your parents like?"

I could have picked any number of pre-set descriptions I had used in the past, but I didn't feel that was fair. I described my father as quiet and my mother as strong, both passionate, both gifted, both virtuous. My words felt flimsy and insubstantial, but I didn't know what else to say. The time had come for me to stop presenting myself and I was just finding out that I had little more to give besides the recycled slideshow I had been using. I had nothing to say about my parents except list off some favorable adjectives about them. I was afraid that I didn't remember what they were and who they were. And if I had, what else had I forgotten?

Covas smiled at me briefly, conceding that enough time

had passed and that we should conclude our conversation. I wanted badly to turn it around and say something worth listening to, but I was out of material.

That night in the holding cell, I spoke to a man, Lawrence.

"Call me Lawry," he said.

"Lawry, what did you do?"

"What do you want me to say? It's them who don't see what I did is good. People disagree, you know?"

I didn't know what to say. I suppose I agreed, but I just didn't know. If I agreed, was I crazy? What was I agreeing with?

"Lawry, what did you do?" I asked.

"I tried to teach some kids a lesson about respect."

Ah. A fundamentalist. I knew what to say.

"Not like it used to be."

"Used to be when?"

"Just when it was more about decency, I guess."

"Decency's nothing. People like to think it doesn't vary person to person, but I think that's bull."

I tried to relate but found myself conjuring up others' opinions, making them my own, trying to care deeply about them. I felt like an unbeliever and a rotten heart. I couldn't decipher what this man wanted to talk about, so the conversation fizzled into, "Yeah that's right," and "Yup," and then a grunt. It didn't seem like he really cared about what I might have to say, anyway. His eyes never landed on mine. They either settled beyond me or just wandered past me. I didn't know whether to pity him or be jealous.

The best part of each day, since I had moved to Earth, was the point in time when the flame finally extinguished. When I ran out of energy, I knew I could feel comfort. I often enjoyed hot nights for this very reason. The point of exhaustion arrived more quickly. And anyway, the flame was a driving agent, turning things into a blur. It was great for going places, but the moment it extinguished, the emptiness was heavy, a clue and an instinct. Much more missing at rest. Very few times I felt a density in this space. Last time was my tour of Mantis Green, a proud review of my designs come to life. Before that, not much. A couple times, when I tried something new. And the greatest density of all, the day I became a Citizen of Earth, even if it only lasted a few months.

Farah Ysvette Mourad Vera

THE EDGE DOES GLOW

A golden curve reflected in his eyes, Milian sat on the dark green steps by the window of his old bedroom, in an enclosure whose squeeze he'd come close to forgetting for good. It wasn't especially comfortable but rather comforting. There was nothing on the walls, and to disrupt the path of echoes, there were just a few pieces of unremarkable furniture. He didn't recognize any of it, nor should he have, for no piece had a single memorable detail on it. Still, the wallpaper made confessions about the place's history and meaning. Milian had hid in here many times, tracing the designs in the wallpaper in a daze. He fell to its siren song now, recalling specific thoughts, music, faces, conflicts…

Bathed in the immediate darkness of the room, the glow of the rim of the Earth seemed a stately and expensive illusion, claiming his drooling fool's gaze, brighter than anything else in the room. At times it seemed to dim, only to freshen its glimmer seconds later, as if the planet itself could breathe. There's nothing more beguiling in the experience of living than seeing a whole planet from far away.

I remembered seeing my own Yarey from Earth, forgetting the stickiness of its spongy marsh, disregarding the memories of its tart rain, singing praises to its towns whose people I had, on a daily basis, wished to trade in for a more idealistic throng of minds and voices.

It was strange now to see such liveliness so still and yet the perception was familiar. Milian had been endlessly ignited as a child, curious and energized; as an adult, he feared almost everything and stopped himself often. He knew the disappointment stemmed from his hesitation, but he dared not defy it and trusted that, in time, it would bring some kind of recompense, be it palpable or mystical.

It had been some time since he had thought of his original dream, a recurrence of long departed nights. In it, he had stood right on the edge of that blue marble, riding it like a wave, sliding down its very face, with soft shoes too big for his feet.

And what would have been the point of stopping?

You go around once, you go around twice, the graceful glow multiplies until you're blind. You stop when you need to or want to and not because someone else told you to.

All this was conveyed within the dream, by way of

implicit logic. And there seemed to be string attachments from the bed of each ocean directly into his veins in the dream.

As a young child, he had known his share of blood transfusions, having had "bad blood" until the family switched doctors. He received his last transfusion a few months before his 12th birthday. From then on, the dream continued the tradition in pantomime alone. The specific sensations of the procedure took a back seat to the sensations of the sport.

And if he ever started to fall, the strings would solidify, crutch-like, to hold him up. Within each dream, there would come a point where Milian knew to make note of any differences. He would catalogue them in a notebook he had learned to summon in these lucid opportunities. Still, he only afforded himself this luxury a couple of times, and had diagnosed the differences as immaterial upon his wakeful review. I wonder when it stopped. Or do I dream it still but just ignore it? Is it always different? Is it ever empty? A trick of the mind to pass over old information.

Adopting fault for his orphaned fantasy, Milian averted his eyes from the glow, feeling its fanciful gaze pointed back on his person. As he gawked idiotically, through the thick of the stars, away from the dearest little planet, he was startled by a shadow. A dark formlessness swinging past the window, then inexplicably inside the tiny room with him, landing a cold heavy hand on his chest.

MANTIS GREEN

Milian thought he was dead for a moment, his tongue swollen and dry in his open mouth, his eyes surrendered, his spine stretched tight and taut. Upon remembering how to breathe, he looked around, saw no hand on his chest, no shadow behind. When he looked back out the window he feared a second encounter so much that he shivered himself awake.

I can't stand those dreams; so real they feel like I've been found out for crimes I can't remember committing. They've come for me, for good.

Hunger.

Is that it?

The glow demanded one more look and after obliging, Milian stood up, bound for the pantry, craving salt.

The pantry was half stocked; mostly condiments and spices, a couple cans of artichoke hearts and a variety of boxed beans. In the refrigerator: bread, half a carton of eggs, milk... a dozen other staples, some leftovers wrapped in foil and a tray of medications. All assuming a continuation.

Bowl of artichoke hearts and a glass of milk. Salt sprinkled on the artichokes. Cocoa powder in the milk. Clink clank, clink clank, clink clank, *Ring*. Clink... They're here.

The hallway leading to the front door was covered in family photographs and drawings (most of them Milian's... age 6 or 8 or 9, etc.) and Milian wanted to stop and look at them again, but the pounding on the door urged him to bypass the sentimentality.

After it's all over, he promised himself.

He caught a glimpse of a poem he had written to his mother on Valentine's Day, possibly age 7. He continued down the hall toward the door, rehearsing a haggard face, exaggerating his expression of grief. He opened the door. Looking back at him—and dreading the encounter half as much—was a plant delivery girl.

"Delivery for Mr. Milian Sieglund?"

"Oh. Thank you."

The girl handed him a pot of red and yellow Lally flowers, smiling. The flowers just as chipper. Milian took the pot, holding onto his frown like a shield.

"Thanks."

The girl scanned through her tasks quickly, making sure she had said hello, pronounced the name correctly and successfully delivered the plant. She smiled again, nodded and turned around to leave.

"Have a nice night!"

"Is there a card or a message?"

"Oh, I'm sorry! Yes, it's inside—Well... let me..."

The girl walked back and reached inside the bouquet to fetch the tiny card. It was smaller than a business card and the envelope was clear. "A terrible loss. Love, Daliya Sieglund."

"Thanks."

"Sure! Bye!" She said and then tottered away with her delivery cart.

He watched her leave, her form melting into a silhouette, then a blur, down the street. Resolving to go for a walk, he set the flowers down on a scratched up credenza, which was nestled between the front door and the door to the parlor.

If anyone showed up now, they'd wait for me out of guilt.

Had everything remained the same?

The inhabitants of this neighborhood were a proud and responsible bunch, not very interested in the Earth-established ambitions, arts, achievements, etc., consistently righteous, but not always kind. Milian spied on some neighbors: an old man and his dog, whose loyalty far exceeded the man's worth. The man ate from a bowl and spat out some scraps for the dog to lick up. It seemed to Milian a gesture of *unnecessary disrespect*.

The street yielded to his every step with its signature sponginess, which he had once despised. Now that he'd returned, there were few things he wanted to do as much as walk on this marsh, barefooted, so that's what he did. Milian sat on the sidewalk and took his shoes off, setting his feet down on the wet road, which sank tightly around his footprint, infusing his skin with its mineral moisture. Unlike the littered streets of his dear planet Earth, the roads back home were pristine and natural, no sharpness or excessive heat to be

176

wary off, no bits of glass or pebbles anywhere, and so Milian walked for at least two miles before the sun shied away from his face. Before turning around to follow his footprints back home, he caught a smell that displaced his thoughts.

Jarcina's had been a childhood favorite. Milian recalled waking up very early to help his mother pick up and carry groceries. He couldn't remember now if it was a periodic task or just a once-in-a-while interval, but whatever the frequency, he remembered the experiences all the same. Getting up that early was a nauseating experience, even though he had usually been awake already, waiting out the rest of the night in bed, allowing time for the sun to dry the coat of mist off the streets. His mother would burst in before the first rays split through the window, revealing the textures and imperfections of the green steps below it. She would sit next to him and run a finger down his face, from the top of his forehead to the tip of his nose, asking, "Good morning?" expecting an answer, eventually.

Yes. Every time, yes. What else could I say but yes? An unfair trick, he thought, but he'd get over it quickly. Soon his hair would be washed and combed, his teeth brushed, clean clothes on and he'd be strolling down the street with his mother, visiting shop after shop, where each shopkeep felt compelled to gift him an old candy or cheap trinket.

They all knew his mother and stayed up to date on

what was happening in her life. It's good that she had so many friends, he thought, but each conversation delayed the shopping even more. Halfway through the series of visits, Milian's stomach would begin to churn. He would double over and swing side to side to signal to his mother that they had overstayed and should move on to the next shop.

The trip always ended the same way: I would be so hungry and angry, I would swear to her I'd never come along ever again. And then, she would take me to the bakery.

"Second batch is the best," *She would say.*

She'd buy an assortment of sour and salty breads, and some sweet rolls for dessert. She'd have the same conversation I'd already heard 6 times, with the baker. Almost immediately after she was asked how so-and-so was doing this week, I'd double over and get ready to swing. She'd call over to me and ask,

"Do you want a cola roll or a palmier?"

I'd stare at the chocolate cookies, wondering if I should risk it, but almost always I chose the palmier.

"You like fancy sweets!" *The baker would say every time, as if he'd never said it to me before. Palmiers had a distinct taste, but I know now that the real ones from Earth taste nothing like the ones from home, and I don't know why.*

I wonder if he's still around.

Milian turned at the corner, where he remembered the bakery used to be. The awning was there, exactly the same and still in almost the same condition, if anything just a little more settled into its frame. The door had changed and the decor too, but not too much. However, the place did seem significantly smaller now.

Before he could register the baker's face behind the counter, he recognized the scent of the assorted breads. His eyes watered and his throat seized up.

"Can I help you?" asked the baker.

Milian swallowed the lump in his throat and covered his face with both hands, pretending to yawn, taking a moment to wipe his eyes.

"Excuse me. So many options." He responded, watching the baker, who luckily had looked away at some point and missed Milian's embarrassing performance.

"Sour round? Cheese fold-ins? We also have some fresh madeleine cookies over there, if you want a couple—I can throw some in?"

"Um... do you have any—" Milian scanned the cases, concerned.

"Cola roll?"

Spotting his one and only, Milian raised his finger and pointed it at the middle shelf.

"Palmier please?"

"How many?"

"Just one."

But as expected, while the baker put the pastry in a bag, Milian changed his mind.

"I'll take a half dozen, actually."

"Oh ok. Any madeleines?"

"Half a dozen of those too."

"Great. Any salty bread? Sweet rolls?"

"No thanks, that's good."

Milian paid for the box of treats, eyes on the baker, wondering if he should say anything else.

"You like fancy sweets!" The baker said.

That's good enough for me.

"I do." He smiled and paid.

"Thank you."

"Buh-bye now."

"Bye."

Milian opened the box and pulled out a palmier to eat. It didn't taste like the ones from Earth but it also didn't taste like the ones he had just reminisced about a few moments ago. By the time he got home, he had eaten one more and was finishing a madeleine, which tasted better than the pre-packaged ones he had tried on Earth.

When he arrived at the house, he saw a note on the door. All it said was: *Missed delivery. Please call to reschedule.*

No one came.

Milian sat back down over the bowl of artichoke hearts and chocolate milk that he had left on the table. The salt had turned into tiny droplets of moisture and a dusty rim of cocoa powder had formed at the edge of the glass. He opened the box of sweets, which he had set down beside it and ate a madeleine cookie in one bite.

Several hours later, Milian was still at the table, in the dark, with his head resting on his forearms, face to the side, eyes open, studying the circuit box, whose little lights flickered in seemingly random patterns.

No one came. I suppose they might have been unaware that I had come back. I didn't have a chance to tell anybody except my aunt, who is not a great keeper of secrets, or so I thought.

Milian dreaded the idea of seeing visitors upon his return, but now that there weren't any, he resented their absence, especially considering the situation.

The phone rang. It was a woman from the service office. Milian made arrangements for his mother's cremation to take place in the morning. The body would be picked up tonight, within the next couple hours.

"She's our last pick up, so we'll definitely be there before nine."

"Thank you."

"Sorry for your loss, sir. Good night."

"Thanks. Good night."

When the pickup arrived, the process took no more than 15 minutes. All the documents had been pre-completed by the insurance company, so all Milian had to do was sign and watch as they took his mother's body from the parlor, placed it in a bag and slid it onto a rack in a refrigerated van. The driver handed Milian a paper receipt for the pickup, and an appointment slip with the address and time of the cremation. Milian thanked him and they were off. He watched the van disappear in the haze, which was thick as clouds by now. He could barely make out the light post twelve feet ahead.

Back inside the house, the emptiness was hard and unforgiving. It's uncertain how long Milian stood against the front door, afraid to journey through the murky hall back to his room upstairs. The thought of being assaulted by the shadows on the other side, although absurd, was a terror growing on his spine like moss on a wet rock.

As a child he had seen his father's dead face across from his own. He had kissed his cheek, not knowing it would be cold and stiff, like chilled chicken meat. The nasty memory had never left him, even though he could never remember any details regarding the circumstances under which such a thing was allowed to happen.

Milian sat on the floor with his back against the door, where he mercifully was allowed to fall asleep. He awoke several hours later, when the night was at its darkest, when the shapes of large shadows were his only tools of navigation. He felt his way around the furniture, sensing the distance between the rooms with the little capability left in his muddy senses. Luckily the stairs were close to the entrance. He found the way up to his old bedroom, guided by the luminous haze glowing through its window. Lamenting the bleak view, he pressed his head against the pillow, sank into it and drifted off to sleep again.

Before he knew it, he found himself outside the window, floating in the haze, unable to make a sound or touch anything. Most things were just out of reach and no movement could draw him closer to any potential anchor. The haze seemed to suffuse with him, dissolving his body and diluting his consciousness. He felt his perspective change to that of the fog's (although upon waking, he'd be unable to reconcile the nature of such a feeling). Time and time again, he tried to grasp himself and remain with his parts incorporated, but the drifting and dissolving overcame his intentions with a natural power.

I can't stop it.

He awoke breathing hard and heavy, with a rush of terror running through him, a searing heat on his face. He felt a ray of sun hot enough to cut into his skin, like a laser. The atmosphere was fragile and he was afraid he had gone blind.

MANTIS GREEN

For a moment, it really did feel like he had suffused with the haze, until a loud noise perked him up: a ring from a clock.

For the first time in years, he had almost been woken up by an alarm.

What a night. And yet I feel so free.

Ashes release me, release us together.

Farah Ysvette Mourad Vera

ASHES

I punished myself by overthinking at night, in between bad dreams. Good ones rarely ended suddenly. There was no wakefulness to contend with, no shadows to squint into static shapes. But I imagined a million ways to turn good dreams into bad, just so I could shake myself awake, afraid that I had died or eager to find myself in a different place. Dreaming seemed infrequent but the terrors were a habit. I didn't have to drift into a fantasy to recall the dread or intimate sadness that exposed me.

The cremation went well, if that's an appropriate thing to say. The morning was hazy still in parts. The Memorial Tower stood amidst—and rose way above—the haze, lending its tenants an immaculate view of the skies. Had any of them still been able to appreciate it, they might have felt like angels. Visitors, however, could enjoy the celestial loneliness hugging the windows of the ornate halls in their own weepy and distracted ways.

Rows of carefully contained remains stretched endlessly along a spacious corridor. A few steps more and there it was: 40-03.

MANTIS GREEN

Milian stood in front of a cubby the size of a shoebox. In it, he placed the sealed urn containing his mother's ashes. A page carrying his mother's skull placed it carefully atop the urn. Then Milian closed the little door, which was decorated with layered strips of crystal engraved with his mother's name and address, and the dates of her birth and death. That was all. It looked like a tiny treasure chest in a glass case, worthy of a hefty price tag. For a moment, Milian entertained the thought of a mindless debutante opening a glossy box of ashes, dirtying herself with his mother's burnt-up bones. He smiled to himself.

The light through the windows was stronger now, filtered by less haze. The mountains were visible, even if only in silhouette.

I haven't been there in a while. Haven't thought much about it either.

He recalled a hike when he was younger. His grandmothers had taken him. They both had worn high heels and had hiked the whole way straight without complaining once. He and his brother had sat down twice to rest, while the grandmothers argued. They argued the whole way about nothing Milian could remember. He did remember, though, that the dirt was very dry. It hadn't rained for months. He had slipped and scraped his elbow and couldn't wait to be back home. The grandmothers argued and hurried along, in their

186

heels, not minding any of the narrow corners or protruding roots, stopping only to tell Milian and his brother to be quiet and keep going. By the time they reached the car, Milian didn't want to go home anymore.

A pharmacy was all I wanted. The sting was sharp and hot.

They went to a pharmacy, had his elbow cleaned and bandaged and then fed him and his brother some lunch. Milian was scared. Always scared.

The scrape healed quickly, within a day or two. He stopped paying attention to it until the scab started to come off in the shower. Then, again, he was scared. Always scared. This time, scared that the scab was just the beginning. Scared of what it meant.

The street had started to fill with people. Plenty of people but not a lot of sounds. Knowing there was no reason to wait, Milian headed the opposite way from home, to the eastern mountains.

I missed the birds. In the mornings, I'd watch them fly over the house. On good days, they would land nearby and I could hear them. But if I slept in too long, I'd miss them completely.

There was a small brook running through one of my spots in the eastern mountains that trickled down from Glecoe Peak, a tall, snowcapped summit usually hidden by the buildings and the rest of

187

the mountains in front of it. It had never made any sense to me that Glecoe Peak was so hard to spot from the heart of the valley, it being so much higher than everything else. The Eiffel Tower is a lot smaller than I thought it would be, but the Peak isn't small at all.

Milian arrived at the base of a hill, where the trail began. He followed it for nearly an hour, until he noticed the rim of the Earth peeking over the horizon on the other side. Milian went on for a few more steps until he spotted a bench, where he sat, watching Earth take a peek over the mountain in the distance. He wondered if anyone was using his name, as he watched. Or if Sylvia had moved. If anyone wondered if he had died.

Maybe I'm still there and this is all a stress-induced delusion.

Milian watched his dear little planet dissolve into the fog. As the rim of the Earth became fuzzier, he remembered the hour-long walk he'd have to embark on before reaching the base of the hill again. He looked down for most of the way, trying to keep track of the road. The fog was dense. It would have been easier to see the trail if he were much shorter. And as it got late, the light cutting through it became warm and diffused. The fog was nothing but millions of little mirrors reflecting the orange light in all directions. Milian couldn't see much. He was happily lost in the fiery cloud. He walked on and on, relying on his feet to stay on the same textured trail until he could hear the sound of the street change. Then, he'd follow the wind tunnels into the city, heading slightly west.

By then, the glare should have gone down and I should be able to see the silhouettes of the neighborhood.

Milian found his way back easily. He had done it many times before, a long time ago. It all came back to him instantly. The landscape was still similar to how it was when he was a child, although he didn't love the underlying scent of the place anymore. Sulfur and mushrooms, nearing a fresh carrion smell. An organic place, rotting here and there a little bit at a time. No one else seemed to mind it much. After all, they probably didn't realize the smell was even there.

Milian recognized the silhouette of his house across the street, but it seemed narrower somehow. He approached it before testing the street lamp with his mother's key fob. When he pressed the button, it flickered three times and he knew he had found it. He was pleased with himself but unsettled at the way he had felt about the house just then. As if the home had been shrinking all along and eventually it would vanish, many years after he, himself, had vanished from this world in some way.

As he readied for sleep, Milian recalled the sound of explosions nearby. He and his mother hiding under the stairs until the bombing stopped, then they had turned on the news to find out what happened. A coup to force the president out. Milian couldn't have understood much about this and what had caused it or what it sought to achieve, but there it was stamped in his memory like a prisoner's tattoo, holding together bits of his history and reasons why Earth had emerged as a solution to the pounding problem. It was hardly thought through, but it made the most sense in an uncertain time.

I was watching the painting on the wall. Violent scenes of a traditional sport, cruel things done by one to another "lesser" living thing. The joy of killing. After a loud blast, I looked at the phone and wondered why no one was calling to make sure we were ok. Were they hiding too? It seemed probable enough that the explosions were much further than I thought. We spent a couple hours under the stairs and didn't come out until we heard other voices outside. Once we did, we emerged, clutching each other, too hesitant to speak. We turned on the news and listened. Calm and technical, the reporters gave summaries of what and why and instructions on what to do (or not to do) next.

Next, we remained silent for the rest of the night. We didn't sleep much. Every sound was magnified in our ears. The shadows of the plants in the courtyard seemed to claw toward me, they seemed so real that I armed myself with a pair of scissors from my desk and decided to ask for a door with a lock for my birthday—if I made it to my birthday. I don't know if the breeze just stopped or if closing my eyes for a while was enough to deter the shadows from grabbing at me, but I must have dozed off because the morning came unannounced and without a gradual change in light. The next day I was very sick.

I had asthma as a child and it was difficult for me to understand the imagery triggered by these attacks. Hallucinations of schoolmates, their skin twisting up tightly into balls and knobs. I wasn't sure whether they expected me to help them or not. I feared getting lost in a fold of their skin if I approached too closely, but at times they seemed to plead for help, so I tried. Finally, a neighbor would come by with a special oil on her hands. She would hold me and shadow me with her hands until I let her enter my vision and take center. She spoke in notes close to one another in a lower register than her normal speaking voice. She almost whispered. Until I heard her, she whispered. I would gradually lose sight of the twisted skins of my schoolmates, and then her face would emerge, gentle and pitying me. "Poor child," she'd say. Her sister would bring me some food, some of the best food I've ever had in my life. They were both big women with very dark hair, beautiful dark eyes, older than my mother. They knew to recite words to banish my asthma, and I was grateful for that.

In the dark fog of the latest part of night, a startling series of crashing sounds nudged me out of a dream. They first arrived as a sudden bombing across a surreal landscape. I ran, steps sinking into a hot sticky tar. Stars too bright to look at, and an enormous corpse *running after me, pale green and sweaty, reaching for me. A blast hit near my face and I thought I could feel its heat burning my hair. I felt the stiff fingers of the corpse graze the skin between my shoulder blades, but just before it could grip me, I woke to find only the sound of frantic pounding on the door. It was my aunt Daliya. She'd showed up after all, not to pay her respects but to announce that my mother's grave had been desecrated.*

When I arrived at the building, a guard was waiting. He said a gang had broken in and smashed open two whole floors worth of tombs.

"But they left the heads at least." He said, consolingly.

I went up to my mother's grave. They had smashed open the urn and taken the box of ashes from it, and yes, they left the head, but not in its sacramental wrapping. They took that too. So I stood there, looking my mother in the eye sockets, wondering if some part of her felt any pain or shame. I reacquainted myself with a deep fear of black magic. Can they harm her in death? Or is leaving the skull an act of mercy?

I wasn't sure what to do.

"Well, take it and let's go to the police." *My aunt said.*

Take it? The head, she meant?

My aunt grabbed my mother's skull unceremoniously, placed it in a paper bag and handed it to me. My arms felt weak and tremulous, like they would crumble any second. Ashes.

We walked for an eternity to the police station. I shifted the

192

bag from one side to the other back and forth, unable to find a comfortable way to carry it. Finally, when we entered the station I sat down and placed it on the coffee table in the waiting room. Immediately regretting the action, I picked her back up and let her rest on my lap. My aunt filled out the report. A policeman came to inspect my mother's skull and had me sign some papers. Then we were off. I can't remember any words that were said, only an echo of drums and prayers.

RESTING PERIOD

Unable to substantiate a place for the emotions I was host-
ing—more because of their variety than their intensity—I sank into
a binge. I ate and ate until my stomach hurt and then I went to sleep
on my mother's bed, with her skull out by the front door. I had placed
it on top of a stack of mail on a little marble-top table, next to my
keys.

The image was familiar. Months prior on Mantis
Green, Gallia had found herself glued in a similar spot. Both
had hauntings to go along with it.

Gallia's:

In the middle of a dark blue night, after swimming up
to the base of a dock, Gallia made her way up what looked like
cement stairs. The steps weren't able to support her weight, so
her feet sank into each one. They became progressively softer,
as she emerged from the water, each step a block of thick, soft
clay. It started to rain. The clay got even softer, the mud mud-

dier. Her feet sank deeper. No sky above, just shards of water trying to pin her down. In spite of the attack, she climbed the last set of mud mounds, grabbed onto a rusty dock cleat and pulled herself up onto the wood. She cut her foot on an old nail, but there was no blood. The wound was a distended gash, stuffed with a brown mass that looked like black mochi dough. The gash produced no pain, just the gummy ooze and its associated discomfort, so she continued walking, without tending to it.

Is it stuffed with mud?

The dock house was much newer than the rest of the structure, but it was still simmered in ocean water. Inside was a small food stand. Fish and rice. Plantains. She ordered and sat down to eat. Then, for one reason or another, she looked down the hall and had the sinking feeling that she had been found. A pair of dried-up eyes stared her down. Then a dozen decaying hands broke through the floor and dragged her down into the mud below. Before her face went under, upon thinking about the approaching possibility of swallowing mud while trying to breathe, she awoke to find the storm system out of control, water creeping into her bedroom.

Milian's:

He was a tourist in an ancient place. Discolored blocks of rock sunken into one another rose up at various heights all over the place, like crystal formations. He looked around for a few seconds here and there while looking for the food court. When he found it, he sat at a table and waited. Just then, a great massive jolt of the Earth shook every structure, old and new. Many people fell to their knees together, in one beat. Milian stared up at a sculpture of an ancient God as it toppled toward him. He tried to calculate the best angle to use for an escape, and was convinced that he had found it until he saw his mother, closing in on him, screaming at his face. He was dead and he knew it, because of her eyes. They couldn't connect with his own. They searched and found nothing to hook onto.

Her helplessness upon seeing my husk.

I awoke from this nightmare to find myself panting and pleading to the pillows. Kneeling before them horizontally, begging them to let me off, like something from an old little book. Then I worried. I worried and regretted until the sun had cut through the haze.

Milian spent much of the following day repeatedly walking past his mother's skull, just to make sure it was still there. He never looked at it directly.

I don't want her thinking I'm coming back over and over just to check. Still, it's nice to know every time I see it that it hasn't been stolen and that it hasn't moved on its own. It's a strange fear I have.

For several weeks, Milian stayed home with the skull, leaving only to pick up more artichokes and Madeleines, which were all he seemed capable of eating. Once he'd tried eating eggs—and on a separate occasion, cheese—and he had buried his head in the toilet bowl until he'd tired himself out. When he did go outside, he would wrap the skull in newsprint and carefully place it in his backpack. When he ran out of newsprint, he used some of his drawing paper. He found the latter preferable because, since it was thicker, it provided better insulation between the bone and his hands, which made the whole thing feel less grotesque.

A week and a half paraded past Milian's attention. He had spoken no words and slept very little, eaten just enough and experienced a series of visions. One particular evening, he had sat in the bathtub until the water went cold. He had lost himself in half-wakefulness. The water felt like hardened cement and he thought he heard an alarm going off, maybe screams, drumming, sirens, thunder, rain. Violent rain. Buckets pouring inorganically. All went dark and he felt cold solidifying rock suppressing his breathing capacity, the deafening storm sounds, mechanical ones, drilling through his ears into his brain. At best, he hoped for a nightmare. At worst, he didn't know what to hope for. Slowly the sounds fell away and the cement turned to sand. It would have been an upbeat ending to the vision, except he could see the rain in the room, accumulated inches of it swelling up from the floor. He thought of Mantis Green.

Farah Ysvette Mourad Vera

IT HAD BEEN STORMY BEFORE (ON MANTIS GREEN)

It started with a long, sustained and exhausted scream. It continued with a yelp and a revved up shout, a discordant, "Ahhhhh!" that resonated against every surface and made it physically painful to witness. Covas watched her from afar. Just watch and wait. And listen.

Fear is a curious and powerful thing. For several nights, Covas waited outside of the house, hoping Gallia would emerge. Inside, Gallia just watched old TV shows and flipped through the same three old magazines. The barley grass machine was caked in green dust and a yellow sappy substance. All of the furniture was wet and on every surface there was mildew. The storm system had been broken for quite some time, but without a formal complaint, no one volunteered to come out and make repairs. It had become too difficult to maintain the gardens. Gallia had requested not to be disturbed, for any reason, until further notice.

"I'll make enough noise for you to know I'm fine."

Covas had no choice but to comply with her wish and take her offer as enough.

Every few nights (or days), the storm system would come on in the entire house. Since the drains were clogged with weeds, the house would flood. Gallia always reacted to it differently. Sometimes, she would scream or cry, and other times, she would play in it, or simply sit in it. If it was too cold, she would sit and shiver on the floor for a while.

Covas was afraid of finding her dead one day. He never saw her anymore, and the only way he knew she was still alive was from hearing her scream every now and again. A terrible thing, that a scream should bring him such relief. He did wonder a couple times, if the sounds were maybe coming from a machine or from the creaking of an unstable piece of furniture about to collapse.

A preemptive court order initiated by Gallia herself, executed and communicated by her estate, kept him from interfering with her lifestyle. He could only respond to attacks from the outside or to specific requests from the inhabitant herself. Or, if such a scenario should arrive, if the habitat monitors returned empty activity reports for the agreed-upon length of time: three days. Sylvia had provided some solace.

"I will come once a month and check in. She doesn't want to be bothered otherwise, no matter what."

From Gallia's journal:

"I engaged plenty. Finally, I'll be on my own land, my own terms, my own process. I can cry and no one will hear. I can laugh at what I find funny. I can dance or sleep for as long as I want and no one can tell me otherwise. I don't have to leave because of weather or pests. I will be at peace, finally. Two more months of this and it's over. No quakes or blizzards or termites or fundraisers or dinners. Just me and this planet at its best, from afar."

Then there were several pages of doodles, poor attempts at figure drawings of herself and the owl. Maybe one of Sylvia on Sondras Alluma—that much could be assumed from her doodle of what looked like the Stratos Station behind the figure, and her poor attempt at sketching ethnicity.

On Mantis Green, she had slowly become accustomed to everything being wrong or broken. She collected piles of notes, scribbles, doodles and drafts. Many of them didn't make it. We found piles of ashes that we later determined were all previously paper or clothing.

She had run out of most food, so she would forage in the gardens whenever she got hungry. She ate some of her clothing, also, whatever she hadn't burned. She had been naked for at least 67 days by the time she died, her toenails encrusted with soot.

LONESOME TARGETS

Lonesome targets can be easier to miss, on account of mercy and the like. Pity, even. A humble awakening. A realization of the self. A manifestation of the meaning of existence. Killing a thing is a spiritual hit. Depth comes in horror, screaming truth at your face. At least, that's how I imagine it would be. Perhaps I'm wrong. But anyway, what business do we have judging the complexity of living and its untimely ending?

Milian thought that, as long as he could forget himself and become who he wanted to be, the hardest questions to answer could be avoided. The overwhelming pressure of meaning would simply squash him on the spot, and so he lingered in a space of survival and held on by one tiny digit on one hand on one arm and was, at all times, about to fall off. Sanity, then, became a struggle and a tedious burden.

In strenuous moments, he wished to yield to nature itself, as perverse and perverted as it is, and accept his place as a tool and nothing more.

Farah Ysvette Mourad Vera

Relinquish existence! It demands.

What lost thought travels? The indignation only stemming from a wish to persist; to endure. The moment where it turns. A dancer often gives in to a dance the same way. "No going-back," they should call it. And for what reason other than it may just be too painful to live through this basic allotment? Pain that may actually kill you, and not from shock, but from its colossal weight.

What tired eyes can gaze upon their limbless, torn body's shreds and live to tell it? This is a hundred times' worth. Dignity and ethics may matter little in life, but history is a funny thing. Reckless and arrogant; an accomplice and a crook, like any of us may be. The specifics differ, but the impact is shared.

What pointless wordlessness to indulge in and pretend with. The better the atmosphere, the higher the value.

New can be very effective. And old can be comforting.

Whatever this means is meaningless.

MORNING COMES AGAIN

In the dream, I was a kind of bird. My wings were heavy and sore. I had recently just got them and had used them for the first time. I found out that although I could fly, I did not have an aptitude for it. I resolved to work at it, hard, until I could fly from one plateau to the other without sinking into the valley in between. The valley was full of trees and vines draped across the spaces and hollows, set up like funneled spider webs.

And in the dream, I noticed a road in the valley that I might try to get to if I fall. All the while, planning not to need it at all. But as I tried to prepare for flying, my wings cramped up, then they hardened, then they fell off, and I wondered what I would do with no wings and no arms. This must be what it's like to be an ostrich. My legs were strong and lean and long, but they too ached when I tried to use them. They became stiff and the feet melted into the ground. I worried that they'd crumble, but they just hardened the same way that the wings did. It would have been more merciful if they'd fallen off the same way, but they did not. Instead they kept me there, swinging like a flag on a pole. I wanted to scream, but I knew I wouldn't be heard. So I tried to sleep and dream myself elsewhere.

When I awoke, I did very little. I stared at the cloud pressed against my window for what seemed like a handful of instants but was actually much longer: at least twenty minutes. Afterwards, I felt too warm, so I changed my clothes and washed my face in the bathroom.

I packed my mother's skull and went for a walk. The haze was still nestled in between the buildings, glazing the rooftops just slightly. I forced myself to look as far as I could and my eyes landed on a patch of purple far off, behind downtown. I couldn't remember what was in that area, so I headed there to find out.

For five and a half hours, I walked straight without stopping and still the patch was there in the distance. When the haze started to lift, I saw it had a texture. The road that led to the center of the patch seemed to come from much further than where I had ended up, so I stopped for a snack and a drink at a place I'd never been: Cifino's Lodge. I regretted stopping there instead of the pizza place I remembered, which was only a few blocks away.

Better stop walking now, was how I put it. I should have followed up with,

MANTIS GREEN

But *what's a few blocks more?*

Oh well, one soggy sandwich later, my head was close enough to the curb to kiss it. I remarked to myself that I had at least chewed my food very well, as I watched it flow away from me. I continued on with an emptier stomach than when I began this interminable walk.

After two more hours trekking, I heard the drums. I followed the sound in the direction of the patch, which was now green and blue and brown and many other colors, except purple. The sun started going down, the fog rolling in. As I got closer, the "patch" disappeared into more of the same land-scape I had been seeing for hours.

I caught a flicker in the corner of my eye; a fire. The drums were coming from there. I followed my curiosity all the way to the source of the fire and the drums, to a beach full of people. The drums were hollowed out trees mounted by three or four drummers each, who banged on their surface rhythms of anger and pain. The one closest to me played a heartbeat, a percussive plea for life. These people had been my neighbors and possibly school mates, but they played with the bones of the dead. Were those my mother's hands drumming? If so, I hoped they drummed the heartbeat. If not, I wished someday they would.

No one on the beach paid any attention to me. What they were doing was that important, or maybe they assumed I was participating, or maybe my presence was merely irrelevant. Anyway, I watched them dance and get loose, fall down and get up laughing, some of them crying on their knees, an older woman praying like the act would physically transform her in any second. I envied her most.

The sky was dark and green now. The air felt wet. And I was too hungry and tired to walk the nearly eight hours back home, so I continued on to where I'd spotted a train station and waited for the next train heading back to my neighborhood. On the train, I saw many blank faces and many lively ones. The lively ones had color and a changing quality. The blank ones were stale and contorted, unfeeling and for the most part, ugly. There were more lively faces than dead ones, but I envied them all, so I could not engage in their dances.

I checked my bag for the skull, finding it exactly where I had last seen it, wedged in a perfect spot that dug into my side at an appropriately uncomfortable angle. I felt the need to rub the eye sockets—something I had felt before but refused to indulge. It didn't seem appropriate or safe to do it on the train, so I waited to get home. Small compulsive urges.

When I got home, I took the skull out and set it on the table in front of me. It felt wrong to prod it, so I walked away to make myself a bowl of artichokes with salt. I thought back to Cifino's Lodge and regretted it again, but most of all I was just glad to be home.

MANTIS GREEN

FOLLOWING A GHOST

Days later, Milian followed the drums again, but he didn't reach the village until dark. It occurred to him that, should anything happen, he could always use his mother's skull as some kind of protection. Either they'd be superstitious enough to believe whatever he said the skull might do to them, or they'd be sane enough to know not to take a chance with someone who carries a skull in their backpack.

The drumming was hard and passionate. The three men playing were focused and at the same time lost, captured by whatever they had surrendered to for the duration of the music (or ritual). A woman came forth. She wore a shimmering white robe. The rhythm of the music changed, as she stepped on the hot sand, near the fire. Swaying along to the music, she took the robe off and threw it near the fire. Milian, the crowd, the woman... they all watched the robe burn. The drummers continued without looking up.

One large flame detached itself from the rest of the rolling fire. All acknowledged it. Even Milian felt its presence.

209

He felt another presence too, that of a face that's been looking at you your whole life. Someone you don't know but whose features you surely recognize. It was impossible to tell whose face it was, as Milian saw traces of it in several people, in and out of the campsite.

Milian slept by a dumpster nearby, in between two garbage bins. He awoke when he heard strange words spoken by a voice he thought he recognized. In his dreams, the voice came from his aunt Daliya. But when he woke up, he found a man he thought could have been one of the drummers, so he threatened to pull out "her spirit."

"I'll pin her on you and she will haunt you if you don't turn away and let me go."

The man had no intention of holding him there. He had simply wanted to verify that Milian was in good health and relatively sound of mind. Both questions had been half answered, which was answer enough. The man watched Milian walk away for a while, until he got lost between the buildings in the adjacent neighborhood.

Milian wandered through the fog. He thought of the night before, those drums. The same he'd heard before, at the police precinct, at the office where he had checked in upon his return home, and even back on Earth.

Had he imagined it? Had he remembered it from childhood and then filled in the blanks? Was silence really more of a constant drumming?

Milian felt disoriented, but he knew to chase the sun all the way home, where he hoped to find something waiting, letters, etc. His mother's memorial was scheduled for tomorrow and he had done a good job of letting everyone know ahead of time. He felt guilty about the way he had handled the cremation, all alone.

After nearly an hour walking, Milian came across a large establishment. It seemed informal, cold and lacking in any sort of character or warmth, but Milian knew it well. It was a Chinese restaurant on a popular shopping street. One of the only establishments with the lights on. His family had come here after the death of a relative. He had seen the old man, in bed, dying, skin scaly and sticky and pale, almost blue, lips crusty.

"Good," He had said before a coughing fit hit, at which point Milian had been ushered out of the room by his aunt. The old man had died shortly afterwards. The family stayed with his widow until she was calm enough to be transported to a friend's house. After dropping her off, they'd gone to the Chinese restaurant.

He ordered vegetable tallarine and some short ribs. First he said to go, then to stay. A bright red apple sauce came with it. He thought he would never taste this flavor again. He had thought so for so long that he had forgotten the joy this flavor brought him, and so he devoured it on top of his noo-dles and then ordered some more. While he ate, he watched the fish in the massive fish tank next to his table. When he was a boy, there had only been one tank, near the kitchen, but now there were more and they contained many more fish than they did then. He remembered his own fish, back on Earth. Won-dered how they were doing, if they missed him at all.

Tired of slurping up noodles, he took the rest to go. He asked for them to put no fortune cookies in the bag, but they thought he asked for extra, so he ended up with three, in addi-tion to the one waiting on the table.

He unzipped his bag to check for his mother's skull, and there it was, smiling at him with all her teeth (she had never lost a single one). He felt calm, so he decided to eat the fortune cookie and read its crinkled little message.

"You will find happiness soon."

Thanks.

He ate the little piece of rice paper, daydreaming about moving to a new planet somewhere. Ideally, he would fix up Mantis Green and move there permanently, developing a self-sustained lifestyle, like those religious homesteading bloggers he'd read about. He would bring in many more animals, of course. Bees, birds, lizards, beetles, spiders, a dog—maybe even Jones. He wondered if other lifeforms would eventually emerge, or whether they had emerged already. After all, Mantis Green had been stewing in its own juices for several months now, abandoned and bathed in life-spawning moisture.

Milian arrived home several hours later. He had left his takeout outside somebody's shack by the Dene river, which ran from the mountains to the ocean, through this side of the city. At this point in the valley, the water flowed through a concrete flood-control channel, which had been built many decades ago. The water was brown and murky. Both sides of the channel were lined with small shacks, assembled by hand with metal scraps and cinder blocks. Some of them seemed to be electrically wired and a few even had satellite hook-ups for their televisions. These people were poor but resourceful.

A young woman emerged from the shack Milian had donated his leftovers to. She was dressed in business attire, presumably having just arrived from work a few minutes ago. Noticing Milian in the distance, she gestured graciously toward him and brought the small bag of food inside the house.

These little shacks by the river formed a skirt around the mountains. Milian remembered how beautiful they looked from above, at night. Whenever he and his family traveled, he loved to see the mountain all lit up in yellow and orange and white lights, on the return flight home. It was a reassuring sight. The lights confirmed the face of the city, its valley with the river running down its side to the ocean, which was all dark, except for the few boats that were always floating on it. It was something else back then. Now, he saw it for what it was: mostly sewage.

He thought of the woman by the river; how clean her clothes had been, good style, fitted and ironed. He looked down at his clothes: a ratty caftan, splattered with vomit on one sleeve. To him, comfort was always a priority, but to her it was a privilege. Something to enjoy in private only, maybe. Even now, he wasn't looking for work or planning on doing much besides sit at the house and think all day. Not that he hadn't worked himself silly back on Earth, but now that it was all rendered so worthless, *why bother?*

As soon as he got home, Milian checked the mail. No confirmations for the memorial. He tried to sleep.

Why can't anyone be reliable in this damn place?

He regretted coming back. He regretted not escaping and hiding out back on Earth.

Plenty of people have done it, he thought.

They got away with it and they're happy. Why can't I do that? Well, no use now.

He was already very far from Earth. Milian went over to the window to see if he could see the dear little planet. The fog was very thin now, so he could spot it easily, and when he did , he noticed that the Marionette trains were stopped.

He looked up the latest reports and learned that protests had broken out on the surface regarding immigration through the ring. They were calling into question the safety and efficiency of the ring as a true border,

Which wasn't supposed to be its purpose in the first place.

Counter-protests were arguing that exact point. In any case, all travel to and from the Marionette was temporarily suspended.

"We are not blocking anyone. We're simply pausing the process, while we work this all out."

There was a news clip circulating that showed a refugee camp forming near the Stratos Station. Hundreds of people, who had been stuck for months on ships in orbit had been allowed to disembark on the Marionette. Many had died on the ships, from starvation and dehydration. Some died from disease, which was quickly spreading. There was even a story going around that referenced an incident of cannibalism involving a pregnant girl. An independent report denied that story but confirmed that two-thirds of those aboard had died already, the aforementioned pregnant girl included. The baby had survived, so the girl's father had bottled some of his dead daughter's breastmilk to feed her newborn child. The bottles had been stolen overnight.

After the incident, Earth's humanitarian authorities intervened, ordering the Marionette to establish a secluded area to host the refugees. Rotari obliged, surely fearing back-lash from the public. Many still criticized the late response, claiming that they had deliberately delayed the order until the population had been reduced to one-third of its original size.

Rotari did not comment on the theory. Instead they broadcast a sanctimonious speech about human resilience and our duty to one another.

I believed the theory. It's always easier to control people, when you have less of them. All governments know that. And I think they all secretly wait for death to take a big enough toll, so that the problem shrinks to fit in their hands comfortably. At least that's what happened here in Yarey. The population was always growing as much as it is now, but people used to demand much more than they have in my lifetime. Now they're happy to build their own tin roofs and they tend to their fruit trees with more care, since sometimes that's all they can afford to eat for several weeks. An apple a day, as they say... but here a day's pay is not enough for one apple. And the doctors are scarce. People here survive like pigeons now. They try to be satisfied. They're resourceful and proud. And they don't sell each other out. But many have stopped expecting what they're owed, and that's how our government maintains its confidence. I don't think it'll be long before another riot breaks out here. But I've felt that way for many years now. Once upon a time, I would have felt validated by such a thing: This. This is why we left.

Instead, it's been a slow wasting away of this place, a long-

term illness. People are as patient as they can be, and patience runs out. There were protests every few months. It was starting to happen on Earth too.

I braced myself to watch both of my planets heat up. Fever is meant to cook off sickness. And there was sickness everywhere again. A cycle.

Milian went to bed. He had a string of nightmares, as usual. The next morning, he woke up with an extremely dry mouth and a ringing in his ears. When he approached the window, he found a large crowd waiting for him to emerge.

"We'll start the procession as soon as Milian is ready!"

He heard someone announcing the plans. Before doing anything else, he took his mother's skull downstairs and placed it near the lally flowers his aunt had sent. Noticing that they were half-wilted, he took some water from the faucet in the kitchen and poured it into the planter. It occurred to him that this was the first time he had watered any of the plants in the house since his return. He remembered his father's watering pot, always sitting on top of the fridge.

And there it was, exactly as he remembered it. He had forgotten all about his father and the plants. Every couple days, his father would be up before the sun, rearranging the plants in the courtyard, angling them toward the spot where the sun would soon emerge. He'd methodically walk between them, watering them and pruning them as needed. Sometimes he'd toss the dirt with a little bit of his homemade compost, to give the plants a boost. His father was very sensitive to the mood of his plants. They influenced him a great deal.

Milian remembered a particular night, mid-summer, when the family gathered in the courtyard to witness the once-a-year blossoming of his father's Night Blooming Cereus. He had spent four evenings watching the long tentacled bud, expecting its debut at any moment. On the fourth night, around 12:40am, as soon as he noticed it starting to open up, he woke everybody up to watch.

It was a quiet celebration but we all felt the honor of being in the presence of the flower. There was something remarkable about being there for its short opening, as if we had waited years to see its face. The world felt a little different after that night. The event had seemed important, and I thought myself lucky for having witnessed it.

While in the afterglow of this reverie, Milian filled up his father's watering pot and then took it to the courtyard, to water the rest of the plants, including the bloomless Cereus. He promised himself (and them) out loud, that he would take a closer look at each one upon his return from the memorial, and take care of any maintenance they needed going forward.

The crowd outside was oddly quiet. Regardless of whether it was out of respect or boredom, it made Milian uncomfortable, so he hurried back upstairs to get dressed. All black seemed appropriate, but he knew that might alarm some people, who would then have gone out of their way to "cheer him up," so he opted for gray instead. He looked in the mirror a few times before going downstairs, remembering the river woman in the pristine business suit.

Before opening the door, he checked the time. 11:01am.

A little early, but what the heck?

He kissed his mother's skull and then poured himself a generous amount of rum from a bottle on the shelf. He let the sweet warmth settle into his stomach and then emerged from the house to face the crowd.

WALKING FOR THE DEAD

The fog was thin by the time Milian joined the group and they all started walking. Everyone was barefoot and dressed in multicolors. Milian's mother had been a pillar of the neighborhood. She had helped and inspired many and was held in very high regard by all. After Milian and his brother left, her shine dulled a bit and the neighborhood found itself orphaned by its vigilant guardian. Life went on, of course, for both her and the neighbors, and she still participated in many of the same things, but from a farther seat in the theatre. Still, the long line of walkers and singers on this late morning were fair proof of her legacy.

"Thought we'd never see you again."

It was Milian's cousin, whom he remembered from his father's funeral, the only other time they had met.

"Hadn't planned on coming back yet, but I guess it all worked out, so to speak."

The cousin smiled.

"Welcome back."

Milian hadn't told anybody why he was back. He felt ashamed that his dismissal from Earth happened to coincide with his mother's death.

Life is funny that way.

He wondered if he would have come back when he received the news or if he would have just stayed in his apartment, stifling his sorrow and quietly processing the loss, sending and receiving condolences, as appropriate, until the noise died down.

I wouldn't be walking around with a skull in my pocket. But where would it be now, if I hadn't come back?

The procession itself took almost two hours. Milian's aunt had rented a space at the park for the memorial. She had asked Milian to speak but he'd declined.

"I'd like to ask one more time…"

Daliya spoke into the microphone, pausing for a moment to look around, scanning the crowd for Milian. When they made eye contact, Milian felt the blood rushing through his veins, a hot feeling crawling up from his neck to the top of his head and spreading all over his face, a bubbling in his chest and the beginning sensation of spaghetti legs.

Oh, please, don't…

And then she continued, as she broke away from his eyes,

"Anyone who'd like to share an anecdote, or just some

221

words about my sister, Dianen, please line up over here to my right. We'll go first come, first serve. The rest of you, please enjoy the food and drinks we're providing here, on behalf of my nephew, who's luckily able to join us for this celebration of Dianen's life. Milian, would you like to say anything?"

Milian's heart raced and for a moment, he felt like he couldn't see beyond the first few inches within his body, couldn't make out anyone's face. Impulsively, he ran up to the stage and faced the crowd, not wanting to expose himself as an intimidated half-child. Once all eyes settled on him and all sounds were subdued, he spoke the only words he could.

"I'm sorry."

The words came out without my knowledge. Always apologize and mean it, my mother used to say. I realized quickly that I had meant it more than ever. Startled by the sound of my own voice, I stood quietly gazing over the crowd, trying to figure out what to say. The hot feeling all over my head was now a claw squeezing my face. I had no choice but to talk through it.

"Thank you for being here. I was concerned that I wouldn't get to see any of you ever again, but as my mother always managed to do, it seems she's wrangled us all together again, to celebrate her and each other. Thank you for joining us. I'll be walking around, so I hope I can spend some time with each of you today, but if not, please come visit me at my mother's house tomorrow or the next day or next week, whenever. I'll be here for a while."

Relieved and mortified, I looked down at my feet and let them carry me off the stage. I was really hoping for no in-depth conversations, and I had already made up my mind to lead any attempts astray. I had no choice but to buckle down and hope to survive the ride. Anyway, a weight had been lifted. When the monster roars, the fear goes away and the adrenaline kicks in. I had only to wait for the rest of the beasts to tear through me before I could rest.

ECHOES

Milian regarded himself in the mirror, registering a foreign acquaintance. Had he ever been anything but a moldable plastic defined by circumstance? Was that different from everyone else?

Later that morning, he heard a neighbor crying. Certainly some kind of loss, judging by the hopeless progression of the lament. Sounded needy and unanchored, emerging from a bottomless well.

A beloved local musician had died. Somebody unknown to Earth, the Athens of galactic culture (or so it would seem). Back on this side of the universe, their music had touched many. Many had criticized and disparaged them, but now that they were gone, those same many mourned their passing, privately or together.

Regardless of everyone's public opinion of the artist in life, in death they were now an icon, a parent gone, a deity discouraged by us, who had finally resolved to abandon us all and leave us to a savage self-destruction.

When an artist dies, a soullessness occupies.

A part of Milian dismissed the whole thing at first, overwhelmed by his own tailored mourning, but he did allow a connection to uproot him from the current place he was in. This musician had done nothing more than uplift and carry by identity alone, a fundamental part of living that Milian had undervalued for a long time. He had preferred the pretense of a chameleon.

He had rid himself of any cultural cadence that would have given him away as an alien living on Earth, but he cherished the moments when he got to explain to a stranger that he had been born millions of miles away.

"I would have never guessed that you weren't from Earth! You don't even have an accent!"

Success.

The chameleonic obsession had always been there. Even as a child on his home planet of Yarey, Milian had often stood off to the side. *Different.* His participation was always limited, as though he were protecting himself from being absorbed by and dissolved into a whole. That was exactly what had happened on Earth, however. It wasn't until this night, back home, that he thought again about his face and voice as isolated identifiers.

The air was thick and hot again. And as he drifted off to sleep, Milian found himself constricted and unable to move.

Figures surrounded him. He tried to open his eyes but he was too tired. He tried to speak but no sounds formed. He managed to see a syringe in the hands of one of the figures.

"It'll be over soon." They said.

"It won't take long."

They plunged the needle into his arm and he felt consciousness draining, losing himself to a neutral grayness.

"Where will I be? What's going to happen to me?"

He tried hard to open his eyes again, but he had no control over his eyelids. They were heavy metal shutters. The sound of the figures shuffling around him was deeper than before, louder. They said things to him that he couldn't understand. He could smell their breath, but it wasn't breath at all, just more of that same hot sulfuric air. He fluttered his heavy eyelids enough to see shapes. Again they sank the needle into his arm, a thicker liquid this time, some kind of oil.

Consciousness. Don't leave me.

Despairing to cling to it, he gasped for air and tried to move, shiver, scream, whatever it would take to stay awake. But still, as if from blood loss, a cold tingle took over, a soggy feeling in his neck and hip, and he melted into the grayness by forced surrender. Mere seconds later, he opened his eyes in the darkened room, mother's skull on the floor by a book. The window completely white from the fog, moonlight shining through, causing a gradient that confused him.

Is that them? Did that really happen? Did they do something to me and then drop me off here?

Milian checked his body, in the dark. He seemed fine, except for some soreness in his shoulders. He wanted to check for puncture marks on his arm but didn't dare move from the bed.

He waited until morning, which wasn't very long, but the active terror coursing through him made it seem like several hours. The trees outside swayed side to side, from time to time, and their shadows' sudden movements sent chills down his spine.

When would morning come? Or is it morning already?

UNFINISHED PARTS

After several months back in my mother's house, my paperwork was approved to return to the Auroral Marionette. The refugee situation had been handled and operations had returned to a more manageable pace, despite rising tensions. At this point, we were all watching and speculating, refusing to fantasize about terrible changes to come from the growing conflicts.

Before landing on the Marionette, I was required to perform my own post-mortem activities on Mantis Green. This meant stacks of the same godawful paperwork, but I was looking forward to seeing, first hand, what had become of my lavish little satellite.

When I arrived, I saw that most of the courtyard was now a marshy jungle. There, I came upon a big strange rock. I leaned on its surface and slipped, taking with me a handful of wet moss. The spot I had scratched revealed a familiar swatch of upholstery beneath the moss. Why this woman pushed all her furniture out into the courtyard I will never know.

As I made my way through to the house, I was over-whelmed by the pressure of its emptiness, much like the one occupying my mother's house now. After opening the big wooden door, which was cracked and water-damaged, I was hit by a moldy smell. She had built large piles of dirt all over the kitchen floor and had attempted to build an irrigation system out of her vitality machine. There was green dust and yellow sap everywhere. To her credit, the black beans she had so carefully *planted* in wads of cotton and then shoved into the earth had grown into some tall sprouts.

The walls were like fountains. Water from the storm system ran down the surface beneath the layers of paint and plaster, forming shapes and filling blisters, some of which looked like faces. They were completely warped and had developed into masses of lumps and crevices. We dug the dirt out of a particularly large crevice that didn't look like the others—it appeared to have been carved intentionally—and found a little box full of wall brine and the small skeleton of Giancarlo, the young owl that Gallia had kept, his feathers in a clump in a separate box, and in a third box, a putrid oily substance.

When we had come up to fix the storm system and clean up the mess of the storm that went out of control, she had thrown us out. I remembered noticing that day that her hands

229

were covered in something dark and thick, and she gave off a particular stench that I dismissed as a newly acquired personal fragrance.

Farah Ysvette Mourad Vera

A DREAM FROM CHILDHOOD

A house on stilts. And it won't stop raining. Among green marsh and water, yellow skies.

A small wet child framed by the door, toes gripping the edge, hands tightly interlaced in front of a slightly bulging belly, pale. From under the back of the house emerges a long dark shadow that moves through the murky water with clear intent, a practical speed.

A shadow that's indigo blue and forest green and black and purple all at once, a color your eyes like to morph into several shades, hoping you're maybe just, "seeing things." Some drifting weeds or dead mangrove roots carried by a current.

Then the surface is disturbed: a small yellow eye pokes through. Very sudden and very quick to disappear again. Did it really happen? Did it have a head?

It's getting dark, and it's still raining hard. All lines and borders are tentative. A dark shadow moves across the water, maybe nine feet in length, maybe twelve.

But just as the shadow moves around to the back of the house and the child's eyes follow, a small dingy kayak approaches the house.

The rain is even heavier. From the point of view of the child, it looks and sounds like a waterfall. The child spots a shadow again, this time very close to the door. Then all of a sudden, a dark thing jumps out of the water and takes his ankle, drags him out of the house. He falls in the water and panics, thrashing around, trying to break free, or at least find the croc's nose to try and rip it open with his fingers, anything he can think of to try and get free. This is it. The last moments. The last chance. As he dives deeper into the water to try and feel for the attacker's face, his hand slides across the crocodile's tail, as it slips quickly through the water. It seems to be leaving him, but his legs are still tangled. It's at this moment that the child is violently pulled out of the water and placed on the kayak, with a man screaming something into his face. He can't understand what he's saying but he's so close he can feel the hotness inside his throat.

In the morning, the water is littered with natural and manmade debris. Pieces of plants, a dead fish, a can of something. A chicken who has learned to enjoy floating on the water, like a duck. A rooster on the shore, calling out into the morning.

The crocodile is sunning himself on the beach. The sky

is yellow and blue. The colors blend inexplicably well with each other but there isn't any green in between.

The crocodile opens his eyes, focuses on something. The child on the kayak. When he stirs we spot his sunburn. Once he starts peeling, he will feed the skin to the fish in the water. For now, the challenge is getting off the boat and not being eaten by the crocodile.

That's where I come in and save the child. This part of the dream is lucid. I don't know if it was ever meant to happen that way and I don't know if I am the same man that saved him from the drowning house on stilts in the first place. I thought the man was a Cuban man. Whatever the case, I am here about to wake the child and take him with me to safety.

The problem is: I always become too aware at this point in the dream so I wake up. I don't finish approaching the kayak. Just as I start to walk down the dock, as I'm about to look up at the sky and take it all in, I'm suddenly too thirsty to keep dreaming. And so I do look up but it's just my ceiling. And I sit there and mourn a little before getting up to have some breakfast.

Last night's dream brought a new breed of shadows. I don't have frequent encounters with said shadows when I'm awake, but something tells me they sneak around and haunt me in silence.

MANTIS GREEN

An old lady's face. It's tan and wrinkled, but the pores are small and the surface of the skin is very smooth. There's a fine uniform layer of fuzz all over the face. Her grimace is pronounced and tired. Exhausted and horrified, actually. I see her in a wider view and she's surrounded by three... no, four young men, who all look alike, except for that each one has different facial hair. They look like brothers, in fact, but upon closer inspection, the traces of different genes are evident. These *brothers* are surrounding this old horrified and exhausted woman. Everyone is tan, with long hair, except the old woman. Her hair is short, wavy and salt-and-pepper. She's lying on the lap of one of the brothers, with a brother by each leg and another one sitting nearby. Does that one have a conscience? They prepare to do terrible things.

When I wake up, I feel exhausted and scared, and I know I'm not directly involved but I still care. And I think about this dream all day and only write about it at night, as I skip dinner and have a glass of wine instead and listen to some mild music before taking a shower.

After I get out of the shower, I look back and see that the tub is covered in dead graveyard flowers. Graying yellow, pink, purple and white petals falling all over the place. Rolled up crunchy dead leaves poking through. I come out of the bathroom, and the courtyard is bathed in yellow sunlight. It feels good, but I know I can't enjoy it. I'm scared and I just want to be sad for a little while.

I dream a lot about being invaded, murdered or flooded. I often dream of massive amounts of water, and recently, dead babies. But dreaming is pleasant to me, even when it's terrifying. It feels like a shower of thoughts and images. Refreshing.

Freedom is an obsession, which negates its whole meaning and purpose. So what is it that binds free thoughts together into dream logic? Why is it that some thoughts travel different trajectories that never intersect? But it's sometimes so obvious when one road leads to another.

Now it's getting abstract and difficult, but this is pleasant, isn't it? A purely thought-ruled habitat, where it's up to thoughts to lead the way. This hurts, actually. Logic is a tough boss.

Thoughts driven by fear now. Fear of judgement and misunderstanding and fear of looking stupid. That's the fear of freedom. Or is that to claim it?

Confusion is an interesting thing. It can even be a cognitive failure of some kind, a by-product of fear or hesitation. Irrespective of whether or not it's conscious or voluntary, it's a way to stall for time while making a decision. People are tricky that way. That gets confusing for me. Sometimes I don't know what my reaction is supposed to be. I don't think I see the world I love in.

Whether "love" was a typo or not in that last sentence, I don't know. This is an excerpt from one of the last letters that Gallia wrote to no one in particular. It wasn't inside any of her journals, just hand-written onto some plain sheets of yellow recycled paper. She had curled it up into a funnel and stuck it into one of the dirt piles. At the base of it were some orange seeds, split open and dried. They had sprouted but didn't survive.

Months earlier, the room had been filled with a heavy light. A trace of green mist, in the air, from the machine. Gallia sat on the floor in her "dawn slip," a cotton garment she insisted on wearing whenever she was up before noon Pacific. A dark reddish brown clay covered half the counter. She was molding it, massaging it in waves, with her thumbs, away from her body, building representations of yet another disastrous nightmare she'd had. She didn't hear Covas come in.

There were muffled sounds in the background, a whistling like the one from the green steam, then suddenly, Gallia felt the warmth and bulkiness of two big hands gripping her shoulders.

"Gallia!" She heard. Startled, she gasped and tilted her face in Covas's direction. Her eyes lingered in the inward landscape a moment longer, and then she looked up, in response.

"I'm having dreams."

She said it like a confession. Covas nodded to reassure her, and she continued,

"8,000 words. I can't move past that. I have nothing more to say, but I keep dreaming these dreams. There's disaster and people are dead or hurting. When I was younger and the Krundians were doing their weapons tests, I used to have similar dreams. But I'm afraid of that, now? None of that can touch me anymore and I'm still just as worried about it."

"Could be genuine concern for the people down there."

"I don't know. That type of caring can be dangerous. Monkeys in the wild will kill each other over reproductive rights. Why would we be any different? What's the point?"

"Maybe you just need better sleep."

That wasn't going to help. Covas regretted saying something so generic, but he didn't know what else to say. He was still holding her in place, as if to prevent her from floating away. She was comforted by the contact but hadn't realized it yet. Her shoulders softened. Covas noticed that she was more calm and present. He let go.

"I can adjust the filters, if you need me to."

"Thank you, Covas. I know this must not be easy."

"It's not. Please take care."

Gallia was stung by the reaction. She thought he should have been more sympathetic. Instead, he made her feel like a bother.

The fact that he didn't realize I said that for the sole purpose of being contradicted...

She was tired and wanted to be alone.

"I will sleep more. Thank you. I'm fine."

She walked toward the counter, to drink her barley grass, which had separated into a layer of liquid at the bottom and a crust of foam at the top.

Her feet were bothering her.

The following night, Gallia got a visit from her mother's ghost, tired and desperate and scattered. As if it had been dragged from place to place, for hours, by horses across miles of hot asphalt. Dead for forty-seven years, never having seen her baby grow up and now suddenly wrangled before her to confess, to ask, to express, to scold, to bond, to *know* her. Such a terrible encounter pushed Gallia back into her hallucinatory hole.

Farah Ysvette Mourad Vera

OH, HOLY NIGHT

Milian's apartment on Earth was a dream. It was located in the Arboretum Circle, a bundle of short buildings that had been built around ancient tree trunks, each between four and eight stories high. Each trunk was hollow and accommodated a lift and a staircase. On the outside, three apartments stuck out on each floor, like oyster mushrooms, natural light allowed to filter into each one through a skylight. The entrance to each apartment started at a carved doorway and continued seamlessly through a shallow hall to the front door, which was made of steel and glass, in sharp contrast with the natural design on display up to that point. The floors in Milian's apartment were simulated rocks and soil, except for marbled gray ceramic in the bathroom and kitchen. In the small foyer, there was a bench where Milian had stacked piles of books and papers. They were hidden behind his winter coat. Some of the books and papers were warped and wrinkled from contact with the snow melting off the jacket. Milian was a destroyer of books. Any book in pristine condition in his apartment had simply not been read.

In the living room, vines wound around a miniature fruit and vegetable garden on the main wall. He had miniature apples, cherries, cucumbers, tomatoes, avocados, oranges, bananas and a few herbs. To the side of the wall, he had a tower of peanut plants in the open glass atrium and in the corner, a dwarf almond tree that grew up close to the skylight, with another stack of books piled at its base. On top of the pile was Milian's head. He stared up at the tree, and through the skylight beyond it, not moving at all, not even to breathe. Falling snow had turned to rain well before hitting the glass above, except for a couple icy chunks that liquified thickly and slowly.

I lie here, watching the strange visiting heat melt snow into sleet, as it falls from above, splattering the neighborhood. I am re-discovering that sleepy peace that comes from exhaustion. No need to express a lie or a cool doppelgänger. The heat, the exhaustion and the neck cramps, the arrhythmic falling of the chunky rain outside, the overcast light propped atop every structure, like a force field, car tires through a puddle, and the sputtering runoff from dusty leaves, as they're shaken by wind. It was in this weather that the police showed up, prematurely. It didn't matter. I had given my fish to Covas. He had also taken Jones. I had no one. Whatever things were left would be picked up by the consignment deposit clerks and kept in storage somewhere until I figured out what to do with it. I couldn't take it home, because it would be confiscated as contraband. I'd have to make other arrangements later, or just let it all move on without me.

"But after three months, if we don't hear from you, it's donate or dump. The guys at the center do an evaluation to decide. They'll call you before they do it, to give you another chance. But if you know you'll want your stuff, call us before the first to save everyone some time. Yeah?"

Everything else was tossed or packed, except for the Christmas tree, which I intended to donate to the curb, baubles and all, in hopes somebody was sentimental enough to rescue it. I hoped that by then the sleet would turn back into snow, so that the tree wouldn't get soaked before someone got to it. And I hoped perhaps, that although it was a Wednesday, the choir at the basilica would sound me an unknowing goodbye.

Instead, all I heard was the raspy ringing of my bell, and after twenty or so seconds, the knocking and the voice of an impatient man. To think I had just thought of the perfect meal to have before filing away. There's a noodle shop two blocks from here, three maybe. The noodles are far too filling but the dumplings they make seemed the most appropriate for the way I was feeling, and their flavor would surely soothe me. I suppose I cannot expect these men to accompany me there now, or come back later, once I've indulged.

MANTIS GREEN

I put down my glasses. I'm the type of person to misplace and lose valuables like that, and yet I had never lost those frames. I'd had them for over twenty years. When I opened the door, two men stood on my doormat, their noses covered in small perspiration spheres that reflected the light from my lamp overhead, like fine crystals. The man in the back wiped his face, smearing all but two of the beads of sweat off his nose, pulling his hair to the side, revealing another cluster of uglier more amorphous beads of sweat on his forehead.

"Ready?" The one said. *The leader, I suppose.*

"Actually I was told you'd be by, a bit later. I haven't quite finished wrapping up here."

Worth a try.

Milian's face changed colors under the even light of his apartment. First, a bluish drain then quickly a bubbling red, clustered in spots by his nose, lips and the corners of his eyes.

The best you can do to express yourself is to repeat what you mean, in your head, several times, before blurting it out, editing as necessary. Use persuasion and grace, and exercise humility. And above all, don't make it about you.

"Coffee?" He said.

"We'll come back later." The leader said, as he glanced to the man behind him, conceding. The man in the back referred to his handheld for the precise time.

New job, I guess, Milian thought.

"Eight O'Clock." He said.

"On the dot." He added.

"Thank you, I'll see you both then." Milian stepped out and started closing the door behind him. The men didn't move. He squeezed between them.

"Excuse me," he said, turning around to lock the door. He walked away and they followed. Once the three exited the building, the two men went a separate way, as if to make it clear to him that they weren't following. It mattered little to Milian if they chose to do it now or later. He expected to be followed.

Milian walked through the streets, watching couples and people with their pets. He thought of his fish Angelo, Sabine and Macaulay, and Jones. He thought of Giancarlo. Gallia. Sylvia. Covas. Then he reached the noodle shop.

He was greeted joyfully by the host, the waitstaff and the cooks, as was customary, no sentimentality. He sat down and looked through the menu carefully, in case he would miss something better than what had drawn him there in the first place. Euzi, a server, came over with some hot tea.

"Thanks. I'll just have some dumplings please."

"Oh, I'm so sorry, we are out right now. Our fryer's broken." Euzi said, pitifully. They really were sorry. They knew Milian and his famous order of dumplings.

Milian laughed to himself.

"I'm leaving town," he said. Euzi wasn't sure what to say.

After a pause,

"I'll bring you some soybeans to start."

"Thank you," he said.

Milian watched Euzi walk away and call a cook over to the counter. The cook glanced at Milian from the corner of her eye. So did the server. Milian stared at them both. For twenty-five minutes, Euzi avoided his table. It was getting late, and he would surely stir up some unnecessary trouble as a result. But this was potentially his last time here, so he thought, *what the heck.*

After a few more minutes, the server walked over with a container. They opened it up and inside were eight rushed and imperfect—but still deliciously plump—steaming and glistening dumplings. Milian looked up from the steaming little pillow, smiling. Euzi gave him a friendly pat on the back, saying,

"They're just pan fried, but they're still pretty good that way, actually,"

"I'm sure they are. Thank you."

They each took a turn smiling, then Milian remembered another comfort from this place,

"The sauce... Ah!"

He found it on the table. Milian and Euzi broke eye contact. When they reconvened, the moment had changed. Just then, a clap of thunder recalled their attention to the outside. Once their eyes met again, Euzi smiled and closed the moment up with that wonderful Earthling phrase,

"Let me know if you need anything else."

Milian watched the rain as he chewed. This moment may as well have been an idyllic snowy Christmas Eve, serene and joyful, a blanket of clean moisture over everything, each bite of food a nourishment for the human soul; even Milian, a naturalized human, welcome to partake.

He had just started on his second dumpling, when a couple walked in. Two women of similar height but drastically different styles. Milian noticed them at first, then looked away again, but soon found himself eavesdropping on them. Mostly small talk, confessions about their displeasure with work, warnings in the way of revelations about complicated relationships with others, attempts at finding a common ground. People are funny this way. They must find comfort first.

Milian continued to listen, as he ate methodically. One end of the dumpling first, then dunk in sauce, then eat the stuff inside and let the skin soak a bit, poke it around a few times, then finish it off. His stare visited three places, cyclically: the rain outside, Euzi's face, the attempting new couple. He paused on each of the three, each time, as if monitoring, and finally, while on his 7th dumpling, at 8:18pm, he spotted his cops outside the shop. They looked in and saw him immediately. Undoubtedly, they had been tracking him the whole time. They didn't seem surprised.

"I'm coming," he mouthed at the silhouettes at the door. The sight of them with the rain falling behind seemed most representative of the night.

"All the faceless judging me."

He ate the last dumpling whole, then drank the rest of the sauce he had poured, then the tea, then the water. He took some cash from his pocket and wedged it under his cup on the table.

Euzi spotted the police at the door, as the restaurant's supervisor approached to find out what was going on. The server managed to say goodbye to their loyal customer before Casey brought the police in.

Milian smirked as he joined them at the door.

"They're with me." He told Casey, the small rugged old man who had owned and managed this noodle shop for thirty years.

The police handcuffed Milian and led him through the rain back to his building. But as they got off the elevator, Milian exclaimed, as if just realizing,

"I got everything I need, actually."

The young cop looked back at him, resentful that they had walked all the way back for nothing.

"Let's go."

SMELLS LIKE EARTH

What I miss most are things like the air. I studied the names of winds when I was young; didn't think anything of it. They were just imperceptible details to memorize. Back then, I thought there was no difference, but now I would love to feel them all one by one, and catalogue them, try to guess which is which.

Milian's trip up to the Marionette had included one intentionally brief but inevitably prolonged stop out behind the arrival chamber. He had built himself a secret pond and bench there, where he could sit and enjoy the smell of Earth, something he'd never forgotten from his days as a child and a tourist, and ultimately what had made him return to Earth for good. There was something cohesive about that smell, as if everything on this big rock agreed. This smell spoke of true equilibrium, even with the political and climate changes, extinctions, disasters (both natural and unnatural), the aging of the soils, and every deceitful difference perceived by those who live here in short spans of no more than a hundred years.

Its smell and its air... it was difficult to see, upon first stepping back into this gassy sphere, what could be so out of line that it demanded a firm complaint.

Although no one else was supposed to know about Milian's pond bench, he sometimes found a candy wrapper or a cigarette butt lying around. This only made him happier. He had made something, kept it a secret, and it had been discovered by someone curious enough to search for—or stumble upon—it. Curiosity was a wonderful and terrible thing, as are all the most authentic things.

Of course there were fish, always fish. Milian was fascinated by their movement and design. Not all fish camouflage, some blatantly show off. Fish have levels of individuality that Milian studied endlessly. And every time he thought he had made a connection with a fish, it would simply swim away without so much as a look back or an intentional flutter of the fin in his direction. It seemed that complexity is not always polite because it's unpredictably complicated.

RECONCILIATION

Milian and his aunt Daliya sat across from each other in the dark, with the bagged skull resting in the middle of the table, equidistant from them. Their silhouettes were expressing heat into the dusty atmosphere. If you'd looked at them against the glow of the front door, you might see the little distorted waves coming off them. Milian took a sip from a glass. When he put the glass back on the table, the map of his hand was plastered on it, exposing where each of his fingers had squished and smeared the condensation bubbles on its surface. Daliya fired a determined exhale through her mouth and was the first to speak,

"She didn't want to hear from anyone anymore."

"She didn't want to speak to me."

"She did. She just didn't know how to tell you how unhappy she was. She wanted you to apologize—"

"I know"

"She wouldn't have asked you to come back—"

"I know that."

I didn't mean to cut her off again, but I felt heat rising from the seat of my stomach to my throat. My words came like a cough.

"What can I tell her now?"

"*Listen.* That's all. We all have our own little world, Milian. That's all she wanted from you, too."

"I didn't want to just give her the same old summary: Yes, everything's good. I did this and this and this. Then listen to her tell me what I was doing wrong. Then what, I'd do her a favor and ask for advice?"

Snide remarks and excuses, etc. Waste.

Daliya sat with both arms draped on the table, eyes down, ripping pieces from a napkin and methodically pressing them onto the beads of condensation on Milian's glass.

"Why are you upset with me?"

"You didn't have to understand each other, Milian. You just had to listen. You just had to sit there and listen and be together for a moment. You think people can relate to each other all the time? Families, especially? These aren't your friends Milian. This isn't a person you're in love with. It's where you come from. It doesn't define you but it imparts a certain flavor unto you."

Now it was Milian who was looking down, watching the soggy pieces of napkin wrinkle up. He felt imposed upon, squashed, force-fed. Daliya balled up the rest of the napkin and tossed it aside. Then there was eye contact, at last.

"I don't know you. And you don't know me, Milian. But I'm your family now. This is it for us."

And there was only one door out of this stale room.

"Will you help me, then?"

Milian's aunt helped him charter a ship that was to set sail in two night's time. The pilot, Mr. Ascilogo Caretta, had been a quiet man of many hobbies, including leisure "astrowalks" as he called them. He had built the ship himself, with help from his son, who was now living on Earth. He almost never ventured outside of the immediate orbit of his own planet, but now that he was old and had no family left in Yarey, he had the courage to watch home grow small and give way to the stars. He had agreed to take Milian to the Marionette and Mantis Green, and had also offered to bring him back home afterwards, if he wished.

"Can move the rock, too. I can build a tow attachment for it, no problem, if you gotta transport it. But I just wanna see this thing first, so I know better what we'll need."

"We'll pass it on the way. I'll show it to you."

"Son, this thing, is it stable enough?"

"Well, no, not right now, it isn't. But that's what we plan to work on first. I just need to get all my permits in place."

"Don't go getting into trouble with those people. You

know how they are."

I know.

"My son can't do anything down there. They watch everything you do, and they don't let you live in peace. He makes very little money and then has to use all of it to pay for every little thing. Water, even. Probably the air, too."

"How long has he been there?"

"Three years already!"

"Well, he'll do better soon. It takes some time."

"I don't know. It's not the same, you know? Well, that's life. We live simply over here. Can't blame the boy for wanting something more to worry about. Keep his brain young. Can't end up like his old man. I wanted to start my own travel company, take people all over the place. Build my own fleet. Well, least I got this buddy here."

Caretta patted the ship on the figurative *shoulder*.

"Gonna get you there. Get some nice views on the way."

He smiled proudly. Milian regretted that he couldn't enjoy the moment as much.

On a gray day, Milian and Caretta headed out. Hardly anything was visible because of the fog, but that wouldn't matter once they'd left the atmosphere.

The house had seemed especially comfortable that morning and Milian had had second thoughts. His mother's words from a long time ago clapped back,

"You'll never make it."

Despite all the signs pointing in the opposite direction, Milian met Caretta at the docks at the scheduled time. He left his mother's skull back home, inside the paper bag, hidden behind the pot of the bloomless Cereus.

Caretta turned out to be a fantastic pilot, and his ship an efficient little marvel. It was equipped and stocked like a commercial ship, but built for only six with a remarkable space-saving design. Milian was impressed and the two passed the time discussing the little ship and its many talents.

"I worked on some of those ships for the satellite commission when I was younger, right out of school. We loved it. My friends and I would just play with these toys all day and collect our money at the end of the week. Blow it all in a couple of days, celebrating whatever. Then they closed up shop, of course, but you were around for that."

"I remember, yeah."

The day they announced that no more ships would be leaving the surface was the day my father found out that he had spent his savings on a scam. He'd tried to contact the people he paid, but they were nowhere to be found. Thousands of people had been duped with the same trick. Obviously someone who already knew what the law would become. Leaving the surface wasn't completely banned of course. Personal not-for-profit cruising was still allowed, but first-time permits would not be granted after 30 days. This was meant to discourage new off-orbit travel, and all the black market business attached to it.

My mother and I watched the last ship launch, along with millions of others around the globe, hoping that something would happen. That maybe they'd encounter an antidote to the current government and help us return to the prosperous and adventurous free place we used to be. Corpo cura couldn't save us now.

Many people risked their lives, leaving in uninspected vehicles without a permit, a one-way trip fueled by a wish for luck. But that became the only way to have a life, if you wanted anything besides the rumbling of hungry existence for yourself and yours. Some had left so they could send back resources to the people back home. A lot of it was confiscated at customs, of course. And some didn't make it anywhere at all. They either got apprehended and jailed somewhere or killed.

My brother and I had barely made it out, but it was even harder for those that left much later. Rumors had spread across the universe that our people were uncivilized and dangerous, and fleeing in masses, looking to steal the resources earned by hard-working people. There was no mention of how many of us had died by the hands of our government. No mention of the silence we were forced to eat instead of speaking. That our news had been replaced by propaganda. That our names had been turned into mere numbers. That our homes were now also used for interrogations and torture. That our children were being taught to fight and reproduce, as their primary function. No mention of the food shortage. No mention of the tainted water. No mention of the bodies stacked, decomposing on the prison floor. Those of us who made it out were labeled as complicit in the violence, not victims of it. While I held my brother's body in my arms, I was just glad that he didn't die with the skin on his back shredded by leather, or with his feet sliced into slaw. He would have surely ended up that way, my hot-headed brother, who would have never shut up for anyone. I wondered how I would have fared. I had made it my goal to survive, and I hadn't even done that properly. But this is also why I felt so compelled to adhere to Earth's values, as I had studied them.

Earth was everything everyone wanted to be. They had freedom and diversity and choice. They had an appreciation for knowledge, and a passion for tolerance.

Having returned home and then left again, I couldn't help but think that the strangest thing on both sides of the galaxy was that life went on, as if normal. Fear stifled expressions and opinions, but the people kept walking and eating and sleeping for as long as they could. No matter how different we sounded or looked or thought. Indifference enabled survival, even if we molted into monsters in the process. The collective urge to surrender and transcend gave me courage, but it also rendered the project of living an eerie abomination.

Farah Ysvette Mourad Vera

THE RATTLE

My head felt like a rattle, and I feared I wouldn't make it through the night. The pressure had a color, blood orange and a smell like smoking meat. If I didn't know better, I'd assume my brain was literally being fried. I tried to sleep but couldn't, so I got up and wandered through the house. The light never changed. Sunny on one side, dark on the other. The refraction mechanism was broken. It occurred to me that I should bring all the light fixtures into the dark side and make it daylight all around, just for fun. Or build a canopy out of all the moss and block the sun on the one side, and sit in darkness. No matter. The pounding wouldn't let me sleep or think properly. It was as if my whole heart in its beating glory had been strapped to my head and made to punch my skull repeatedly. My ears clogged and unclogged as I breathed, and every time I moved my head, it sounded like I had sand wedged between the bones in my neck. The crunching was startling and didn't go away for hours. The next morning when I awoke, the headache was gone but the sand was still

257

there. Crunch. Just like sand inside a clam.

Every time it happened it was the same thing. I studied my symptoms and tried to explain the headache to myself, even narrate it. Now the ears pop, the rattle swells up with water, the neck bones crunch, the bone of the eye sockets, inflamed and stretched, grinding and squeezing my eyeballs. And what was this for? It was a game too silly to smile at. Waste. How can I live like this week to week? Will it ever stop?

I drifted off to sleep in a corner while watching my feet. I had picked at a callus on the side of my big toe. Its jagged edge looked like a laughing mouth against the light of the fire. I felt small and torn up. The pounding must have either exhausted me or lulled me to sleep. I awoke with a stiff and sandy neck and sharp pains along my spine, from the twisted knot I was in for what must have been at least four hours. But the light never changed. And I didn't check my watch all *night*. So I had no idea what "time" it was, or how long I had slept.

There was a warm light filtering in and I knew it was time to go. I looked at my hands. They didn't look mine. They were gray and desiccated. I touched my left palm with my right middle finger and where I touched, the skin turned to dust. Both my palm and my finger had eroded at the points of contact. In a panic, I rubbed some more, and more of my hands disintegrated into the air. I watched my flesh-dust float down to the floor in a million specs. I rubbed some more off my palm and two of my fingers fell off. They dropped to the ground faster than the rest of me and as they hit the unyielding surface, they burst into gray expanding clouds. My hands! I rubbed what was left of them together until all I had were stumps. Their dust covered my feet. I crouched down to blow it off, but as I did, I watched my toes go up in a mist as well. I had been found. I had been punished. Ashes release me. Die so that I may wake. Lucid.

I awoke with my hands and feet intact. They looked like old friends. I spent a few hours in the garden, collecting whatever had sprouted after weeks of waiting. There wasn't much, and the more I dug in the dirt, the more afraid I became that I would pull my hands out and find no fingers.

After a while, I was too tired to finish, so I went to take a bath. I ate some fruit and sat by the fire. A bed of ashes lay at the bottom. I felt their wasted nature, their freedom, their stillness, their volatility. Release. I took a handful of ashes in my hand and walked it over to the vent. Watching the black sky through a little window, I stuck my hand into the chamber, then flipped the switch and released the ashes into space. I watched them float for a short time, then saw them disappear into the infinity. My legs felt heavy, my spine a frayed rope. I went to sleep for several hours, resolving to get off Mantis Green within a week.

TO LOOK FORWARD

Awaiting the arrival of Mr. Caretta's ship was just me and the handful of bird bones. After all these years rejecting the culture I'd been born into, here I was, inadvertently embracing its oldest and most nonsensical customs, abandoning possessions and collecting the remains of the dead, so that they may be put to rest with more dignity.

I spotted the ship in the distance. They would be traveling in my direction for a few more hours, so I decided to spend some time on the other side.

The sun flickered a bit. My eyes felt heavy and my lips were sticking out. I felt my jaw clench even harder, my teeth grating on one another. The pressure rising from all places to my neck, to my jaw, to my nose, to my eyes, to my head. What can I do to prevent or cure the feeling?

My mind felt doughy and stuffed up. I wouldn't be allowed back on the surface of the Earth. How close was this? Close enough? I had already applied for a permanent visa to Sondras Alluma, with sponsorship from Sylvia.

It was actually easier to visit the Marionette as an alien tourist than as an Earthling. Given the nature of the place and its boundaries, the screening process was simpler. Being cleared to visit the Marionette didn't clear you to visit the surface, where there was less containment and monitoring. When we designed the ring, we didn't envision it as an alternative destination for aliens, but they almost seemed to prefer it. It was a stable environment, with a surplus of amenities, no weather to worry about and splendid views of the Earth. One of the first things tourists do when visiting a place for the first time is find the highest point of observation. The Eiffel Tower, the Empire State Building, the Space Needle... people have always had an obsession with looking down at a whole city and no trip is complete without some version of this accomplishment. The Marionette was all that.

The flex-axis of the ring ensured different views of Earth throughout the rotation. In a week, it was possible to see a little of each continent and ocean, including the poles. The day it opened, most news outlets made some allusion to Saturn's rings and suggested that Earth had once again made an improvement to nature itself. There had been plans to build two more rings at least, but legislation still had to be worked out. The governing bodies had to come to a series of agreements, and most of them had already signed off on many, except for Venezuela, and more recently the US, who had either denied or deferred approval of all proposed agreements, under a new wave of nationalism. That same sentiment kept a lot of people from leaving the hot and stale comfort of the surface. Most people who adamantly opposed going up to orbit used the same two excuses, which had also been used by US leaders in official travel warnings to the public:

"What if you end up stuck up there?"

"What if they run out of air?"

These weren't real issues, but messy legislation and poor regulation were. And the same US leaders opposed the enforcement of regulation in general, so go figure. They were not, however, opposed to extensive monitoring of the population, and in some cases had asked that Rotari share metrics with them. While I was still working with Rotari, I know they had refused, but that may have changed. The monitoring systems on the ring were part of a robust tracking network that followed everyone and everything. It was fully automated, but no one was solely responsible for resolving any exceptions. These tools were designed to *assist* intelligent and well-equipped security personnel, not to replace them. Almost immediately, they went from being security instruments to statistics tools. Like everything Rotari got their hands on, it was all about the vanity points. If the door looks strong and shiny, people will feel secure.

Rotari spends a fortune on protecting your safety while en-

suring your satisfaction.

It didn't matter what the complaints said. People were still lining up to empty their pockets because Rotari allowed them to be certified citizens of luxury and perceived quality. I knew first hand that their advertising power came from the customers themselves, flaunting the shiny souvenir, showing off the exhilarating experiences they enjoyed thanks to their brand. And if anything went wrong… well, here I am. As an independent contractor, it was my fault. The good people at Rotari are just as appalled as you. Help them, please. They need you now more than ever.

It occurred to me that I had started to complain too much. The initial shock and dismay of being stripped of everything I'd ever wanted and everything I'd ever worked for had started to wear off. My mother's death had started to become a defined paragraph in the book of my life, and Mantis Green had been laid to rest in my mind. Why didn't I feel the clutching and the squeezing and the tentacled darkness around me anymore?

My nightmares were more utilitarian now. A simple maneuvering problem. Could I steer a ship through a door? That was it for dreaming, one night. It felt terrifying in the moment, but if I described it to someone upon waking, they would have found it rather boring. Even as I thought of it now, I was ashamed at my limited imagination within that dream. A dream, I called it. Not a nightmare, although as it developed, I felt scared and uncertain. Uncertainty was peeling off its fear suit.

Still, I worried about what this meant. I had been on Mantis Green for a few months. I had seen no one and nothing but the landscape on this rock. I felt healed back into my usual apathetic *cuero*. What would I feel if my feet sank into the marsh of home again? Would the pain return or would I remain "in peace," like now? Most of all I was concerned with deciding which one would be best, and how much of it I could endure.

A HOLIDAY

I thought in spirals again. A tear in my fabric had stripped me of the medicinal apathy I suckled at. Anxiety was back, like a sudden urge to pee. Worry, vertigo, a need for sleep, a fear of dreaming, tossing and turning to survive. I slept and slept until my aunt and Mr. Caretta arrived. I thought that maybe I should be thankful for the conflicts ushering purpose back into my daily life. Once the concept of being useful is fully digested, an unearthly way of life seems irresponsible.

They were announced by the alarm. Not the most practical thing, but I felt too weak and impatient to rely on my eyes and thoughts. I walked out into the station and opened up the gate. They had gotten out of the ship and looked eager for a tour. I obliged.

As we walked through the garden, my aunt stopped.

"How does this get maintained?"

"It's not very practical. Pretty much have to vacuum the pollen and do the bees' work yourself."

"Probably better off just buying the fruit from a store and shipping it up. Or does that spoil it?"

"Well, the change in pressure affects it a little bit, but no, not really. The woman who commissioned it just wanted a garden to look at. Her homestead took care of it for her."

"Why are you keeping it?"

"I don't know."

Milian led his aunt and Mr. Caretta into the house. The old man looked behind him once more, conceding (*or condescending*),

"It's beautiful."

Mr. Caretta lived and worked out of a small wooden house near the water. He was a part-time repairman, but also operated a little restaurant in the afternoon, where he served the fish he had caught and the mussels he had collected right on his own little stretch of beach. He had inherited the restaurant from his mother, who had inherited it from her parents. The same tiny house had held at least five generations of the same family. Mr. Caretta was in awe of the size and elegance of the house on Mantis Green, but he hid it, for fear of being judged a simpleton and a loon.

"You did a nice job here."

"Thank you. Probably wasn't the best use of my time and efforts, but here it is."

"Nah, you ought to be proud. Anything you touch, whether it succeeds or not. Movement is what keep us going."

Caretta was ashamed that he had let himself get carried away. He believed that life was a mysterious and wonderful mess, and that the only purpose of living beings was to move.

The moment we are inert, it means we're dead, he thought. Milian was familiar with the sentiment. He smiled at Caretta, who was already tinkering with Gallia's old barley grass machine. Milian answered the unasked question,

"I couldn't get it to work."

"That's ok. Just a juicer. Blade mechanism's probably broke in there. Too much buildup."

"I don't think any of these things were made to be very durable, anyway."

"No, nothing is durable on Earth. Cheap and shiny's what they do best."

Milian agreed but he was a little offended nonetheless. Daliya could read him immediately.

"Don't worry, he would buy this stuff too, if he could." She patted Milian's shoulder as she said this.

"The hell I would!" Caretta added immediately. He was a nice man, but he didn't like to be misrepresented.

The three of them shared a mild chuckle, as they moved out onto the porch. As they exited the house, they all looked up at the stars in silence. For a few minutes no one spoke. To Milian, the stars looked more majestic than they had throughout his entire stay prior to this day. He appreciated their shine tonight, in the company of the other two people.

"They look kinda weird, right?" Caretta said, to which Daliya responded,

"Just rocks."

Milian's heart sank.

Quietly, he led them through the cave, which Mr. Caretta seemed to dislike. It did look false and phony, when considered through his eyes, which had seen so many real caverns and was acquainted with true comfort. Milian's aunt, again, picked up on his distress.

"The pool's so blue." She said.

Milian looked at her.

Please, don't.

They walked back to the lemonade porch and looked up one more time. Milian quickened his pace until they reached the front door of the house.

"Where's your stuff?"

"I got everything."

Caretta and Daliya looked at each other, then down to the ground, as they continued to walk. Milian followed. He shut the door, although upon doing so, he realized how ludicrous an action it was. He had hoped to find himself a home on this rock and now he was going to suggest to the legislative committee that they just blow it all up. Build something else. Maybe a lake or an amusement park, a promenade with cafes and gift shops. Whatever. Mantis Green would soon be gone and with it everything that had defined Milian up to this point.

When the ship landed back home, the first thing Milian noticed was the humidity in the air. Mantis Green was wet but not like this. This was a delightful marsh. He was happy to put his feet on the spongy ground again. The fog was warm and comforting. Mr. Caretta offered to host Milian and Daliya for lunch the next day. They accepted.

Milian walked home alone. He could hear the drumming in the distance. It was familiar but uncomfortable. The street lamps were invisible in the fog, except for the orbs of light themselves. He walked through the white mist, following the lights. It was as though he had been lost in some space.

As long as I can feel my feet touch the ground, I know I'm still here.

He thought of his mother. He thought of Gallia. He imagined disintegrating into a storm on Mantis Green.

It was hard to tell if he was going the right way, but somehow he ended up back at his mother's house. The skull was where he left it. He had feared that it would be gone, stolen—or run off by itself. The bloomless Cereus seemed to relax, as if giving up its vigilance. Milian pulled Giancarlo's bones out of his pocket and placed them next to his mother. Then he put a small towel over it all and went upstairs.

Milian took a long hot shower, changed into some clean clothes and went to sleep. He was dreaming, almost instantly, that he was back on Mantis Green, but it was nothing like the place he had just left. It was much larger and there were people everywhere. The baker from his childhood shop was there. Covas and D'Alsace. Sylvia. His two partners from the Marionette proposals. A lot was going on, but no one could see him. They thanked each other for doing this or that. They were all enjoying everything. The porch, the pool, the stars, the fireplace, the stained glass. They ate fruit out of the garden and napped in the pod and the hammock and the bed. They watched TV and played piano and read inside the room, *that* room. The one that had always scared everyone. But none of them saw him and when he tried to speak to Covas, Covas walked away. D'Alsace served an indulgent dessert, but he forgot to give Milian some. Milian went up to ask for his share, but there wasn't any left. Before he even asked, he heard D'Alsace in the kitchen, announcing triumphantly,

"We had just enough for everyone!"

Why didn't they see him or hear him? He thought he saw Sylvia looking at him, wondering if she should say something. *Yes.* He knew she had seen him. He knew that she knew. When he woke up, he wanted to call her and ask her. *Why, if you knew, didn't you say something?*

SLEEK AND SLIMY

The next day, there was a bizarre mood in the air. Milian and Daliya had lunch with Mr. Caretta at his restaurant. The fog didn't clear at all, even when it got hot. The heat just turned the mist into a glue that covered everything. Skin and hair and everything was sticky and slimy and sleek. Things were different at home. Milian was unsettled by this and what it meant. He felt like the gooeyness of the atmosphere had seeped through his ears and into his brain. His thoughts couldn't move through their natural course.

I can't finish any old thoughts and I can't begin any new ones.

He was afraid of being left behind but couldn't find a way to participate in the conversation with Caretta and his aunt. They seemed so suddenly eloquent and he so dumb.

A sack of nails could think more than me right now.

Waste.

"So, what's the plan now, boy?" Caretta asked.

"Well, I don't know. I guess I have to call some people

and see what we can do."

That was vague, even for Milian, considering how much time he had spent on Mantis Green by himself, and how very anticipated his feedback was.

"I thought you were gonna be talking up a storm. What did you do that whole time? Do you have to go back, finish anything?"

"No, it's done. I don't know. I'm sorry. I really don't know."

Daliya looked down at her food, then the water lapping up on the shore, passersby, anyone and anything, except Milian. Caretta was carefree and animated, like he had no idea. He just ate and ate, retelling anecdotes about a friend of a friend and back in the day and then another time. Milian was quiet and detached. After the meal, he and Daliya thanked Mr. Caretta and prepared to go home.

"Don't worry. You'll be fine, both of you."

Who is this man? Why is he so damn calm? My brain is fried and this man is calm. I don't know what this is. I don't know why. I just don't know.

Caretta had nothing and still he wanted very little. Small moments of joy were a feast to last him days, and they seemed to be plentiful. All it took was an amiable encounter or a good bite of food. According to some of my aunt's old friends, he had been through some character shifts throughout the years, but since he found himself without a family, he settled into his most sanguine humor yet. He became everyone's friend—everyone still willing to partake—and resolved to expand the reach of his simplest daily routines. He took the long way to everything, did much of his work for free, and fed the hungry, regardless of their ability to reciprocate. It's a common phase for many people everywhere, but Caretta did it differently, without any effort at all, and it always seemed like it was everyone else seeking him out, rather than the other way around. Did he derive a lot of pleasure out of being wanted like this? I assumed he must. Seemed to me like an addictive situation. Maybe Caretta *was* selfish, after all.

As I went through my thoughts about Ascilogo Caretta—carpenter, engineer, astropilot, fisherman, cook and neighborhood sweetheart—I felt worse and worse. Tarnished and guilty. Idle and fat. Poor. Inanimate. Undignified. I wanted more than anything to tear him down somehow, in a small enough way that would go unnoticed by most, to uncover his corrupt sense of self-importance, to expose him as an opportunistic vampire, to call him a parasite until he confessed to an insincere motivation for his jovial behavior. People don't change. But they must.

Cynicism is true evil, and I must belong to him.

PROMONTORY

Home can be lost. You can lose the connection to your-self. The thing that makes you beat as you. The substance in the tube.

A few weeks after I'd left Mantis Green behind, my aunt and I rode with Caretta to the Stratos Station, where we met up with Covas and D'Alsace. My approval paperwork had been delivered to customs by Sylvia's people, along with tem-porary permits for Caretta and my aunt. We planned to stay in the same building as them, which was owned by Clarence Bing. It was small but posh.

Too many amenities, I thought, at first. But then, I found myself eating a freshly baked muffin in a plush bamboo robe, while playing a game on the console. Pampered little freak. I felt like an alligator in yoga pants.

And once again, I'd left my mother's skull back in the house. What if the place got robbed? How could I sit here en-joying myself while she was over there, in danger of being stolen, crushed up and drunk with coconut water on that beach with the drums. But maybe she'd like that. To move beyond the idea of being just a skull.

From my room, I could see the immigration compound on the other side of the station. Hundreds of people like me were lined up, arriving from the same holding facility I was in, down on the surface. The news claimed that most of these people were criminals, but I could see a lot of them were children and elderly people, quiet young professionals, a handful of them seemed to be nurses or doctors, still in their scrubs.

Things had escalated quickly since I'd been kicked out. At least they gave me some time to gather my things and a scheduled appointment to be escorted out. Looked like a lot of these people had been picked up in a raid and brought here directly. I watched one of the nurses leave her place in line, asking each person for something no one had. She held a piece of paper in her hand and would refer to it each time she asked.

From my window, it looked like most of the buildings were already full of people who were awaiting approval or denial on a case, or presumably just waiting for a ship to take them wherever they were going. Some officials were setting up tents in the assembly space beyond the little complex of buildings. This part of the Marionette looked more like a war zone than the orbital airport terminal it was intended to be.

But I suppose that was just what they had told us it would become, eventually.

On New Year's Eve, Caretta asked us all to join him in his apartment. His son had planned to visit, but his work permit was up for review still. He was afraid that leaving the surface would cause problems, so he had cancelled his trip. Caretta was upset, of course, but he still wanted to celebrate,

"New Year's Eve is the most direct holiday we have. Done with this; let's go with that! I don't like to waste it. Come over. We'll make some food and have some drinks. Oh that young cook… The cook, your friend's boyfriend, he's making some sort of cake. And wow what a talent he has! I haven't tasted anything like it in my life! A real wonder! Come on down Milian. Ok? Alright, son! See you in a bit."

I think I only got to say,

"Hello," and then,

"Ok."

Caretta had assembled us, his bucket of characters, in the little cubby, for a New Year's Eve celebration. It was the two of us, my aunt, Covas and D'Alsace, Mr. Bing, and Sylvia, who had recently sublet a space on one of the small satellite clusters near Sondras Alluma. I feared some uncomfortable conversations would spark over the table, but none did.

MANTIS GREEN

With my aunt's help, Caretta made a dish I'd forgotten all about. My grandmother had fed it to all of us on cold rainy days, or when we got home late after traveling. I knew it well because I'd made it for myself many times, back on Earth.

I was convinced that the trick was to make the whole thing using only one fork. That was mythology. The secret, of course, was the balance of flavors, but I had believed (and still believed) that the single tool used to prepare my grandmother's signature rainy day meal was the magic wand that imparted its unforgettable flavor. Seeing my aunt and Caretta make it for all of us, it was easy to see how culture travels. My grandmother made it for the entire family, and each member of the family made it for everyone they knew, and now strangers were carrying it on.

It wasn't anything fancy. Pasta with a cream sauce made of pasta water, butter, powdered milk and grated parmesan and romano cheese. The smell would tell if you had made it right. And although I wasn't at my mother's house, surrounded by the footprints of my upbringing, or in my apartment on Earth surrounded by my evidential identity materials, I caught a scent of my core through that creamy pasta dish we all had held onto generation after generation. Even after I stopped eating animal by-products, this dish was home to me. I regretted all the times I had ruined it with mushrooms or peas. I resented my tendency to make it only to medicate my depression during stressful times. I was grateful to know it and remember it until now. And I was happy to taste it from the hand of someone outside our immediate family. To see my grandmother's expression on a plate, on a ring of satellites orbiting the Earth. In a way, she had made it out, too. We all did.

The counter in Caretta's cubby overlooked the fireworks in London. I ate my meal silently and watched. I imagined the fights going on. The kisses, the break ups, the cancers eating people up, how grateful or resentful the hosts of the numerous events taking place would be, the political crackling between public figures involved, various ailments and behavioral faux-pas that were going on down there. I watched and I didn't know how to feel. At first, I despaired about finding an appropriate match for the scene within my empathy bank. But in the end, I saw that I gained nothing by living two minutes ahead in the future. And I went back to my plate and savored it. And then I looked up and wished I could be down there again, and hoped that one day, perhaps, I would. The cloud generators were working properly, producing enough fog, not the kind of velvet fog that forms in Yarey every night, but a fog that was softer and less predictable. Just as you got used to it, it dissipated over pockets of light.

"Milian?"

I looked up from my empty plate to find Caretta and

his bucket of characters staring at me. I cocked my head sideways but forgot to speak. Bing intervened,

"We don't know what time it is up here, technically, but London just had their midnight, so we figured—"

"Lisbon's next. Or Morocco, you said, right?" Caretta was drunk and jolly. He was enjoying the geography game.

"Dublin, too." Covas chimed in.

"How is that? Isn't that pretty much the same area as London?"

Covas and D'Alsace drew a map on a piece of paper for him, and showed him how some time zones curved. Caretta was on the floor, laughing.

"That's so silly! I don't understand—ah-ha-ha-ha-ha."

"You're out of control. Get up." My aunt had become Caretta's keeper at some point.

"No. Come sit over here, my time zone! Everybody! It's New Year's Eve down here in my time zone! A toast please!"

Covas and I chuckled. He was serious, though, and wanted us all to sit on the floor with him. We obliged. He sobered up and made us all hold our hands out, as if waiting to receive something.

"Fill these hands with every good thing you can fit into a year, Earth year or Yarey year or whatever year. Give thanks to every day for the new trinket in your hands. At the end of the year, look at your hands again. They will be full. Look at everything you collected throughout the year…"

He paused and looked at each of us, dead serious.

"And EAT IT! HA-HA-HA-HA-HA!"

Nobody *got it*, but he enjoyed it so much that we all laughed along with him. Some people have that contagious joy that you can never explain to anyone. Being swept up by their current can be like a weird high, and you know you can never repeat the experiment in your own lab.

"Cheers everyone! Happy New Year!"

"Happy New Year!"

"Happy New Year."

"Happy New Year's!"

"Yay! New Years!"

I looked out the window, where the fireworks were happening all over Western Europe and Africa. It would be a few hours before they reached across the Atlantic to New York and Quebec, and almost a half a day before they got to Howland Island, though I'm not sure they do fireworks there. The other side of the ring would certainly see Honolulu's fireworks a few hours before that.

Just like that, the year was gone. And I did hope to fill my hands with something more than ashes.

MANTIS GREEN

TAKE COVER AND HOPE FOR HALLELUJAH

I was up anyway, but when the rumbling came I really woke up. The Marionette was under attack. There was yelling and gunshots and smells I hadn't encountered since I was a child. Suddenly, I was staring at a painting on the wall again, crouching on the floor. I had ended up hugging my knees again, completely involuntarily, like I had never fucking left this place. There they were, these ghosts: the stairs. Right next to me. The smell of my mother's perfume. My wet hair from having just showered after volleyball practice. My hands. They weren't my hands. They were a child's hands. My arms were squeezed together by some force. My mother. My aunt. My grandmothers. The neighbors. All here with me. My aunt saying that they had bombed the heliport, which was just a few blocks down the road. But I had been there again. I had gone back and seen that it had been reconstructed and expanded. *What do you mean, this is happening again?*

"Did they get him out?" My mother asked. She meant the President.

"I don't know. I had to leave when they started driving the tanks down the street."

I remembered the tanks. I had seen them. What in the world was happening? I had the sudden feeling that I was trapped in my child body. That I had lived out my whole life in that one moment. Was I about to die? Was this it? Is this how I rationalized dying? I would move to Earth, pursue some career, fail miserably at it and then die the same way anyway. Or had I really avoided that?

Yelling. Yelling in my face. My life was a daydream. Could that be? My aunt was yelling right at my face. Her eyes were beautiful amber yellow, almost green, with a cataract over part of the left. A matter of age.

I looked down at my hands.

There was blood.

They were my hands, not a child's.

Scratched and bloody.

"Milian! Come on!"

I followed her and Caretta out of the building into the back of the hive. Covas and Bing were stuffing sacks and bottles and other things into Caretta's little ship. Hot orange flashes and gunshots were everywhere. D'Alsace was inside on a mat with a twisted grimace on his face. I helped my aunt and Caretta into the ship and then brought in the rest of the bags that Covas and Bing had left by the hatch.

MANTIS GREEN

D'Alsace was lying with a pool of blood around his hips and legs. Bing and Covas tended to his wounds as Caretta and my aunt got the ship moving. And I was there, repeatedly checking my hands to make sure they were mine. Where were we?

As we took off, I looked out the window and saw the attackers destroying the structures. A massive chunk of the Stratos Station was propelled into the atmosphere by an explosion within the tunnel. The debris would hit the surface within minutes. I would have hoped for it to land in the ocean, but even that would produce massive tidal waves and who knows what else. Could this really be happening? Who is doing this and why?

D'Alsace had been breathing hard and crying from the pain for a while but now his face was sagging. Covas held him tightly, unaware of his surroundings. I had never seen that face on him before. Covas was the most stable and rational of us all. Now he wouldn't stop looking at D'Alsace like he was waiting for an answer that wouldn't come. Bing seemed confident that he would make it, but I suppose that's not something you can prove. D'Alsace looked up at Covas and turned into him. Cradling his head with his right hand, Covas closed his eyes and took a deep breath. Bing reached out and gripped his ankle. They exchanged a look. With me, too. My aunt and Caretta focused on pathfinding.

I looked back out the window and, unaffected by all this, on the other side of the hot orange flashes, was Mantis Green. It had been detached from the Marionette for some time. I wondered if it would eventually drift away, lush and uninhabited.

I looked down at my hands again. They were mine.

HOME

I woke up and we were on the marshy beach by Caretta's shack, which had been robbed during a riot that had broken out while we were gone. Much of neighborhood had been burned down. We'd gone from one pile of ruins to another, but at least this one wasn't hovering over another planet.

"No matter. It happens… No matter."

He walked through the modest remains of his home, studying the damage for a while. They had taken a few things he never thought he would lose. Things he thought no one would want.

"It was just a small thing. A poem from a friend from when she left to move to Earth."

"Oh. When—"

"From when we were kids. She never made it there. I didn't even find out til nearly 30 years later. Thought she just had never thought of me again, being over there with all those better things."

"I'm sorry."

"No matter. Just a little thing. People go, you know."

He pointed at my bag, where he assumed I was still carrying my mother's skull. I didn't have it, of course. It was floating around in space, mingling with stardust.

Caretta looked at the top of his hands, inspecting the papery skin over his knuckles. Then he got up, touched my shoulder and said,

"Come on."

My aunt was outside inspecting D'Alsace's wounds with Bing, guessing at his chance of recovery. He seemed to be breathing normally. Covas was more or less back to his pragmatic self, quietly taking inventory of the supplies we had so hastily packed into the ship.

We hid in my mother's house. At the top terrace, there was a shed with a well inside it. We went up in the dark, filled up some canteens and then headed back down to the basement through the courtyard, where the family had gathered years earlier, to watch the blooming Cereus.

All night I heard the symphony of drums, D'Alsace's heavy breathing and Caretta's snoring. I felt safe enough for now, but I was afraid to sleep, and then to dream of the ghosts I remembered on the Marionette during the attack.

The next morning, I awoke much earlier than everyone else and walked through the fog to see if the bakery was still intact. It seemed that my old neighborhood hadn't been hit as badly as Caretta's. The bakery was open but only half stocked. I managed to persuade the baker to sell me enough cola rolls and salt rounds for all of us. He was trying to enforce a one-per-customer rule, but since they were smaller pastries, he let me take them.

"Haven't been able to get enough butter lately. If you hear anything…"

I promised I would tell him, although he was certainly more likely than me to get news of a black market source for butter. No matter. I appreciated that he thought of me as someone who would know these things.

As I walked back to the house, I glanced toward Earth. It glowed dimly through the gloomy fog that still hung in the air, spurts of glittering lights exploding here and there, but I knew it wasn't fireworks.

Farah Ysvette Mourad Vera

LOS ALMACENADOS (SQUIRRELED AWAY)

We stayed in the house for several days doing as little as possible. D'Alsace slept a lot while recovering from the injuries he'd suffered. A piece of metal had been embedded into his back. Removing it may have killed him, so instead we hoped to let it live in there. Covas stayed with him most of the time, while perusing through my father's old horticulture journals. Bing and Caretta drank together and took care of the ship, while my aunt went out on a couple excursions a day, trying to secure provisional visas for Taianna Lune, a small planet that had recently emerged as a neutral place for people to hide out. It had been uninhabited until very recently, when a small group of refugees settled there, less than two decades ago. It was a small colony with limited resources and very tight security. They were more flexible with people who were fleeing violence, but unless we could find someone to vouch for us, they were likely to turn us away at the dock. We would try anyway. If we couldn't make it there, we'd have to find a bigger ship and aim for Mars. Earth's sister planet was overcrowded with refugees already, but at least we knew they were more likely to take us. Getting there from here would take more time, meaning more supplies. With six of us on board, we had barely made it back here from the Marionette on Caretta's little ship. We'd need more space to store water and food, and depending on how soon we left, we'd also have to account for medical supplies for D'Alsace. He was doing well, but it would take a while for him to recover fully, and we had to keep his torso properly cleaned and supported. I suppose we could've gone in separate ships, three of us in each... in any case, my aunt was figuring all of this out. I was unofficially in charge of the food. I'd always been a lazy cook but I loved nutritious food, and I think it did us well to eat only vegetables from the house garden and Caretta's fresh fish for a few days. Caretta and Bing had been by his shack every other day, to salvage what they could and catch some fish for us.

"What was he like?" Caretta asked, tugging on his hand line.

"Who? Art? He was sweet."

Bing smiled, remembering his old partner.

"Sweet man—bad temper sometimes, you know, we all get sour. He was sweet though. Took care of everybody he liked."

"Where'd you meet?"

"Oh we knew each other for a long time, since we were

kids, pretty much. We didn't go to the same school, but we lived nearby and we did a lot of the same things in our free
time, had the same group of friends, pretty much. It just made
sense for us."

Bing recalled a time when he and Art had set up a little
door to door business. They had asked their parents for a loan
to buy materials for weaving blankets and hammocks. They
had weaved for days without stopping. Then, they'd gone
door to door selling what they had made. The hammocks had
been more popular than the blankets, but they were much
harder to make and hardly worth the money they were selling
for. They abandoned the idea for a few years, but then Art had
picked it back up. He had asked his sisters to join the endeavor
and the three of them weaved hundreds of hammocks and
hammock chairs. They made enough money to buy a set of
two industrial hammock looms. Bing had reentered the business, per Art's request. His sisters had claimed one of the
looms for themselves and branched off on their own. They
were still at it, apparently. Two old ladies in a cottage somewhere, weaving hammocks and living off the profit. They had
also built a handful of schools on Mars after partnering with a
transportation company that wanted to advertise its tours on
their hammocks. The old ladies didn't care much for advertising normally, but in this case, they had taken it because they
were offered free travel to and from the red planet. How else

could they have afforded it? Anyway, Caretta was beside himself after hearing about the old ladies.

"My mother would have loved them."

"I'm not so sure about that. They were pretty aggressive. Art left home because of them. They were always picking on him, taking his stuff. I don't know how he put up with it for so long, but he moved in with me... let me see, I think it was when I had just turned twenty-one. Yup. Because I remember I filed my taxes that year and I had to do a bunch of new stuff because I had turned twenty-one."

Bing wanted to keep talking but Caretta had apparently shut off. It happened very seldom, but he hadn't been feeling very confident about the way his life had gone. He had stayed safe and sound in his shack by the water—the gift his mother had given him—and now he didn't even have that and it was like having nothing at all. Caretta watched his hand line just dangling limp, more debris than tool.

I visited the baker again the next morning. He was standing behind the counter, eyes down. I walked along the narrow space from the door to the register. An old lady was securing her purchases to a small shopping cart. She looked up at me, questioning why I watched her. I looked away. Once she had finished securing her items onto the wheeled contraption, she rushed inelegantly out of the bakery.

"Do you have any palmiers today?"

"No. Sorry, sir."

Sir…

"Okay, thanks. I think I'll just have three regular loaves."

"Sure thing. I've got some rainbow meringues, if you'd like? Fresh, actually."

"Sure, I'll take a box. Thank you."

I thought they would be appreciated back at the house.

The baker explained that his suppliers were still short on butter and milk.

"But plenty of eggs and sugar. The butter I do get I gotta use for regular bread, you know? That's what people eat to live. Everything else… I miss making it, but hey! Soon enough, man. This can't last forever."

I had been gone for under a year, but things were getting worse fast. People were more fearful than before. And more suspicious. The streets were emptier than they had been during my months of mourning after my expulsion from Earth.

I broke away from the baker, awkwardly, and went on to visit the fruit merchant, who had always been less personable but still easy to talk to. Within a few minutes, I was on my way back to the house. The fog was clearing up and it was relatively quiet, save for a few excited murmurs that escaped here and there. The neighborhood was grim, like it had been on that day of the coup, when I was a kid.

All day the sky was orange and gray. We all ate in silence, in the room with D'Alsace. After supper, I watered my father's plants with his can. Some of them had dried up in my aunt's absence, but a few remained remarkably alive. The stillness of the house pressed the silence tightly to my ears. I thought I might put on the television, even if it was just the one man talking nonsense for hours. Maybe they would play some old nature shows eventually. But I didn't dare be the one to break the silence because it seemed like no one else was bothered by it. Instead, I went and sat on the green step at the window of my old bedroom upstairs and listened to the quiet of the house. As the sun went down and the fog thickened up again, the drumming emerged. Night after night I had peeked out the window and seen no Earth and heard no drums. We had been locked up tightly, as if under water. But now, although I still couldn't see a thing, I heard the drums again. And for the first time since we left the Marionette, I felt safe. I feared everything but the nest of these sounds, which contained and guarded me. They were insulation between me and everything that wasn't me or mine. And I was humiliated when I realized that my comfort came from this place. That I wanted nothing more in my scope than the familiar, the established. The very things I had renounced before. The very things that pinned my dear planet Earth against me and those like me. I found myself unable to speak coherently for days, maybe weeks—and obviously, I stopped tracking time and stopped analyzing things.

Some events have a way of correcting your apathy.

A CUP OF COFFEE

Sylvia had booked a seat on a volunteer rescue boat that would take her out of the flooded city. Her loft was filled with people. Gallia's house, too. Debris from the Marionette had scatted and fallen violently throughout the Pacific. Hundreds of thousands of people had died. Archipelagos, islands and miles of coastal land were under water. Millions had survived but were now displaced. Billions of people were short on resources and patience. And billions had resolved to do something about it. Millions more would perish for one reason or another, throughout this transition to the new design of the planet. Government and law enforcement had little to do with the way it would all shake out, though they sure would try their best (or worst) to control it.

Sylvia, like millions of others, sought a way out. She had booked a seat on this makeshift rescue boat that would deliver her to meet with a high-end pilot, who would fly her and a few dozen others to Mantis Green. The pilot was a family friend, who had flown Gallia to remote places all over the planet. He'd been tempted to decline the request, but Sylvia had offered him several times the usual fare, and this was no time to turn down money.

As she approached the boarding area, all Sylvia could think about was having a cup of coffee. She'd been drinking it daily for sixteen years and the last three days had been a throbbing nightmare without it.

The coffee shops in her neighborhood had been ransacked, like most other businesses. She was hoping to buy some from someone on the boat, or at the very least, to find some along the way. Gallia's manor had been taken over by a large mob. They'd built a sort of ancient Rome inside. This was an exhibit of people the way people used to be thousands of years ago; the way, perhaps, they'd always been. It's possible that all along since then, it had all just been an act. Times of scattered values and disorder like this came along frequently in different forms and with different advocates, which was understandable, considering that people were only here for a hundred years or so. Volatility was natural for us.

Often times, Earth responded to large scale destruction with solidarity and structured leadership. Other times, it reacted with fear and ignorance, reducing the complexity of its civilization to the territorial conflict of tribes at war. And the leadership tribe locked itself up to maintain its power and resources, ignoring its duty to those it pertains to represent. This has often been the case in the blue marble Earth, and elsewhere. In a way, it was good to know that *some* cooperation was still taking place somewhere in the midst of this global self-composting. Almost natural.

Sylvia watched as two women beat a man to death with his own shoes so that they could take his tent. Soon the rain would come, followed by sleet and snow, so those sleeping on the elevated bits of street that peeked over the water were desperate for shelter.

In a few minutes, she would reach the spot where she was supposed to hop on the boat.

"If I don't see you, I'll keep going. Wear yellow," the captain had said.

He had been specific and clear and she would be there in a yellow shirt, just as he asked. She passed an aid truck that was distributing supplies to the anemone of desperate arms that had pressed itself against the back door. Small bags filled with items, she couldn't tell what, but also cups of steaming liquid. Coffee. She thought she could smell it. Dark roast, black, a little watery but fresh. Soon.

If I had known this would happen, I would have gone up there with her. She would be up there with me. The owl would be with us, too. I wouldn't be down here, with those two murderous old ladies, with the mass of reaching hands, the dozens of people crammed into my tiny tri-loft, like in an old tenement or an asylum. Gallia's house packed like a Las Vegas casino on a holiday weekend. Worse. What was left of the world as we knew it turned into a sprawling refugee camp, but with no one to provide assistance. It could be that if I had just held on a little longer, this all may not have happened. That I was selfish under the guise of independence. That I was selfish but claimed I was only freeing myself from the confines of... what? This woman I loved and despised. I had felt such relief after she left for Mantis Green. And I had felt relieved again when it swallowed her up. Selfishness. And nothing more.

The boat arrived on time, and Sylvia hopped right on. Inside were about eight others, some well dressed but distraught, some barely clothed but calm, most of them looking down. There was a little kid covered in dust and some kind of dark liquid.

At first I thought it was blood, but it was actually oil. Strange thing, but I supposed they still used gas in some parts of the world. They had come up from South America, where the ocean had washed their entire village down in a gulp. They held onto a billboard for days, and had used other pieces of debris to row until they saw land.

"And the smell. Very bad smell. You know, fish and farts kind of smell."

"Egg farts." The kid added.

"Oh yeah. Strong acid smells."

Sylvia offered a sympathetic smile, but she wanted desperately to exit the conversation. And she wanted that coffee now more than ever.

"You like coffee?"

"What?"

"Coffee? You like?"

"Uh, yes, but…"

"Hey man, can we turn up here and get some coffee and bread?"

"What are you talking about?"

"Tengo un amigo por aquí que se me hace que nos puede echar unos pedazos de pan y una botella de cafecito, eh?" / "*I have a friend around here that I think might be able to give us a few pieces of bread and a bottle of coffee. How about it?*"

"Ah sí? Ok man. Here, call 'em up."

The captain tossed the man a flimsy little phone. Soon enough, the man was speaking into it, in a language that nobody else understood. The other passengers were visibly uneasy, scanning each other's faces to see if anybody knew what the man was saying. They looked at the kid, too, but she wasn't paying attention. An older gentleman tried to wave her down. As the boat hit a piece of debris, the jolt made him kick the child, by accident. The man hung up the phone. He checked that the kid was ok and then shot a look at the older man across the way. Then he told the captain to make a left.

"What language was that?"

"Gahardi."

"Are you two aliens?"

"Originally, I am. She's born here. Well, in Caracas, but you know what I mean."

"No, I don't."

"She's from Earth. I was born in Gahar, Thila, which is pretty close by."

"What's your profession?"

"I'm in sales."

"Sales of what?" The older man chimed in.

"Household goods, pillows, tables, all that. I coordinate between stores and distributors."

"That doesn't sound like a profession."

"How did you get your papers?"

"I was a singer before."

"And now you're a salesman."

"Yeah. My vocal cords got damaged and now I'm a salesman."

"We should get out of here. Look at the street he took us down to."

"It's a bad neighborhood."

"They're all bad neighborhoods." Sylvia spoke out of nervousness. Trying to diffuse the tension.

"It's right up here. Come on. You're getting nervous for no reason. These are normal, good people."

But the passengers weren't having it. They didn't know what he had said to the person on the phone and in their minds, judging by the tin rooftops and the sidewalks filled with tents, he was clearly leading them to some kind of black market organ trafficking situation. Best case scenario, they would be killed and cremated and their ashes would be used in black magic rituals, or as medicine.

The captain stopped the motor.

"Get off."

"What?"

"Get off the boat, man."

"Please. No. Why?"

"I told you there's no guarantee and I'm not taking any chances."

"Sir, please!"

"Don't call me sir. Get off the boat with your kid."

"Ask your friends down the street for help." The older man chimed in.

Sylvia didn't want to have to participate, but she knew she would regret saying nothing.

"Please, just keep going. It's just a misunderstanding. We can find some food later, ok? We don't have to keep going down this way."

"Yeah, it's ok. We don't care. I can call my friend and tell him we're not stopping anyway."

"So you think we're going to let you call him again? And you're gonna tell him what? You think we're stupid?"

"Sir, please!" Sylvia pleaded.

"Do not call me sir, lady! Off now, man. You and the kid. I'm sorry."

The kid, suddenly realizing what was going on, exclaimed,

"Please!"

"You can't be serious!"

"I paid you. Please!"

"Get off and I give you your money."

The man and his kid looked at the other passengers, pleading. They were met with silence. They got off the boat. As they were about to swim away, Sylvia got up.

"I can't believe this."

"Be my guest." The captain gestured toward the water.

Sylvia got off and joined the man and the child floating on the side. The captain handed the man his money and took off.

"Hey! What about mine?"

The driver kept going faster up the street and vanished.

"Never you mind about that money. We'll get you

some more somewhere."

"It's more the principle of the thing."

"Those people have no principles. You hungry?"

"Sure. Do you really have a friend up here?"

He was visibly hurt by her comment. She regretted saying it, but she was angry, and it had just come out that way. Nothing she could do now but swim up to the embankment with these two strangers and make conversation. His name was Alit Santoner and the child was his daughter, Nico.

They arrived at a family-sized tent, bleached by many months of sunlight. Inside, it was a cozy home. Clean and organized. Appliances, TV, a computer, a sofa, everything she had in her own tri-loft. And nowhere near as crowded. And nowhere near as loud. Or hot.

Two old women and an even older man were sitting on stools around a set of portable stoves, atop which were a coffee pot and a pan covered with foil and a loose lid. Sylvia, Alit and Nico joined them.

"Hola linda, bienvenida al abode." / *"Hi beautiful, welcome to the abode."*

The smaller of the two women spoke to Nico in a singsongy voice, as she handed her a little notepad and a pencil.

"Dibújame un fantasmita!" / *"Draw me a little ghost!"*

Nico was bashful but excited. She took the notepad and teased at it with the pencil. Alit took the opportunity to tell them about what had happened—and to explain how Sylvia ended up drinking coffee and eating pan biscuits with them that morning.

"I don't know what's going on with people. I'm sorry."

"It's ok. We'll figure something out." Sylvia replied to the old man, Fulgencio, who had emigrated from country to country since he was fifteen.

"Would you want to join us?"

Fulgencio's eyes lit up. The two old women watched him and looked at each other.

"Vaya hombre. Por qué no?" / *"Come on, man. Why not?"*

"Ah! Que va!" / *"Oh! No way!"*

"Vamos mijo. La vida es una sola…" / *"Come on, son. You only live once…"*

"He want to leave for years, but no money and now so old, no work."

"Ya mujer!" / *"Stop woman!"*

"Que no te lo van a pedir otra vez, mi amor." / *"They're not gonna ask you again, my love."*

"Ya si, pero ya, ya…" / *"Yeah, ok, but, ok enough…"*

"Y ustedes?" / *"What about you?"* Alit asked the two women.

"No gracias mijo aqui ya estamos acostumbradas." / *"No, thank you, son. We're already comfortable here."*

MANTIS GREEN

"Y a mi no me sacan de mi tierra." / *"And nobody gets me off my land."*

The older woman had been born in the US, first generation, and she refused to leave, even if it meant a better life—although most places left at this point would have been more or less the same, especially for two elderly women accustomed to living in a tent in temperate weather.

Fulgencio knew this would be his last chance to move again. And anyway, he had been staying with the two ladies for a long time, now. Their comments were a clear message. He accepted the invitation and the three of them planned to go together, further up the neighborhood, to see a former army lieutenant, who had an in with some private long-distance colony charters. Sylvia had volunteered to pay for passage for the four of them. But first, they shared a meal of pan biscuits and coffee.

Coffee. All I had wanted all day was this. And it was so much better than I had expected. The warm spiciness traveled through my body, in a solid string. I could trust myself today. And I had to get us all out before things got worse. Was it selfish to leave? Or could I do more from afar than by staying here?

I sipped my coffee, pairing each sip with a thought and savoring it. Soon, we'd be on Mantis Green and I didn't know what kind of mess we'd find up there. Most of the plant life had been composted and resown, and the structures repaired, but nothing had been main-

tained since the post mortem.

Another sip. I'd bring some coffee with us. And one of those backpacking stoves, just in case.

Fulgencio finished his meal outside, fidgeting with his luggage. He laid out his possessions on a piece of tarp and arranged them into puzzle pieces, separated from each other by equal distance. He was the type of person who re-arranged the route maps on buses, so that they're all organized. Nico watched him from the edge of the tent. She was the type of kid who preferred playing alone, so that she could pretend to be grown up.

FROM THE FARTHER POINT

Covas had found a way to pull the signal from one of the satellites on Earth, so we finally got to watch some real news on a portable device. Fire and water mostly. Masses of people asking each other for help. Journalists sharing equipment and supplies. Unsurprisingly, a lack of response from top leadership but plenty from those in the periphery. We even caught the tail-end of a Rotari ad calling for volunteers.

Bing remained stoic,

"It's what we do best. It'll pass."

D'Alsace propped himself up to speak,

"It's never been like this, though. This is something else. This isn't the usual destructive impulse."

"It's just destruction."

"I—What do we do?"

He looked at each of us, begging for an answer that none of us had.

Covas took his hand and gestured for him to lie back down.

It was an indescribable type of disaster. They had destroyed themselves while aiming for us. It wasn't a new concept, but the scope of it had changed what it meant. It was, still, the same mentality that articulated evil in stories throughout time and all over the universe, the same sentiment of avarice, that same angry group of people who refused to relinquish their advantage in a changing world, the raging fire on a sinking ship. If we can't have it all, then no one can have a damn thing. Those people came and went, but the damage they did to the world scarred it deeply and shaped its future.

Now, we were here, in my mother's house. The ring I had built around the Earth was now missing its station. D'Alsace wouldn't be back on his feet for several months, maybe years—maybe he would never walk normally again. Covas and Bing were lost in some philosophical place. My blue marble, Earth, had suffered disastrous tidal waves, following the fallen debris from the Marionette. Its people were crowded on top of each other, unable to discern anymore who the "real" citizens were. Many parts of the planet were now underwater. Mountains had softened and crumbled. Valleys had turned into massive saltwater lakes or swamps. And I won't even mention the fish…

From this point, farther than most with a view of Earth at all, it still looked the same shade of blue. And I wondered if maybe this had happened many times before, without the rest of us noticing. That maybe I had witnessed a great tsunami or hurricane, and oblivious to its destruction, assumed all was well still. Maybe Bing was right in saying that it is what they do best. I knew what he meant because I felt that way about my own birthplace. But disengagement frightened me. Much more could happen while we slept.

STIR IT

The sky went from pitch black to yellow, mottled with tiny clouds in bold patterns. No Cloudi generator had accomplished such a work on that canvas. Sylvia had been up for some time, watching it turn colors: black, navy, steel, rust, orange, warm yellow, lime green, cool yellow. As the light intensified, the water, and all the debris floating in it, reflected it back. Lights dancing across the landscape, where streets had been, shining orbs of white and yellow onto the tents on the embankments. In the distance, a sort of iridescence hung in the air. It would be time to leave soon.

As soon as they wake up.

Sylvia and Alit went looking for Alit's army friend. Apparently she had moved.

"Don't smell right."

"Well, could she have just left, maybe?"

"She wouldn't leave like that."

They looked and looked but couldn't find her tent

311

anywhere, nor anyone who knew—or would admit to knowing—where she had gone. Eventually they came upon a
spot, far north in the neighborhood, where several buildings,
including Gallia's old beloved book store, had been burned
down. *Maybe she left in a rush when this all went up in flames.*

The truth was less cinematic. Her name was Benata,
and she had been tied up and tortured in a basement nearby.
She had suffocated to death when the fire overtook the building, along with three hundred or so others, who had also
been "found out" by police and brought down there. They'd
been detained for different reasons. Some of them had committed crimes, violent or nonviolent. Some of them held phony
immigration papers. And some of them had simply refused to
cooperate with the police in catching others. Among the char-
red remains were people ages 3 to 87. All walks of life. Missing
limbs, torsos, heads, dismembered or attached, lying amidst
small piles of teeth and phalangeal bones. A scene that almost
anyone would assume could have only happened elsewhere,
in the far and brutal past of a less advanced society. Surely,
eventually, it would be memorialized by way of photographs,
in a clean-aired room, dramatically lit, with an audience at a
quarter of their attention, drunk on local wine. And they
would agree on the degree of horror exhibited, maybe one-up
each other in a frivolous discussion about the aesthetics of the
photograph and how they support or detract from the mea-

ning of the "piece." And then take another sip. Sleepy eyes. Hoping to get drunk soon. Thinking about when to go home.

Sylvia and Alit had no idea that the bodies were underground, but it still didn't sit right with them that an entire part of town had been burned to the ground overnight, so they explored the ruins trying to make sense of them.

Sylvia found a poetry book, whose 3-inch core had survived the flood and fire. She was able to read a few words from the center of each page.

"Better than nothing, I guess." Alit said, then added,

"What's it say?"

"Let's see..."

She scanned the round little pages for something comprehensible.

"Though / in the allied / for as it / discontinued interests / effort alone / tramps and flowers / their eagerness / endless / alone."

"It's about giving up." He said, as if playing a guessing game.

Sylvia smiled and dismissed it. It wasn't until they had moved on after walking through the ashes that she saw how gray her hands and feet were. They'd been walking all day and the sun looked like it might go down soon. For days, the sky had been orange and cloudy, not in the pleasant pre-storm way that she loved, but because of the terrible pollution. She hadn't seen the round shape of the sun for several days, nearly a week. Near the coast it was worse. Everyday, hundreds more people arrived from all sides of the sea. And they all arrived searching for heat and food. Bonfires raged for days along the new beaches to sustain the immediate aid required by the newly arrived masses everywhere.

When Milian & company saw the images from the satellites, it looked like new Earth had miles of fluorescent lava outlining each new continent.

Farah Ysvette Mourad Vera

I FEARED INDIFFERENCE

The drumming wouldn't leave me, but still I felt uneasy. The political environment had never been stable, and every few years it bubbled up like a natural disaster. Then, the flooding receded on its own and no one demanded any kind of clean up. People eventually stepped back onto the marshy ground and spoke to each other with the same presumptuous attitude. They were jovial and inclusive, and at the same time strict and judgmental. My mother had written me once that she thought I had lost myself while adjusting to Earth. I replied to her that I was fine.

Now, I had been back here and tried to adjust again, but the most natural place for me was outside my window, well above the ground and away from the drumming. In the middle of the night on Earth's orbit, I had enjoyed the strangeness away from the surface. Lighter than some days. Clear. Back home, it was nothing but thick white. And although my skin and my eyes felt infinite relief in this environment, even without the aid of lotions and eyes drops, I couldn't help but

315

miss looking further up with nothing in between. I missed the —often unnoticed—act of perceiving the space between my eyes and the stars. So far that they took on that false shine and the rest went completely dark. How blinded we can be when what we see is so flashy.

BABARATA

Sylvia and company arrived back at the top of the road, where they were greeted by a tin gate engraved with the word, "Babarata." This neighborhood had been a small isolated community during the week, and a breakfast haven for outsiders on weekends, when the market was open. It was part flea market, part promenade. Many of the stalls were built with pieces of plywood and tin and the food was cooked on makeshift stoves. The inhabitants were skilled inventors who had acquired and developed their multiple talents in times of need. The weekends were a chance to showcase their achievements and make money.

Now, the market was open every day, given the unprecedented flow of desperate people. Most stalls made no profit, but Babaratans weren't concerned with money beyond survival. And anyway, the entire social dynamic had shifted, maybe temporarily, but at least for a long time to come, until resettlements were possible again or until the population decreased. Either way, the Babaratans had been through many crises be-

317

fore and were prepared to help others get through theirs. Naturally, some people were dubious. One of those was Sylvia, though she would never admit it.

Sylvia liked to think that she had struggled and persevered, but the truth was that most of the struggle had usually fallen on those around her: her parents, Gallia, Milian & Rotari, etc. She had been shielded from a lot, and as a result, her own life had always happened somewhat outside of her reach. She was in between spaces. Never out of control but never at the wheel. With Gallia gone, her choices had no other recipient, and accountability was fully hers. Gradually, she eased into this new practice.

The air smelled rotten and it was hot again. Some days were cold. Some days were hot. Sylvia had once preferred hot, but now hot brought with it a stench she couldn't bear: unwashed flesh, decaying fish and rancid milk. Soon enough, they would be up and away from it, she thought, but then what? Would the stench follow? Maybe it had nothing to do with the neighborhood, or with the millions of organisms decaying in the hot sun for miles and miles around the world. The gases collecting and hanging like clouds over every place. No, maybe it wasn't that. It was exhausting to try to visualize how far the smell went, or pinpoint where it started.

Sylvia refused to indulge further and crawled into the

tent to sleep for a while. Outside were Alit and the old ladies. The kid was next door, in a makeshift yard, fenced in, where they grew some of their fruits and vegetables. She was playing board games with the old man.

"Okay… okay… tienen todo, then?" / "Okay… okay… you have everything, then?"

"Si mama. Estamos bien. Ya para arrancar y no ver más pa tras." / "Yes, momma. We're good. Ready to take off and never look back."

"Ok mijo se cuiiiidan eh?" / "Ok son, take caaaare of yourselves, ok?" The older lady said, in her musical voice. Sylvia wondered what she could be saying in such tones.

"Si viejita. Por mas que sea, la chamita no me lo aguanta todo… ella sabe hasta dónde alcanza." / "Yes, old lady. Anyway, my little girl can't go along with everything… she's aware of how much she can take."

"Tu también?" / "And you, too?"

"Claro viejita." / "Of course, old lady."

"Ok que los acompañe el lucero de la mañana. Que los lleve a la asunción con buena vibración y total que bueno pues aquí estamos, si no." / "Ok, well, I hope the star of the morning will accompany you. And that the ascension brings to you good vibrations and well, ok, here we are, if that's not the case."

She laughed heartily at herself, waving her hand back and forth, like she'd spoken too much nonsense, and looked up at Alit, smiling. Alit regarded her the same way.

"Take care, baby." The other lady chimed in.

"Asunción divina, mi amor." / *"Divine ascension, my love."*

One more good wish from the matriarch.

"Thanks mama. Gracias viejita." / *"Thanks momma. Thank you, old lady."*

He kissed them both before slipping into the tent, where Sylvia was now pretending to be asleep.

"Did you get to say goodbye?" He knew she was up, but she still didn't respond.

"I'll come wake you up when it's time." He slinked back out and into the little yard, looking for his daughter.

Sylvia heard the commotion next door. The old ladies bringing their cushions back into the tent, the old man prepping the bedding and boiling some water for tea. Father and child recounting their days to each other. And all filtered through the empty space of her own little tent, which they had graciously provided for her to use for privacy. She wished that she had done a million things differently, and eventually, while deep in her cloud of regrets, she fell asleep. As had been the pattern for several nights, she awoke in the morning, as if the night had been no longer than a minute, certain that she had not rested even a bit.

The sun wasn't up yet, but the little community of Babarata had already begun the day, with small and simple conversations about the night's rest and how much good it had done to some people, as well as a sharing of food and what smelled like really great coffee. Sylvia got up with a craving for it. The occupants of the big tent next door were all outside, including the old matriarch, and the kid, who was feeding some pigeons and pigs. The other woman, Alit, and the old man were sitting together, sipping coffee and planning out the day, the kid drawing fantasmistas near the water. Sylvia emerged fresh-faced, despite firmly believing that she had only slept for one minute.

"Happens when you're really tired."

"I know. It just feels the same way every day now. I don't know if I'm actually sleeping."

"You are."

"Maybe I'm not."

"You are. Don't worry too much. If you need to sleep, your body will do it to you."

PACK UP AGAIN

D'Alsace was stable enough, at last. For several days, the streets had been unusually violent. We were rocked to sleep each night by the rumble of bombs and gunfire, and we awoke to sounds of mourning.

There was no easy way to discern when the people's discontent would manifest itself. The town had been burning at the busiest spots for at least four days now, but the upcoming holiday week promised a possible cease fire. Even in times of street combat, the people of Yarey took time to drink and celebrate. That's when we planned to make it out on Caretta's scrappy little ship.

For days, we had been trying to scatter ourselves throughout the streets, at different times of the day, when it was quiet enough, to bring our cargo onboard the vessel, little by little. Some days it was a full pack, but on more dangerous occasions all we could manage to carry inconspicuously was a small paper bag or two of food or fuel. We were rarely stopped by police or neighbors, regardless of the size of our carry-bag, but we feared the encounters nonetheless. Once we did get stopped by one of my aunt's friends,

"Milian?"

"Oh hi, Narie."

"I didn't know you were still in town. I thought you left."

"No, I just had to take care of some things, but I'm back at the house. You should come visit sometime."

I felt Covas freeze up with the same discomfort that I felt snaking up my spine. I spoke the way I thought would seem natural… but it was patently unnatural for me to say such a thing to such a person. This lady was a nosy congregation leader who had stopped by my mother's house, uninvited, on several occasions. She would surely do it again, sooner or later. She regarded Covas curiously. He was obviously *different*: a short blonde man with a light complexion. If he hadn't been with me, she wouldn't have concealed her accusatory stare with phony playfulness.

"Yes, son, I'll stop on by just as soon as all of this passes. It's hard enough to even leave the house these days, you know?"

"Yes, it's very dangerous."

"Well, you head on home soon. Both of you. I'm sorry, I don't think I've met you. Are you—"

"I'm Covas. Milian's friend. Just visiting."

"Oh nice. Nice to meet you."

"You too. Take care."

Covas was much better than me at breaking away. I smiled at Narie and walked away before she could say another word—and I knew she wanted to say plenty. There's a certain look of excited concern that the people back home get when they think they've *caught* you. It was best to part ways as soon as possible.

Covas and I made it to the ship without any further stops, but we still thought it best to wait a while before heading back to the house. To pass the time, we had a drink. It had been several weeks since I had tasted any alcohol at all, so as I drank it, its effect wiggled through my legs to my feet at full tilt. Weak and sleepy, I told Covas about my mother and how her bones had been stolen and used in the rituals. I told him about the drums and asked him if he could hear them. He could not. I wasn't sure if I could hear them myself at that moment. But I assured him that I'd heard them plenty, in nights past.

"Where do they come from?"

"People over by the water, near the hillside. Medicine and whatnot."

"Have you ever joined in to see what it's all about?"

"I've watched them."

He looked at me, waiting.

"I don't know. I probably should have left her skull back there."

"It's just bone. She won't mind."

She wouldn't mind even if she did know. The point wasn't that she would mind, but that I felt guilty. I had released her to release myself and in so doing, I had trapped myself in my own hands. I looked down at them. My hands. Covered in metallic dust from Caretta's ship.

FOR DAYS, IT RAINED

It rained for several days. Something that hadn't happened naturally for almost a decade. Some of the tents were waterproof, but others had to be covered with tarps, boards, quilts made from rubber sheets or in our case, taken down and set up again beneath some form of shelter. We had left early before the rain started, so that we could get a spot inside the market.

The roof of the structure was tin, and it was as loud as it was cheap. However, by the third day, the noise had become nothing but room tone to us. Still, the loudness of it kept us from talking much. Mostly, we slept and ate and read. I didn't have much to browse through, aside from my legal papers and a couple of old journals, so I borrowed some old nature magazines from the hosts. One of Gallia's articles was in one of them. It was about recycled wood from old canoes. I couldn't read past the first couple paragraphs. It was like having her here, demanding my attention, no matter what she was saying. I felt the heaviness of her presence, like an angry ghost waiting for recompense. For the first time in a while, I felt guilty and that made me afraid of being here still. I kept flipping through the magazine, but it all felt like her. She watched me from those pages and knew that I was thinking about her.

It rained for days and the rain kept me in that tent with Gallia's quiet ghost judging me. No one else paid me any mind. They all took the time to internalize, meditate, rest, whatever one does while wholly self-absorbed. Even the child spoke to no one. She played by herself near Alit, who read nonstop. A thick historical fiction novel about nouveaux missionaries in a nearby colony—his home perhaps. I would have asked him for more details, but the noisy rain on the roof made it too awkward to talk. It was the noisy rooftop also that kept us from hearing the rest of the people in the market. Or were they all just as silent?

After a few days, I was afraid to speak. If I did, would I throw everything off-balance? Would they find my voice disturbing? Would we find out that it wasn't raining at all anymore?

For days it rained and we didn't discuss a plan for leaving. More than ever, it seemed like we would stay. I was afraid of the idea. It had started to seem like a nice prospect.

MARIONETTE PIECES

We landed back on the Marionette, near Mantis Green. It was full of people and garbage. We exited Caretta's little ship, one by one, stepping into the street, where we were gree- ted by an unfriendly marshal named Ted.

He led us into a holding area filled with dozens of others, who were bent over their registration forms, trying to decipher what to put for this one or that one.

What did you put?

Is that going to hurt my chances of staying?

Should I say more or leave it at that?

People frantically searching their bags for documents— or money, perhaps. Most of the population in this area simply didn't have the buying power of those beyond the makeshift gate. Caretta and Covas knew I was considering bribing somebody, and they were against it. D'Alsace was with me. Bing was prepared to do whatever we decided,

"So long as it's sound."

"We might not get through this until three days from

now, at least. We're not even in the thick of it."

"Where is it that we are going?"

Covas thought this was all a mistake. It might have been. We could have stayed in my mother's house, but if we were going to be killed off by a mob, I'd rather die here than there. Caretta wasn't short on candor.

"It's the same shit, son."

"Yes, I suppose it is."

"I think we best just wait our turn then. Can't see we're gonna do much better than this once we get through here."

Why, of all times, do you pick this time to be pessimistic, old man? People have a thing for untimely flare-ups. I had loved Caretta very much the past few months, and if it weren't for him, I would have certainly died or lost my mind, at least twice. But on this particular day, I really wanted to tie him to a rocket and ship him far away, like in those old cartoons. However, with my luck being that of the same cartoons, he'd probably show up in front of me, again, like nothing happened. And I'd go crazy, with spirals in my eyes.

My aunt had stayed back. Spongy marsh. My mother's ghost. The plants and their nighttime claws. The drumming. So loud and so faint at the same time, and at no point did the beat of them leave me. Having my aunt there re-assured me. Something of me was still present. Even if I could never re-claim ownership of the house or the things in it, as long as she was there, they wouldn't touch it. As soon as the last family member passed, the house became public property, along with everything inside it. Even the plants couldn't lay full claim to the pots hosting their roots.

But this too was an endangered and unfriendly home. This place and the blue ball it floated over. Gallia had made this happen, and if she had seen it develop, she would have claimed to care and then dismissed it in her own mind. She would have sheltered herself. She would have moved away, further up the inhabitable zone, to any place that would let her have more than a fair share and some excessive privacy. She would have never made it back in Yarey. The drums, the processions, the music, the shopping would have all been too much for her. I hated her more now than I ever did. And I never knew I had hated her at all before.

I thought of Sylvia. What was she really like? Was she still alive, down there or up here? I wanted her to live, to be fair—she would still have a chance to right some wrongs. But I didn't want her to be safe. And I didn't want her to get away from all this. I felt guilty for wishing torment on her, but I thought it was only fair. For I can't say how long they had lived with such comfort (or homely discomfort) and indulged in their criticisms and complaints. Now maybe they'd have to let nature take its course, let life live through them instead of the other way around.

I was a furious thing and I didn't have any business filling out my paperwork like a responsible creature. I felt Gallia and Sylvia judging me. I felt my mother's pity. And my aunt's. I knew Caretta's patience was at an end. And that Covas would be less sympathetic to me, and even to D'Alsace. D'Alsace and Bing would be fine. They're true resilience, alive and breathing in bodies. Their expectations were little more than getting through the gate alive, together. Once past that, we'd huddle up and figure it out, or go on our separate ways. The rest of us were much more anxious about our possible fates, and especially how we related to each other. Favors to be repaid, jobs to fulfill. Identities to maintain.

I calmed myself down and filled out some of the paperwork. When I looked up, I spotted a lizard on a nearby rock. It had something stuck to its face. A bee. Food. This lizard had no idea how it got here, and it paid no attention to all of us. All that mattered now was getting something to eat. It wasn't until now that I realized how hungry I was. Suddenly, eating a bee made sense. I have always thought, though, that insects are too small to be enjoyable without some sauce. Apricot sauce or maybe cayenne and ginger.

What would we eat when we ran out of rations? Hopefully, we'd be out of the holding area by then. But maybe we would not, and if that was to be the case, I wanted to be better than prepared.

331

MANTIS GREEN

We slept in the ship that night, like most of the other people nearby. D'Alsace had trouble getting in bed, stiff leg and all, and Covas resisted the urge to help. I say it that way because Covas is not capable of turning his back on anyone, no matter what. Caretta snored all night, made it feel like we were back at the house. In the morning, it'd be time for madeleines and watering the plants. And maybe do some planning for turning Mantis Green into a nomadic satellite.

As I surrendered to sleep, I tried to absorb how my companions felt, hoping to feel it all myself. I knew very little about what provoked me to do this, but I'd done it all my life, inherited habit from my mother and father. I searched for concrete definitions and found only anger and loneliness and a deep want. Translation and performance were phony connections. Covas and D'Alsace, my aunt and Caretta, Bing and everyone. Just me. Just Sylvia.

BETTER HERE THAN WHERE

Sylvia craved a cup of coffee again, on a day when the two old ladies refused to get up. The old man only offered tea. Sylvia dared not ask for coffee for fear of insulting him. When he handed her the tea, she added far too much cream and sugar and ruined it. But she acted like it was the best tea she'd ever had in her life.

"I don't know a lot of people that do milk in their tea."

"I've always liked it like that."

"I knew a guy like that. He added something to EVERYTHING."

Sylvia chuckled to humor him.

"He still didn't like it, though. Everything was always wrong."

"Some people are like that."

"You like that?"

"No. But the woman I used to work with was like that."

"Why'd you leave?"

"She died."

"Oh…"

"It's ok. She was ready. For a while. She's the woman that died on Mantis Green."

"Oh, what?! Oh my goodness! You never told me that!"

"Yeah."

"Why you never tell me that?"

"I don't know. It didn't occur to me to talk about it until now."

It took a few more days, but finally Sylvia, Alit and the two others were off on a small ship. They docked on the side of the Marionette.

"Thank you."

"Thanks, man."

"Thanks man!" echoed the kid.

"Yup. No problem. If you need to go back or you know other people trying to come up here, send them my way."

"Of course."

The pilot, Garelle, was one of the cooks from the market. She had learned to fly from a friend, who had started a small tourism agency. They'd owned three shuttles. Unfortunately, the friend's health took a turn and he had to sell his company off. Garelle bought one of the ships with money she had been saving to migrate back to her ancestral planet. Like most other inhabited rocks in the neighborhood, Garelle's home had been engulfed in civil war, which resulted in a mass exodus. The tensions arising between the minor planet and the other worlds nearby (mainly Earth) precipitated great hostility against people like her. She worried about being detained or deported, so she thought it prudent to own a private ship, and anyway, her friend was grateful for the money he earned in the speedy transaction. He was able to go in for treatment, which would have added several years to his life had he not died from being struck by a sudden wall of water and debris, as a chunk of the Marionette fell near the clinic mid-way through his appointment. Garelle held a private funeral for him, in her mind, as she flew the ship over the area in the subsequent days. If he had survived, how would she have explained to him what happened? It was an odd form of daydreaming.

Sylvia and her companions stepped out into the mass of people awaiting admission. A row of guards or police or officials of some kind were making their way through the thickness of bodies, tagging and numbering them as they went along. They struggled to avoid questions, giving some people non-answers and others just a standard push.

"They'll help you with that up at the gate. Hold onto your tags."

It could take several hours to get to these officers. Then several more to reach the gate. The gate itself was more or less a relief, until people found themselves waiting another few hours just to speak to somebody. And then it would still be days before they were released into the makeshift processing complex past the gate. Half the people didn't make it in and were instead held at the camps on either side of the gate, waiting for a way back to the surface, crafting a second try at getting through the gate, or in some cases, making arrangements to migrate elsewhere. Over the sea of heads, Sylvia spotted the first officers and estimated they might reach her in a couple hours. It ended up being four Earth hours before she was handed a set of tags with numbers and letters on it.

"Tag yourselves and your belongings. Assume you'll be separated."

And after that they moved on without looking back or confirming that everything was clear and fine. Just like that. Hours of waiting. They came and went and then there was a lot more waiting up ahead.

Surely, soon, we'd be hungry.

Farah Ysvette Mourad Vera

BELOW, THE CLOUDS MADE EARTH DISAPPEAR

The surface was completely covered in clouds for at least three days. We slept in shifts, since most people had given up on the whole night and day concept by now. D'Alsace was sick, surely his body was overtaxed with repairing itself in addition to the trek and ordeal of trying to get back to headquarters. And you'd think that if anyone were to get through right away, it would be Bing. After all, he owned a great chunk of the place. But I don't think anyone expected him to fight for special treatment. At least not right away.

"We wait our turn and turn up the heat once we get in the right room with the right people."

I didn't like the political side of Bing. It was bitter and manipulative and forgot that it once liked you, as a friendly acquaintance at least. Now he was a sort of patronizing overseer, directing us to sleep or distribute food to the others, and in this case, to wait quietly, despite our standing.

I didn't want to fight with anyone. I was unnerved by

all the waiting, but the idea of claiming preferential treatment was a humiliating notion. In a time of such evident despair among masses of people, playing with status was vulgar. Still, Bing and I maintained our friendship, even if Bing felt the need to condescend and commandeer me and the others throughout this slowly developing situation.

When I slept, I dreamt in fragments. Gallia was there sometimes, Sylvia too. Birds I had to take care of would suddenly die. My teeth were made of bubble gum or paper. We were underwater and no one knew what the rules were. The waves were coming. A bridge onto which we could throw bag after bag of supplies, and it would never sink. My feet sank into mud, however, time and time again. And time and time again, my mother would come after me, headless, rotting, running with split legs, covered in hair or torn newspapers, with the drumming in the back. And every once in a while, a trumpet player.

La Trompeta was a music shop I used to go to. As a kid, I tried playing guitar and the four-stringed guitar, a local favorite. Twice a week, after school, I would go to *La Trompeta* for guitar lessons. I only went for three months and then gave up. But I would return in the evenings on the weekend sometimes, when they would move the racks and shelves off to the side to accommodate a small crowd for concerts. The cashier's desk would transform into a bar and a band would play on their little stage in the back. I'd met a few new friends at *La Trompeta*. We'd share snacks and a dance or two, but we didn't get along very well outside of the dark little shop. Still, we had a good time together at *La Trompeta*. And I did enjoy several of those before they were forced to close down, shortly after I'd bought a set of replacement strings that I never ended up using. Surely they were still at my mother's house, rusted or even fossilized.

And speaking of fossilized, it was my turn to wake Caretta, who slept much more deeply than the rest of us. We had brought a small tent, where we each took turns napping. Two hours and your time was up, at least for another eight hours. That seemed to keep us going ok. At least for the past three days.

I thought about my fish. My aunt had kept them at her house, in a little pond. Surely, they'd be happy there—unless the house got attacked, of course. And as soon as we passed through this gate, I planned to look for Jones, or at least find out if anyone knew what had happened to him.

THE GATE

Slowly, each group made its way up to the gate, unaware of the other. Both Sylvia and Milian were consumed, rehearsing how they planned to secure passage for their companions. It was very unlikely that they could make it through without their help, except for Bing and Covas.

None of them wanted to sleep anymore—or eat, for that matter. It'd been at least twenty hours since any of them had eaten anything or slept. Nico, despite her young age, was the quickest to observe the pattern.

"They ask them and then they take the person behind them and bring them back out later and then they ask the person behind that person and then they take the person at the front of the line. That was the person they took *before* before, when there was someone else waiting at the front of the line."

There were three separate interviews, it seemed. First, presumably for basic information, biometrics and whatnot. Then, probably some kind of filtering process, where some people were sent back or admitted to the front of the line. Finally, an admission decision.

We couldn't see it before, but at the front there were three spray painted lines. Yellow, pink and blue. Shoddy work, crooked and uneven, oversaturated in spots. Caretta was driving me nuts.

"This is something else. If we had known what awaited, eh?"

"Better here than over there."

Covas was gracious enough to present him with the facts. Riots had broken out back home, yet again. This time big enough to be reported by Earth's news sources. There was fire everywhere, luckily more or less contained by the daily arrival of the fog. There were several dead and hundreds wounded, including a young cadet who had stolen a plane and tried to assassinate the local dictator. I wondered why everyone resisted calling it a civil war. The government was at war with its people, as tends to happen everywhere, from time to time. But my home planet hadn't seen this kind of violence for a while. They were peaceful and cautious people, even if they were a little nonchalant when it came to politics and the law.

Three hours later, a fight broke out at the gate. Gunshots were fired. A burst of blood spattered into the air and stained Nico's shoe. She glanced down and then looked away, breathing in sharply. Alit asked if she was ok. She nodded and pretended to brush something off her shirt. As soon as he looked away, Nico positioned herself in a way that hid the trail of blood from Alit and the others. She refused to move until it was time to step further up in line. Sylvia looked down at her and noticed the blood on her shoe. She called her over to her side, but Nico refused and started to make figures with her fingers, as if engrossed in a fantasy. She didn't want anyone to panic and was hoping to delay the drama for as long as possible.

When Alit noticed the blood, he was horrified. Nico blamed Sylvia for giving it away.

"What... they kill somebody?"

Fulgencio had been aware of the whole thing, too, and he also had been hoping that no one would make a big deal out of it.

"Mijo, ese está bien, a lo mejor se lo llevaron a la enfermería. Yo lo ví moviéndose." / "*Son, he's fine. They probably took him to the infirmary. I saw him moving.*"

"Ah si? Pero a dónde se fueron, por todo esto?" / "*Oh yeah? But where could they have taken him, through all this?*"

"Ah no se hijo. No se preocupe. Ya pasa la cosa. Sabe cómo es la gente de torpe, ignorante, impaciente y malcriada." / "*Well, I don't know, son. Don't worry. It'll pass. You know that people are dumb, ignorant, impatient and spoiled.*"

"Así es..." Alit was stunned and displaced from the

scene. He looked down at Nico, who was still pretending to play with her hands and now with a colored pencil, too. Her index and middle fingers walking the length of it, like a tight rope.

"La fantasía de un niño." / *"The fantasy of a child."*

The old man spoke, smiling warmly, to comfort Alit, who couldn't register the gesture. He looked at the child but didn't exactly see her, or anyone else. He was silent for the remainder of the wait until they reached the gate.

THEY ARE DIFFERENT FROM US

A similar thing happened to persons throughout. Although the Marionette had no defined nationality, the officers at the gate were stopping all who were not from the United States. Bing, Sylvia, and Covas had all passed their first two interviews, but Milian, Alit, Nico, D'Alsace and the two old men were still held inside tents, on their second interviews. Alit and Nico were refused. So was Caretta—no surprise there, as he had gone off on the guards about the superiority of his home planet and gotten himself immediately dismissed. D'Alsace made it through. Milian and Fulgencio remained.

I was joined, in my tent, by two others: a woman in a large sweatshirt, maybe late 50s and another one, couple decades younger, with long braided hair and a bad sunburn. They smelled sour and musty. It occurred to me that I hadn't thought about my own smell in a long time. What did I smell like? Smells traveled differently on the Marionette. Still, these women smelled to me and I hoped I didn't smell to them. They say you can never really smell yourself—not your true smell, at least. And I knew it to be true from traveling between planets. They also have smells. Atmospheres are like the inch of air just above a freshly poured soda. The fizz of the surface has a strong and distinctive scent.

You will not believe it, but as I battled the smell of these two women, I heard the drums play. For an instant, they both looked like my mother, staring at me, asking me what I was doing here.

"Go home," *they seemed to say.*

I'm trying.

SONDRAS IN RUINS

Bing was granted access to Sondras Alluma, where he set up Covas and D'Alsace in a small apartment at the edge, near the connecting tunnel. Fulgencio, Alit and Nico remained at the complex and would try again to get in. Caretta would, too, but begrudgingly.

The entire half of the rock by the station was in ruins and covered in sheets of titanium. Much of it was little more than a dark can full of debris. Part of it had survived, and in exchange for passage, Bing had been tasked with helping to prepare it as housing for more people coming through the gate in the upcoming days. Most of the satellites were full by now, except for Mantis Green, where a storm was still raging.

After four more days, they came to get me. And just in time, too. In those four days, the two women had ripened even more, and I wasn't sure how much longer I could take it. Bing came into the tent with the two officers and explained that he needed my help fixing up the station and its connecting areas on Sondras Alluma. I accepted. They had me sign a stack of paperwork that had been produced in a rush, typos and all, some stating my provisional permission to remain on the Marionette based on sponsorship from Bing, another actually declaring me a partial stakeholder, and a few others related to liability and accountability and all that other shit. I signed them all without reading them too closely, and left with Bing, craving a bed to sleep on for a few hours.

Sondras Alluma was a mess. Even the area we were in had been hole-punched by gunfire. The walls were stained with blood and other various shades of browns and yellows. And from a window, I saw the only thing that could be worse. Earth was a horrid greenish brown. That pristine blue marble was now stewing in its own sewage. I wondered if anyone down there could care. What was it like?

I thought of my fish and Jones. They had been in the now-can-like area of Sondras Alluma when it happened. In the same room as my things. The tank had exploded, but the fish had survived, in a small puddle. I had scooped them up in a thermos and brought them with us. Jones was nowhere to be found. Had he made it out alive? And there it was… in the darkest pit of the can: the drumming.

Jones. Where are you? Jones. Mother. Sylvia. Jones. Gallia, why are you doing this?

She had perhaps cursed me and everyone else. Could she have known that her passing would cause the end of Earth as she knew it? Her precious swamplands just sediment at the bottom of a thick salty sludge. The melted cities she frequented littered with bodies, dead and alive. The bacterial air she dreaded permeating every nook and crevice of the planet, making it sick.

Sylvia thought,
If she could see all this, she would just say that she's glad she died before it happened.

I fear sleep because I fear seeing her face. She wants to get to me. I'll have to describe this disaster to her in vivid detail, the way I used to do with the environmental updates before a conference. Sit her down and talk at her. Have her not listen. Memorize a few things, only. Things she can then say, feigning passion, to everyone she comes across that night.

And then, waiting for her to get home, to comfort herself with me. To wash herself with my hair and massage herself with my hands. To rinse her shame with my submission.

I looked down at the brownish surface of Earth and missed my apartment and the coffee. It'd been almost a week since my last cup, but I'd gotten used to the headache by now. Still, I hoped it would all be over soon.

Farah Ysvette Mourad Vera

OUTRAGE IN SILENCE

The stage was Forgiveness and I wasn't ready for it. For months I hadn't felt or seen rain. For weeks, I hadn't even looked down at my dear little planet to see how she was doing. Everyone still left on the surface had most likely found a solution to their problem of survival or passed on and abandoned their claim to resources. Some of those who had left the surface had been admitted to the Marionette, and many others were still waiting at the stations, some on their third or fourth appeal. Others had taken flights to nearby planets, trying their luck there instead.

How many had stopped by my planet? Anyone? Would they consider trading the limited land space on Earth for civil war?

I found that I had a lot of contempt for people. How could they be ungrateful, dismissive, complacent, full of judgment and yet so fearful and spineless?

Up here, in my tiny live+work space, I had plenty to busy myself with. I started growing some plants from seeds I

349

found, no clue what would sprout. It was hard to tell how long I should keep the lamp on them, but I tried to give them equal parts light and darkness.

"Twice the light."

Covas knew much more than me about growing plants on these satellites.

"Keep them on a 24-hour day. Like when you go to sleep, put them to sleep too."

"I don't sleep a lot."

Little known fact. The days on my planet are much longer than the nights. Genetically, I need between 70 and 140 Earth minutes of sleep a night to be healthy and alert. I prefer the lower end. Too much sleep makes me nauseous.

Sylvia was nearby, but I didn't feel comfortable reaching out—I didn't have a method of doing so, either, besides making a public announcement. Communications on the Marionette were almost completely down. Only the mass public resources worked. Every morning, there was a report. Shortages, news from Earth, new services offered, service announcements, and at the end was a lost and found section for persons looking for other persons. I submitted a query about Jones, which had aired for several days, but I never received a response. I could only hope that he hadn't fallen to Earth, trapped in a bundle of debris. Maybe someone had taken him and wasn't willing to give him up now. I could only hope.

The lost and found queries included a time and meeting point, usually what had been nicknamed "town square,"
which was an empty stretch of land where a flea market had
previously been. It had been completely trashed in the attacks.
Afterwards, the debris had been swept into the dumpster and
pulverized, to make space for new arrivals to meet up with
their loved ones, and for mass distribution of resources.

I got the feeling that although people preferred being
up here in the clean air, they resented the way things were run.
Many demanded special treatment, usually folks with money
or what they considered unique situations. Under different
circumstances, they may have been offered preferential treatment, but this was a galactic disaster and whoever didn't understand that should be added to a SPECIAL TREATMENT
DENIED list forever. At our level, however, we did make certain accommodations for some people. Primarily, we took care
of people with timely health concerns, disabilities, advanced
age and maternity cases. People who applied for expedited
service had to provide a reason, and if applicable, attach supporting evidence. We made no exceptions for two popular
"Reasons": "I am [name of prominent person]," and "We have
children with us." We did take a moment to explain to the
prominent people that we simply had to take care of others
with health concerns, first. Usually, this embarrassed them into

hopping back in line. The children were young. They could use their springy little legs to wait. We gave no further explanation for those.

I've always been surprised by the elite status that children have on Earth. After surviving birth, if no health problems are present, children are extremely resilient and know to wait their turn. If they're taught to. Many a brat and a malcontent are created by being granted this royal treatment based on a low number of years lived. The idea that your rambunctious eight year old should be admitted into the mess hall ahead of this diabetic man, who very well might die if he doesn't get food and medicine in a timely manner, is ludicrous.

"I'm sorry. Please return to your seat."

"My child has to eat."

Your child is playing with a stranger's skirt.

I really wanted to say so many things to so many people over the last few weeks. I thought about it incessantly. Oh, that someone would challenge me! But no one dared. Things were too dire. Admission could be rescinded immediately over any conflict, as deemed necessary by an authorized person. Every day, we had a reminder of this. It also applied to authorized persons. We could be kicked off the Marionette too, but the case had to be reviewed and approved by six people from a separate department first, to avoid any abuse of power and eliminate petty retaliation cases.

Farah Ysvette Mourad Vera

At the end of each day, my head felt like a soggy mushroom. The migraine was nearly continuous now. Nothing made it better and everything made it worse. It also didn't help that the Marionette had almost no humidity. Water was scarce, at least until they could finish the clean-and-transpo system to bring water here from the surface. For now, I dealt with the headache in the only way I could. Freezing and eating tomatoes and dunking my head in ice water twice a day. It didn't banish the pain but it dulled it enough to live with.

TOO QUIET

We had a good thing for a little while. People were more or less properly accommodated and supplied with modest but appreciable consumables, and the infirmary was emptying out slowly. Down there it was still brown. And Mantis Green was blue. The opposite of what it had been several months ago.

After a few weeks, we got Fulgencio, Caretta, and Alit through with work permits. Nico came through as Alit's dependent. We planned a dinner to celebrate.

D'Alsace fixed us up some dumplings. Fulgencio filled us in on what went on at the complex.

"It was strangely calm. You'd think it would be running and screaming all over the place at all hours, but people had kind of started rebuilding their own things, with whatever they had."

"What about the dead?"

Covas looked up at us, as D'Alsace spoke from the

doorway. He had made a new hobby of lurking and picking fights.

"They're down there." He added, motioning toward the window facing the festering planet.

They were. Decomposing slowly, back into the Earth. Dust to dust, as they say. I wondered if perhaps the brown tinge of my dear little planet was partly due to blood and rotting flesh. I hadn't thought about it that way. And why not? Was I that enamored with the idea of a pristine surface? One that had never been crawled on by billions of two-legged things? The two-legged things, and many four-legged things and other legged and un-legged things that were now fallen and not crawling any longer.

On small stretches of land, they were shoulder to shoulder, straddling each other and trying to survive, as if petrified. If the entire planet were fossilized, its new soil would be shaped like bones. Surely others would land on it and do with it new things, soon enough.

Until then, I had nothing else to do but reconcile the changes I had witnessed. And although reason tells me that it hardly makes sense to feel this way, I often worry that my little entourage and I had been catalysts in these fatal changes to Earth as we all knew it. Gallia most of all. Or maybe it was me most of all. Or Sylvia. Or Covas. One of us could have stopped the rest.

MANTIS GREEN

We confused caution with indolence.
Our hopeful hesitation brought us ruin.
I can list it all, again and again. Try to understand.
But what use is it to analyze it now?

Farah Ysvette Mourad Vera

IN THE MONTHS THAT FOLLOWED

Sylvia and I met up in the ballroom of the station, a space to be repaired. Covas had cooked a squash stew for us to try. Bing had convinced him to start growing whatever he could on Mantis Green, where the underground farms were still very much alive and plenty fruitful. He had found that he could grow three types of dwarf squash and a lot of baby cabbages. Miniature vegetables were faster and more economic to produce, and anyway they were the only seeds we had, which I had brought with me from my apartment on Earth to my mother's house, and then back to the Marionette.

After they'd sprouted, I had given the potted plants to D'Alsace, but I hate to tell you he was no longer with us by the time we cleaned up the path to Mantis Green and went over there to plant them. His mood soured more and more until it poisoned his spirit. We found him dead in his chair one afternoon. I grabbed his naked shoulder and was immediately reminded of my father: the cold chicken meat. No hideous wound this time, though. Just an empty bottle on the floor by

357

his gray foot. A more merciful scene for one to find, I suppose.

Covas was not surprised, but he was desperate for comfort. He led us back to Mantis Green the same afternoon, where we planted the seedlings in the underground gardens. We parted ways and left him there. Alit and the two old men had been contracted to help with the gardens, but they wouldn't be around all the time.

For several weeks, we didn't see Covas at all. He sent evidence of his wellbeing, however. Snapshots of a sprout here and there. One day, the bud of a small zucchini blossom. The next day, a few more. On the day I met Sylvia, he showed up to serve the stew himself. He had lost some weight, but otherwise seemed healthy. His skin was especially plump. I envied it. The Marionette was incredibly dry still, even after the conditioning system had been fully repaired and improved for the increased population.

We ate the soup and were nourished by its natural sweetness. There was much to say but neither of us knew where to start. When he returned from the kitchen, Covas brought with him a bowl of beans and nuts and a dark brown loaf of something.

"Algae bread. Imported." He pointed down to Earth.

It seemed Covas had established his own business on the other side of the Marionette. He had built a small community that converged around Mantis Green, with the help of some marine farmers he had encountered in the crowds at the gate.

Sylvia, Covas and I worked on a proposal to show the orbital ministry stationed at the gate. They'd been the spokespeople for the U.S. government, which was still theoretically governing the Marionette from the mess down below. We planned to make Mantis Green an official port, and to encourage trade between the ring and the surface, as a way of supporting survival efforts in both places.

We'd hired Nico to deliver handwritten correspondence between us. That way, we could all watch over her, while Alit was traveling between Earth and the Marionette. She stayed with Fulgencio and Caretta, who were sharing a small cubby near Sylvia's.

COVAS TO MILIAN

ED:Monday, August 12th
EP:13°51'17.6"S 171°46′00.8"W below standard meter

Dear Friend,

I think we should start to encourage more pickups by offering a credit or bonus. We're losing a fraction of valuable food while waiting for those ships to make their way back to us. And even when they get here, there's only so much they're willing to carry. I've spoken to some of the other producers and they suggested delivering some things themselves, if we can get them the clearance. I feel obliged to tell you they were deported from the surface a few months before the event, so they aren't without direct motivation. However, we do have more compost than we know what to do with now and it's affecting the rest of our petit environment. It would be helpful to engage a few more folks in an effort to keep this stuff moving, even to other planets, if that's an option. I look forward to hea-

ring your thoughts. I know you will lend me due considerati-
on.

Send news when you can.

Love,
Covas

MANTIS GREEN

MILIAN TO COVAS

ED: Saturday, August 17th
EP: 45°28′22.1″N 0°29′50.1″E below standard meter

Covas,

    I received your letter this morning and I will speak to Bing when he's back from the surface on Tuesday. He will have a better approach, as I don't deal with those people at the gate often. As soon as I have a better idea of what the next steps should be, I will write you again and let you know. If you don't hear from me by the end of the month, it may be that something is stuck. Write me on the 1st so that I can have evidence of urgency. I'm sure we'll need it, if we can't get some form of response in the next two weeks.

    Hope all is well on the little rock. I caught a glimpse of a clean green patch down below. Looked like an old vineyard.

Sincerely,
Milian

PS. Is the cave still usable or too overgrown?

MILIAN TO COVAS

ED: Tuesday, August 27th
EP: 45°54'44.7"N 1°21'32.5"W below standard meter

Dear Covas,

We've been given until the first of October to share a proposal with the gatekeepers. I hope to see you and Alit soon. Sylvia and I will be at the complex in Sondras Alluma for the next few weeks, so it should be easy to find us, but if you'd like to set up a firmer time and place, do let me know.

Thank you,
Milian

Farah Ysvette Mourad Vera

COVAS TO MILIAN

ED: Wednesday, September 4th
EP: 13°45'42.7"S 171°53'50.2"W below standard meter

Dear Friend,

According to the meter, I've just started sailing over the South Pacific. It looks a little bluer here. Almost like places I remember. It could be a trick of the eye, of course. Some kind of light and water game inside the atmosphere, filtered through my own little membrane on Mantis Green—a truly magnificent "rock," as you call it. All is well, except I feel that I need to tell you about some bad dreams. In them, I watch a fire roaring and Gallia's face appears. She watches, waiting for me to look away. And then D'Alsace is with me, in his original sweetness. But he turns sour. I don't know exactly how else to describe it, except for that my skin feels very dry when it happens. And then he turns to ash. And my hands freeze in place until all of the ash has piled on top of them. Once that happens, my hands are no longer frozen, but I dare not move them. I want to keep every grain and speck of ash that I can. I name it D'Alsash (the me in my dreams is a morbid person). But I get rewarded for holding it, for the sweetness returns. And it makes Gallia, in the fire, look away and mind her own business.

I feel simultaneously accomplished and defeated when I wake up from this dream. And it's hard to shake the feeling. I also hear the phantom noises you told me about: airplanes, cars, clinking silverware. I know it's nothing more than an illusion, of course. But I do concede that it's a disquieting experience to hear these things so vividly.

I found mushrooms growing inside the cave. It's not too overgrown otherwise. But I did have to drain the pools. I'm now using that area for more compost. The cocoonish environment helps out nicely and speeds up the process a bit, although it does trap the stench. I don't go down there for any other reason (except to pick mushrooms now).

I moved the hammock into the house. Hung it up in the kitchen, actually. I realize it's an unusual place to take a nap, but I like sleeping with the sun on my face. Now that I think of it, that could be why I keep dreaming of fire. I may be getting too much radiation, even through all the filtering and sunscreen. It's a soothing room, actually.

The porch I find to be too lonely and I wanted to ask if you or anyone else has ever felt that way about it. I never thought of a porch as a place to be alone, but it's impossible to escape the screaming solitude of that little bench. The stars look strange and dull. And the size and impact of your own existence is clearer here than anywhere else on the "rock." I suppose many people must enjoy contemplating life from that point of view, but I've never cared for it. I do not mean to sound unappreciative. I do enjoy the pristine night it affords. It was just something that occurred to me last time I sat over there and watched on. It may be different beside another body. We should maybe all try it together some time.

Thank you for securing our meeting. I look forward to it very much. And I look forward to seeing you and Sylvia and Bing. I'm sure Alit is looking forward to it too. He's been training new staff, so that he can spend more time with us up here and see Nico more often. We'll be sailing over the Pacific darkness until then.

Love,
Covas

COVAS WALKING IN DARKNESS

I knew from their personal accounts that both Gallia and Milian experienced some discomfort on Mantis Green. However, I viewed myself as more logical and less dependent on lifestyle attachments. I focused on having as little of a footprint as possible, and I didn't allow for many things to leave their footprints on me, either.

"That we have lived here before."

He told me last night in a dream. We have, in a way, but in what way did he mean it? I suppose I should say,

"In what way did I mean it?"

No matter what the answer is, I am first and foremost aware of the futility of trying to hold on to Earth times and days. And even if we were to continue using the same yardstick, we'd have to alter the notches on it eventually. For me, time is standing still right now, has been for what I think is at least a day. Or maybe it's only been a few hours. I don't know. It never happened like this before. I could easily recall how to convert time units for Earth into time units for these satellites. But the logic of it escapes me now.

I felt it was essential for me to stop digging around in this mine of muddled details, so I went for a walk. I hadn't walked the surface to the cave in some time, I think, and as I came upon the hill, I thought I saw the shadow of a small bird flying overhead. I felt a strange drop in the pit of my stomach, a premonition that didn't shrink down until I arrived at the observatory. Through the telescope, I spotted a meteor, aiming to kiss me on the nose in a few days. I photographed the item and wrote a communication to send with it. I sent it to the folks at the gate, my folks on the nearby rocks and the folks down on the surface. While I waited for anyone's response, someone else took action. Seems that the meteor would have likely missed all of us but then it would have hit the people of Kacin—a small nearby planet, which was now on high alert due to the newly arrived Earth refugees and their drifting space debris. They had been monitoring the skies in our direction since before the attacks. The Earthly habit of pollution had forced Kacin to establish a process for keeping our garbage out of their immediate vicinity. All of this and more I learned from my surface friend Thario, who had been born in Kacin and only moved to Earth two years ago, to farm and export sea vegetables.

I had offered him a spot off the "coast" of Mantis Green in exchange for seeds for my garden and sea veggies for the

Marionette. He agreed to work with me if I could help him secure visas for him and his family. I got them provisional approval and brought them up here with me. We would eventually need to attend a series of meetings for each of them to be allowed to establish permanent residency or to willfully withdraw from the Marionette. Fortunately, that wouldn't be for a long time. And anyway, with the amount of people needed to build out and set up two other rings, they would surely be allowed to stay.

The question that kept coming up was this:

"Was the Marionette considered "Earth"?"

To my knowledge, the Auroral Marionette Treaty hadn't been altered yet to account for an increased number of permanent residents. Considering our future configuration, I'd say we might become a sovereign state instead. We'd make the moon envious.

I do feel a certain pride and patriotism towards this ring and its rocks. Something I didn't feel down there, though it certainly hurts to see her swallowed up in mud and trash.

I looked down to see what colors were there and saw nothing but black. A few days more, I thought.

When I arrived at the cave, moisture hung heavy in mid-air. I emerged with an armful of very plump mushrooms and decided to grill a few over an open flame for dinner. I did it on the porch, where the smoke could drift easily up to the

A/C vents. I burned my tongue with the hot liquid from a mushroom. Eagerness. If I'd been able to taste, I would have praised their sweetness probably, but since I couldn't taste their flavor, I savored their texture: soft and meaty, crisp and chewy at the edges.

SYLVIA TO COVAS

Dear Sir,

I hope this letter finds you well and I look forward to seeing you in person next week. Time has flown by, but we've accomplished a great deal already. It's difficult to be cheerful, of course, but I do think it's worth mentioning anyway. Thank you for including me in your plans. I'm sure we will be able to do a lot of good through it.

And please, if I do ever turn blind and cheerful, remind me of my dues to you and Milian—not that I'm accustomed to taking things for granted, but I've seen it happen to people with values stronger than mine.

Thank you again for the supplies you sent Monday night. We've been able to keep more people satisfied for much longer because of your efforts, so thank you also on their behalf.

Farah Ysvette Mourad Vera

I wanted to ask if you could bring back some photos of the place. We've been discussing a possible tour for the gate-keepers, so it wouldn't hurt to give the place a once over, de-sign-wise, if it needs one. What do you think?

Greatly appreciated.

Your friend,
Sylvia

MANTIS GREEN

DEAR SYLVIA

I took some pictures of the house, but most of them are actually of the gardens, as I imagine this will be the most attractive feature to show. I've been tinkering with the storm system, but it doesn't seem to like me much. It's making me work for it, I think. I'm not sure if it's smart to get it running again, but I would like to see what that rain is like and whether I can use it to grow some more plants offsite. Some of the bigger trees thrive when their roots can dig themselves deeper and further without too much constraint. It might be a good idea to remove part of the house, in fact, and leave more space for the plants to grow. Speaking of growing, the grotto is proving to be a wonderful mushroom farm. I'll roast some for you and your guests when you visit.

Something I am concerned about, and I hate to bring this up, but it has been a popular topic on this side of the ring: the treaty. Some of the producers I work with have temporary paperwork to continue to supply the Marionette with their products and services, but as you can imagine, the resources are limited and many of them are weighing their options, in regard to the future. I think we may lose vital resources if they aren't offered a proper arrangement. The people on this ring will need a stable source of consumables, and so far we've been able to deliver a large part of that. But the pressure is on now and I was wondering if maybe you could bring this up to whoever you are speaking with next week. I've sent a similar request to Milian (though it was just an idea at the time, before tensions started to pile). Would you please consider it? Any suggestions or information you may have I would be happy to relay. I've maintained a more than amicable relationship with most of the people I have in my little satellite network, but I would like to do for them whatever I can, especially considering how much they've done for us already. One of them, I found out this morning, is from Milian's corner of the universe. Please let him know. I await both your responses eagerly.

Love,
Covas

I put the note in its sleeve and left it on the kitchen counter, next to the console, planning to give it to Nico in the afternoon.

I made a cup of toasted rice tea and sat by a small aquarium containing two little fish Alit had brought me from Earth. They were similar to Milian's old pets: silver little swords of flesh. Can fish smell smoke?

MANTIS GREEN

There was a tiny fire on the porch, started by a cinder from my mushroom meal. I put it out easily. Smoke travels much faster in this enclosure. For days, it smelled of fire. And that affected the plants and me. But not the fish.

I dreamed that I'd picked some peanuts and suddenly they'd turned into hot coals in my hands, falling onto my lap and burning through my clothes. I dreamt that I'd woken up under dunes of ash, a black and gray desert all around me. I dreamt of rain and its source was my own body, evaporating inside a newly formed ball of fire. I thought I heard a tiny voice on a tiny planet, suddenly exclaim,

"A new sun!"

And it was me. It was us. On Mantis Green. The new sun.

And all along the fish didn't care at all.

Farah Ysvette Mourad Vera

THE TRAITS

SYLVIA

We'd been staying with Covas (with his permission, of course) on Mantis Green.

In the dream, I heard a laugh (more desperate than that) or a cry (more animated than that). A loud cackle-yelp propelled violently forward and out. An unanchored wildfire. A bug in the code. An unnatural joy-fear that turns the stomach sour as if eclipsed by acid fog. A familiar sound.

I breathed deeply. I had been alone in a room before. I had been alone in a room in her house before. I had been alone in her room before.

But this was disappointing. This mildness.

I'd been afraid before and it wasn't like this, but "unsettled" wasn't disturbing enough. I stood between wanting to wake up to find my situation as Gallia's ornament unchanged; or I wished to watch her get dragged down to the mythic flames of hell and be destroyed, certifying my freedom at last.

Luckily, neither one happened. But instead I was here, in the mildness. Its gray duller than shrinking rain clouds in the desert. If it were a ghost, it would certainly smile differently.

I resented them for trying so hard. And for sticking together, and helping me off the surface. When we met, we were all on different surfaces. Now after this little train wreck, we're all on the same flat noodle of a world surrounding a world that used to be everything. And they continue on and work on things and give a shit. And all I can do is resent them. I have no space for anything else. All I ever wanted was given to me and then some. And I resented them for orchestrating it.

MILIAN

All night I wanted figs. Finally, after a long traverse through time, by which I mean, crossing the Pacific for endless days, I thought of how hungry I was. When your basic needs come back to you again as the headlines instead of the funnies, you've made it over a hurdle. You can see what's next but aren't able to discern where "next" ends.

The figs were downstairs. I don't know why, but now that I was here with others, I was hesitant to move around the halls and rooms by myself, something I had done numerous times, before and after Gallia Sinlava occupied them. It occurred to me that the house had four guest rooms. Surely, she would have never filled them, but I'd liked to have known if she had plans to try. In that sense, it was a sad story. She was never cured of her fear fever. Waste.

Gallia looked into what she thought was a telescope but turned out to be a mirror. And she ran after that image on the other side. Had I known then what I know now... well, I bet we'd all say that and mean it. Even she herself had rubber-stamped her fate (and ours) with sticky red ink. Waste.

COVAS

Alit would be back the next day. I hoped they would be able to secure more soil. Without that, we'd be ruined. Nothing would grow unless we replenished the soil. The compost had helped a little, but that wasn't enough.

I didn't sleep at "night" every night. It seemed like when you left the surface, you left its thinking behind. All the parameters that we existed within were no longer norm. They could be upheld artificially, but the body moved on, regardless.

It adapted.

For the first time, the most secure thing seemed to be obeying instinct over logic.

I worried. I worried often and very much. Would the

deliveries be stopped by the new leadership party? I'd have to come up with plans to satisfy them. I'd have to stop my research. And I'd probably have to hire their people. Hell, they'd fire me and mine, once they were done setting up.

And if that happened, maybe I could move to Milian's hometown. I know... "the grass is greener on the other side" and that sort of thing, but I thought I could make a comfortable living there.

Milian would be all set. He owned the Marionette's design. He had Bing and Sylvia to help. Perhaps Alit and Nico would join me and we could secure voyage for the others, too.

I would declare that I had had doubts about being here. I'd felt terribly afraid the day we landed and saw the mass of people ahead of us. I didn't want to be here. I'd wanted to hide back in the fog of Milian's home planet. I'd hoped, as we got closer to the gate, that we would be rejected.

The gardens were good to me here. I enjoyed their company, but I wanted to leave now. From here, it was hard to tell where that little planet was. It could have been any of those tiny white spheres I'd been watching. The one that flashed at me.

Farah Ysvette Mourad Vera

MAN WAS WITH AND WITHOUT

"Things look better in the morning. Don't worry about it. And don't pick!"

My grandmother's words of comfort after a long hike in the mountains. I must have been nine or ten years old. My feet were blistered. Hers were not. She had worn heels up and down the mountain. When we got home, I sat on the floor in the parlor, took my shoes and socks off and refused to move for the rest of the day. She walked upstairs to the third floor to grab the laundry… in her heels. Then she went in the kitchen to grind up corn for the week's bread. Then she went up the street to meet with some friends for a procession. And off they went, singing through the fog as it thickened. She never once took off the heels. The next day she wore the same shoes on our weekly walk to Chinatown.

I find it interesting that our Chinatown was exactly like some of the ones on Earth. It offered the same comforts: knick knack shops, seafood stands, restaurants, bakeries, tea houses and ice-cream parlors. Once a week, we'd go eat there and my mother and aunt would buy pounds of fresh fish and shellfish to stew. They'd work on it for a whole day and serve it to the neighbors at one of their evening gatherings.

"Best fish is in Chinatown." Always my mother would say. And the crowd agreed.

"I can catch you some."

He always chimed in, this old man. His name was Brauglio. His wife and child had been killed on a train during a government raid. They had been searching the cars for anti-government protesters and when a fight broke out, they panicked and fired at the closest group of passengers. Five died that day, including Brauglio's wife and seven year old daughter. After two years trying to recover, he stopped going home. He vowed to make merry until he died.

"In their name, Maria."

He called everyone Maria, including my mother, even though he knew that wasn't her name.

"Please give me a kiss."

My mother never confronted him about it. She'd just smile and walk away. Then my aunt would start.

"Brauglio! Go away! Who do you think you are, coming here with all that Maria Maria give me a kiss trash? Enough!"

And she would sense my mother watching, mentally begging her to desist.

"Go!" She'd yell again and walk away, taking my mother with her.

"He's drunk."

"He's always drunk."

"Maria, please!"

They'd snicker softly together.

Brauglio would be walking down the street, hunched over, touching his face frequently. He hadn't slept in his house in years. And he hadn't bathed in it either. My friends and I (and the generation after us) thought he was a vagrant. We'd see him bathing at the fountain near school, some days. Other days, he'd be up the mountain, dipping himself in the river. In addition to the empty house, he owned an apartment near the lagoon two hours away, which was also empty.

"I don't even know what it looks like, anymore. If I had to go find it, I probably couldn't."

My mother would talk to him sometimes.

"Maria, thank you. I'm so lucky you talked to me today. I thought I was going to die."

"Don't say that, Brauglio. I just think you need to calm down and enjoy yourself. Make other people happy by letting them be, you know?"

"Yeah. I'm sorry. I just get so happy I want a kiss."

"It's ok. You going home, tonight?"

"Maybe."

And he'd drift away. His smile would freeze in place as his eyes traveled rapidly through memories he preferred not to linger on. Then eventually, as if released from a grip, he'd breathe in and look up.

"Well… I'm off. Chao Maria. Have a good night."

And he'd blow her a kiss and immediately "catch it" and stuff it in his pocket, wagging his finger at it.

"No, no, no!"

My mother would wave goodbye. I'd wave goodbye as well, from my bedroom window upstairs. I don't know if he ever saw me.

I struggle to remember what the facade of my mother's house looked like. Some things you never think about from certain angles. I know the inside of that house very well, but not the outside. What color was it? What was the roof like? The windows? The outside of the front door? I remembered it from inside. It had a large thick pane of glass at the top that I worried about constantly.

All someone would have to do is break that and we'd be done. Invaded and surely murdered within the next few minutes. I'd be smelling my own blood. And all we had to do to avoid it was get a solid door.

Sometimes at night I'd sneak out of bed and fall asleep on the floor, where I could see the door. If someone did attack, I planned to run upstairs and wake everyone immediately. I'd

work myself up into hyper-alertness and stay up, almost gasp-
ing every time a shadow passed. And sometimes, I swear, they
were trying to look in.

    Aye! Oh let the well empty

         That tiles of tears pave my road

         That sunny be the beach

            upon which

                    I perish.

If I write poems continuously from now until the end
of the year, I will have been writing poems for two thirds of
the year. The other third of the year, I tasted no letters. But this
would be an improvement in the sense that I finally recorded
and quantified it. For less and less words in your day will
eventually yield numbers. Now, before we file away between 1
and 0, let's not forget to wave goodbye.

These small things are amusing to me, and they excite
me. I hope to meet you someday, and listen to your small
things.

APOTHEOSIS

When a mosquito bites, you end up slapping your own skin.

I stood in a room filled with brick-a-brack. Things I recognized. Candy wrappers from when I was small. A collage I'd made out of ice cream cup tops. The older ones made of a flimsier cardboard than the newer, more durable kind. A shoe I dropped under my bed, never to be retrieved, because I was too afraid to reach for it. It was folded into itself, like a piece of paper. A doll I'd hidden in the shed, because her eyes were too real. It was back on my shelf. A dress that my grandmother had sown for me, before my mother ordered me to stop wearing it. I'd worn it while rock climbing one day and scraped up my knees pretty bad. My mother blamed the dress. She ordered me to wear pants.

"They're just more comfortable, don't you think?"

She herself preferred pants to skirts, claiming that,

"Chafing's not worth it. Oof! You ever been chafed,

Milian? After that happened to me, I stopped wearing all that immediately."

I appreciated her trying to make it about herself. And perhaps that's the greatest thing she ever taught me. Reveal yourself when the spotlight's on somebody else, preferably the one you're speaking to. That way, they aren't tempted to find you out. And you live another day.

I looked out the window and saw the water. The street now a riverbed. A chicken was floating placidly, like a duck. She seemed happy with her new life.

Just behind her, there was something else bobbing in the water.

Apples, I thought.

But as they bounced up and down together, at the steady rhythm of the polar molecule's nature, I dared question them.

There must be more beneath the water.

There was: a crocodile, whose eyes I'd been observing. They floated in the water like apples, and they could see me.

I considered swimming onto the crocodile's back, before it could leap at me. How impressive a feat that would be. But I should do the sensible thing and wait for it to swim away. The water was deep, so it was possible that I could lose sight of it completely, if it submerged itself. I looked around for something to use as a floating device. If I strapped together some books, maybe. Books I'd never read.

I awoke to the sound of a staff alert on the public communication system: precautionary measures were now in effect due to a growing demonstration near the gate.

"Stay indoors, if you can. Otherwise, please listen to the following instructions…"

I glanced out the window and saw that it was raining hard on the surface, couldn't see anything beside knots of white and shades of gray. I slipped back into sleepiness and into a memory about a flood; one of the worst that we'd experienced back in Yarey.

It was raining hard. My father was late coming home from work. We would later find out that his car had filled up with mud and he had to wait to be rescued. Our neighbor's daughter, Merced, was posted up at the top of the street, keeping watch, readying to signal to the rest of us that the rushing water was coming. Standard communication methods were down, as usual. And Merced's signal would only serve as confirmation of what we already knew. The water was coming. It had rained for days. It was the time of year, and the unofficial flooding holiday had passed two days ago. It happened every year. I was tasked with moving as many of our things upstairs as I could, which I had been doing for almost two hours. Electronics, papers, clothing, my father's plants, some food, anything I could think of that we might need, or that might be ruined by the brown water.

My mother was perched on the windowsill, watching Merced. Suddenly, we heard pellets of ice falling on the roof. I ran to the courtyard, lifting up the bottom of my shirt into a wide pocket, to catch some.

"Don't eat that!"

I heard my mother say, as two gray pellets fell into the fold of my shirt. I ate them. There were crunchy grains in them that grated against my teeth, like tiny rock shavings.

I heard my mother cry out,

"It's coming! Milian! Upstairs!"

She rushed to her bedroom downstairs, pulled a thick wooden board from under her mattress and carried it to the foyer. She opened the door. The first wooden board had already been jammed into the tight iron channels on the inside of the doorway. This one would go on top of that one. Merced met her at the door, water rushing halfway up her shins, to help her secure the second board. Then, she made her way across the impromptu river, now rushing past her knees, and hurried up the fire escape across the street to her apartment on the third floor. I watched her appear in the next window. She changed her clothes and then perched at the window sill, like everyone else, watching the brown water rush by. She had a small white mouse, who was also watching the water from the same window sill. It had been *my* mouse, Cicero, until the prior week, when my mother had tossed him out into the street after he bit her. She had told me he was dead, but I never saw the body. I intended to confront her after the flood.

It didn't stop raining for several more hours. The water was about to come in through the windows. It was ankle-high inside, just from the rain coming in through the courtyard. And it was hotter now, so the small clumps of hail that had accumulated were almost completely melted.

A thunderclap set off several car alarms and made the neighbor's dogs go hoarse from howling so hard. I worried that the water would reach the second floor. Then what? When my mother came upstairs, I knew there was real danger.

The house was flooded all night and into the next day. Finally, in the early afternoon, we heard the thirsty gulping of the drain.

I stood by the kitchen counter inside the house on Mantis Green, remembering Cicero, when a rumbling started. I mistook it for my stomach for a moment, before the pressure in my head mapped the sound outside my ears. Low and slow at first; like clattering junk metal afterwards. Crisp claps, thunder-like, adhered themselves to my eardrums like bubblegum bubbles snapping on your face.

The most familiar feeling I knew had returned. A knowledge that in a short time from this very second I'd have to find courage somewhere and use it—like a drug—to flee. As always, I wasn't ready (who is?). I left the memory of my old pet hanging, like a gas, above the table and followed the drums.

Mantis Green was lovely today. The light was warm and the air condition was stable. It would have been a nice day for a picnic, or a drink with friends, music, whatever it is that people do when they enjoy each other. I walked out of the house, saving myself from its pleasant air; walked through the courtyard, holding my breath to avoid its soft earthen fragrance. As I stepped into the tunnel to exit the rock, I saw plumes of smoke near the gate at Sondras Alluma.

A sea of people was in front of me, looking the same way. Some had been demonstrating earlier today, some were headed there now, to make their voices heard. Motives were plentiful and justified. I saw faces of every kind: fear, indignation, ecstasy most recognizable among them. And as I followed the snake of bodies, I saw a small loud crowd parting in the distance. High-pitched sounds echoed one another as the bodies squished together to let something through: Covas.

He was approaching Mantis Green purposefully, with the type of determination that would have pushed the crowd aside. But they didn't need pushing. They moved aside willingly. As he drew closer, I thought he must be carrying something. His face was red and swollen and his shoulders were slumped.

As he emerged from another mass of yelping people I saw the limp arms and legs of little Nico swinging from his arms, her head lolling side to side with each step. His expression was hard and tight. Hers was the kind of neutral you only see once on a person.

The distance between us was too long. I watched him and he watched me but neither of us said anything. And as he drew closer, I was glad we hadn't tried to communicate over the congregation between us. They offered their own works of acknowledgment. Whatever we may have had to say to one another would have been redundant. When he was only behind a few rows of people, I saw that his eyes weren't looking at mine. The last few rows of people were not as loud as the rest. They were eerily quiet, respectful.

The crowd stood still, as he approached me, still looking straight ahead at nothing in particular, and said,

"Alit?"

"He's not back yet."

I was a clown. Answering instead of asking what happened. Covas granted me a formal closing glance, then hugged the girl close to his chest and disappeared into the hall toward the house.

The crowd watched me, waiting for an announcement. I apologized. Whimpers, words (unintelligible but accusatory), sighs, gasps, hot air and sweat and salt from human bodies. I turned around and began walking down the path toward the rock.

"Justice!" A woman chanted. The crowd joined in, eventually rhythmic.

When I arrived at the house, I followed the sounds of mourning into the kitchen, where Covas stood holding the lifeless girl, squeezing her tight as if to keep her here.

My breathing was loud and I thought I might disturb him, but he looked up at me with gentle eyes, lowered his shoulders from his ears. The girl's body shifted in his arms, all gravity and no muscle. He swept one hand under her knees and lifted her, placing her carefully on the counter. With a jolt of pain, as if suddenly impaled, he collapsed to the ground beside her.

The girl's face fell to the side, facing the window, and I felt an impulse to close the blinds a little, to protect her from the harsh sunlight.

The minuscule mirrors in the dome shaped the sun's rays into the cruel slant of a pretty afternoon. Covas was shielded by the shadow of the kitchen counter.

"Where's Alit?"

"Should be here soon, I hope."

"They did it to send a message."

I knew they did. It's what they'd tried to do to me and my brother when we landed. They got him before realizing he was already dead. Then a twister of bodies swallowed me up, the sound of yelling all around me, and eventually within a few months, I was safe in the back of a lady's car, bound for foster care.

It's what was always done at borders and on beaches. And what they'd been doing since the gate filled up with refugees, from Earth and everywhere else. The enforcement agencies and their benefactors made a fortune processing everybody, but every once in a while the crowd became impatient, or grew into an overwhelming mass of hands asking for help. They'd fire shots to hide them again, keep them in their pockets. They'd shot Nico in the back, between her shoulder blades, as she ran through the hordes of people, looking to deliver a parcel. She had died long before Covas reached her.

Covas and I looked up, when we heard loud stomping approaching, dragging behind it echoes from the crowd's wheezing laments outside.

"Alit—"

"What? WHAT? No! What? Oh my God no... no! no! NO!"

He threw himself on top of the girl and heaved wildly, making guttural noises so miserable they were almost humorous. Covas squeezed his shoulders and cried quietly. I stood in the doorway, unsure what to do, presumably blocking it all out. I don't know. Feeling this pain would mean feeling my own and I'd outrun it thus far… Waste. I felt sick for feeling jealous of their free-looking sorrow. I'd wasted myself away, letting warmth expire. It wasn't lack of feeling. Only a pathological inhibition that kept me from expressing it.

I stood watch, as Covas and Alit grieved together all evening, on the floor, next to little Nico's makeshift altar. They were good hosts to their grief. I'd never felt more hopelessly alone.

The next morning, Alit awoke screaming.

"What is it—Nicolina, no! Please!"

Covas held him until he found a way to stop. The scene repeated a few more times. We could offer nothing more than scraps of comfort. I was frozen in place with them on the floor, and the girl's body still on the counter.

People left notes and small offerings outside the gate. I made them something to eat. Brought them into a room to sleep. And then I called Sylvia.

"I'm on my way. Bing is talking to police. We don't know what happened exactly, but he and Caretta are down there still, so hopefully—"

"Thank you."

"See you soon. I'm so sorry."

MANTIS GREEN

In her dark small apartment on Sondras Alluma, Sylvia had smothered herself in a fragrant skin oil that Gallia used, as if donning war paint. She'd loaded a small backpack: three liters of clean water, iodine tablets, a bag of nuts, a packet of ground pepper, a lighter, a small bottle of hair spray, a long screwdriver, a paring knife, a mobile device, cash money, two forms of ID, and a fresh bundle of socks and underwear. After slinging the bag onto her back, she had placed the keys on a little table in front of her small sofa-bed and headed out.

The street was empty but not quiet. A few hundred feet behind Sylvia, the uproar at the gate was growing. A voice on the loudspeakers failed to come through clearly. Instead, a score of yells and cries were amplified and the assembly of bodies repeated the sounds, like a tormented church congregation. Sylvia picked up the pace.

She'd arranged to meet Fulgencio and Caretta at one of the smaller stations on the far side of Sondras Alluma, where they would board Caretta's little ship and fly around the ring to Mantis Green. Bing planned to join after meeting with the police.

I watched Covas and Alit holding each other, thinking about my mother. As a child, I'd been affectionate, but as I got older, that impulse faded. My brother had grown out of it much faster. He'd sparked the hesitation in me, one day, when he rejected an embrace from a woman who lived down the street. She used to swap produce with my mother, when food started to become scarce. On one occasion, she'd dropped by unannounced. My brother and I were home alone. She seemed to know him well, I remember. His taste in food and the way he ate spaghetti.

"He slurps it down whole, like it's a worm! I've never seen anything like it!"

She giggled, reaching for his hands. Going on and on.

"Sauce everywhere! Hahaha!"

He pulled away from her each time, glancing at me as he did it, lips tight. She opened her arms into an arc, expecting him to curl in. He bent down to pick up the bag of potatoes she'd brought and hauled them off to our kitchen, then refused to come back out, claiming he wasn't feeling well and had to go to the bathroom. She'd come back later that night, stood outside our bedroom window with a flash light, shining it through, trying to wake him up. But my brother slept like a rock. I shuffled over to the window to find the light had been turned off and the fog was completely still, undisturbed. For years I thought I'd dreamed the whole thing, until my brother explained what it was all about.

I'd tried being affectionate with people on Earth, trying to reconcile my fragments, only to find too many people were suspicious of that expression. I understood that, so I stopped.

By the front door, I kept a little jar of cloves. An old superstition. Supposed to cleanse the energy entering the house. Also my family's go-to during funerals and vigils, as a breath freshener. I picked up the little jar and put two cloves in my mouth. The bittersweetness of their oil was perfect. I offered some to Covas and Alit, who both took some. Alit smelled them first, curling his upper lip to cradle them up to the tip of his nose.

We sat together beneath little Nico's altar, Alit letting me hold his hand, Covas breathing rhythmically with his eyes closed. Exhausted. Time and silence were fantasy elements. Mechanical sounds layered atop one another, amplified to a point that felt like being inside a washing machine. And the storm system wasn't even on.

When our friends arrived, we welcomed the extra sounds with near-joy. Sylvia had brought water and food. Caretta and Fulgencio brought candles and blankets. They'd also brought in some of the things the crowd had left outside: artwork, toys, religious figurines, books, a pie that Caretta couldn't refuse.

"I know the lady. It's good. I forget what's in it."

"Rhubarb."

"That's it!"

Fulgencio and Caretta seemed settled into each other,

warm and pleasant. I suppose when you've been through enough, you learn to take what you can and enjoy it.

We held a memorial for Nico. The crowd outside was invited to come in and pay their respects, offer their sympathy, share their anger and pain with us and each other, whatever they needed to do. Mourning is multi-purpose.

I was suspicious of an older woman that was asking Alit too many questions. She wanted to know where they were from, where her mother was, why she was at the gate today, what she had done, where he had been when it happened. I realized that I'd been in a vigilant state of mind since I was about five years old. It had never stopped. First it was tanks in the streets, fighter jets in the sky, bombs raining down, provisional military governments, dictatorships, fleeing, flying, my brother dying… laws and paperwork, money sickness, a death threat from a xenophobic neighbor, homelessness, my eighteenth birthday, my first work permit, education, on the up and up (for the nationalists too), Rotari, my apartment, citizenship (barely squeezed through), the Cloudi mess, The Marionette, Gallia and her bird, citizenship undone, exile again, my mother's skull, the rest of her stolen ground up and made into a tea, more in the graves than on the streets, everywhere a protest, a piece of hot metal ripping through flesh, boiled blood. Everywhere I went, no home. No rest.

399

I kicked the woman out.

"This is no time for this."

"Darling, I'm just…"

"Don't call me Darling—Don't call me Honey or Sweetie or Baby or whatever it is that you think will make you sound most harmless. Leave this house. Now."

"Milian—" Caretta was scared. I understand. It wasn't like me to act this way. I was embarrassed but I couldn't stop.

"No. I'm tired. You come in here, pretending like you give a shit—Everything! Everything you have, and it's still all about *you*. *You* have to be answered to. *You* have to be *thanked*. Please…"

Waste. I couldn't finish a single thought. There was so much I wanted to say to her and it wasn't all for her to hear. I had decades of unspoken thoughts to fire at this presumptuous self-aggrandizing false-heroic medal-collecting cookie-munching dirty-conscience phony selfish spineless crawling irresponsible wasteful judgement-obsessed artificial-intellect immature-emotion consumer of a vampire of a being. My face was hot and my whole body was shaking and I couldn't say one more word. Covas escorted her out.

During the hot pink flash of time that followed my misplaced outburst, Bing arrived. He'd filed a report with a clerk at the police station, but due to the activity at the gate, he'd been guaranteed a delayed response.

Nico was laid to rest in the garden at Mantis Green, at the base of her favorite tree, whose leaves she used to polish with a wet napkin. She'd murmur things to it, fully engaged, as if she heard the plant's reactions to her words. My father used to do the same thing. And briefly, during my third or fourth year of life, I did it too. As the story goes, I had a small tomato plant in a tiny pot that I used to carry with me everywhere. Plants make special friends, completely ego-free. They're great listeners and trust you to care for them. I don't know that we can achieve the same kind of fulfillment between animals. The most optimal evolution belongs to the leafy ones. Eternally patient, appearing to stand still and dying a hundred deaths, they understand and accept everything as it comes. They shed and renew and provide comfort and life to countless others.

After we buried Nico, we all fell asleep together in the living room, watching TV. Nothing but news coverage of the altercations at the gate. Several injured. At least a dozen dead. More refugee ships refused docking permits, forced to try their luck on a nearby planet. Many of the smaller ships weren't equipped for longer journeys. They'd eventually turn into mass coffins drifting through space. Every week, one or two ships would be found without a heartbeat on board. The only concerns left, in regard to these vessels, were pollution and collision risk. No matter. Surely, the problem would fix itself, if we hoped hard enough.

It was the most wretched sleepover. We assembled a massive mattress out of all the pillows in the house. There were drinks and snacks and tissues all over. We fell asleep in shifts, awoke hungover and exhausted, drank and ate some more and watched some more TV. Covas and I took turns washing dishes and picking up trash around the ball of bodies. Caretta and Fulgencio cycled through conversation topics endlessly, with Alit chiming in between naps. Bing and Sylvia spent a lot of time discussing the events on TV. They seemed to have a solution to everything. If only someone would listen.

I couldn't bear to eat another handful of dried fruit or nuts, so I decided to cook a meal for us. I threw together a stir-fry of spicy chard, soy curds and yams, with some orange slices on the side, rolled in a tamarind powder. Fresh ginger tea with lemon. Some of it was grown here, the rest was on Alit's book of imports. I found myself missing cinnamon, saffron and cayenne pepper. Mangoes. Fresh coconut water. Those dumplings from the noodle house near my old apartment. The madeleine cookies from the bakery near my mother's house. I was hungry.

We ate silently. There was a weird rhythm in the room, from all the clinking utensils and chewing and slurping and sipping and sniffling. Was it the spice or the grief? No matter.

We didn't look up at each other, out of respect.

The news finally changed into a pathetic little movie called WESTERN CORNERS. It was all about a large happy affluent family in the U.S. who all suffered different degrees of psychosis, leading to a multiple-murderer bloodbath. The kind of stuff without substance that makes enough money to allow the creators to continue to do more work in the future. I had something like that. It was called *"And On This Day..."* and was a string of loud installations in a handful of second-tier cities, where tourists and locals alike could pretend to be on the front page of local news. A code on the plaster surface told the camera to pull the latest top news and send a final image to the customer for their personal use ("all rights reserved"). The program was smart enough to adapt to their experience in the world, but that feature didn't end up being used, as nobody wants to be publicly shamed about their point of view. I thought it could have been an interesting social experiment, but I was too optimistic about the popularity of thoughtful conversation. Instead, I ended up looking like a cuff link shopper pretending to have a youthful sense of fun. But it did convince Rotari to award me an apprenticeship, even though I'd already graduated, effectively building a bridge into my next life. This movie was somebody's bridge and nothing more, regardless of whether they saw it as a failure in all other areas. When the kid no longer spills their drink, that's when you let them hold their own cup.

Alit had raised a strong smart child. She'd been taken, anyway. It seemed to me, at times, that life is most terrifying when things don't line up. Eat more chard; it makes your heart stronger. Swim in the ocean early on in life to stave off seafood allergies. Sleep at least eight hours every day. Eight Earth hours?

Why shouldn't we be shamed for our point of view? We fall, we learn.

After a few more rounds of snacks and two more movies, it was my turn to sleep. I'd barely made it under the velvet curtain, when I was suddenly roused by a ringing in my ears.

Blast.

Colors flashed through the windows, as we scrambled to exit the pillow pit, getting tangled up and stumbling over each other. The emergency signal was blaring and I couldn't hear much else. Tiny specs of dust, or dirt, or fragments of wall and ceiling, were falling all around us like a drizzle. Rain! I missed rain!

Blast.

Covas and I helped Alit gather the emergency supplies, as everyone else followed Caretta to the cave. We tried looking outside to see if anybody was there, but it was all smoke. Covas wasn't looking on with me. He also wasn't packing anymore. I put my hand on his shoulder to wake him up, if he had drifted. He was conscious but frozen. All we'd been through and this was the one that did it. Blast.

I looked on the other side at my dear little planet, Earth. Her face was a checkerboard of white and ultramarine. The muddy greens seemed to have gone away entirely.

Blast.

Caretta and the others came rushing towards us.

"Son, we have to go."

"Where?"

"Down."

"We don't have enough fuel to go anywhere else."

"Down?"

Blast.

Specks of wall and ceiling. People mouthing words and not reacting to each other. Ringing. As if drawing spheres with the vibration. Pounding in treble notes.

We saw movement in the grayness outside. Blasts of color silhouetted helmeted heads. Suddenly, the outdoor sounds were inside and Covas was collapsing to the floor. A chunk of ceiling fell between us. I saw in the corner of my eye a uniformed person yelling words that would have been loud, if my ears weren't trying to protect themselves. Fulgencio was dragging Covas out into the courtyard, when four other uni-forms marched in. I saw a gun pointed at my face, right before multiple hands pulled me out of the house.

"Close it!"

I hit the button to cue the closing of the gate ahead of us and we ran for it, heading for the bridge, where we could hop on Caretta's ship and take off. Covas was alive but unconscious, so Bing and I had to carry him. Alit and Sylvia hurried Caretta along, as Fulgencio followed close behind.

"Are we gonna make it down there?"

"We'll make it."

Alit wasn't in the mood to explain how or provide any additional assurance. Trying not to yield to panic, I urged Bing to walk faster. Just as I thought I had stepped on some kind of rubble—a broken rock or something that wasn't supposed to be there—I found myself thrown several feet from my companions, as if teleported. Sylvia was next to me, yelling at Alit's face, glancing at me a few times. I wondered if I was dead. As I stared at Sylvia and Alit, trying to make eye contact, Alit's face turned in my direction. His eyes were vacant, but his hand was moving. I thought maybe Sylvia had been making his hand move, as she held him up. But then he got up, on his own. He looked at me. I wasn't dead.

A stampede of people followed, uniformed and civilian. Some fought, others fled. The uniforms did the same. It really was oddly natural, and I didn't like that it made sense. You've seen an image of aggressive behavior, and in the end it's wrong. This aggression is primal, and it feels sadistic be-cause *we know better*. I had several people looking at me like I had strangled their family. I had others plead with me or wish me good luck. Some more lost than others. All lost in different places. Everyone scrambling for shelter. Safety. Comfort: the final wish.

Blast.

"Hey!" We heard an unfamiliar voice yelling from the house. Then a cloud of blood misted the air, spraying the mass of panicked people. Caretta emerged from the crowd, drag-ging Fulgencio by the leg. Comical and terrible. Fulgencio's hand had been shredded by the explosion. We watched Bing running the other way, waving us off. A child was put into his arms. Clearly, he'd continue his fight up here.

Sylvia and I reached the ship first and started loading it. Alit was dragging Covas and yelling at Caretta to hurry up. Fulgencio was barely awake, his head lolling, the grip on his wounded hand loose. Caretta's face was red and wet.

After we managed to load Covas and Fulgencio onto the ship, I ran to the bridge door to press the trigger for the gate lock. A heavy metal gate came crashing down to the floor, locking away the raiders for the time being. Caretta fell back.

"Oh no."

"Where do I start it?"

Alit struggled to remain in control of himself, as he

flipped switches and toggles on the console of Caretta's ship. The old man had built it quirky and illogical. Made it more fun, I suppose. It also kept other pilots from knowing how to fly it.

"Please?"

Sylvia shook Caretta, who was fixated on his friend's face.

"Help him. I'll take care of his hand."

Caretta went through the motions of starting the ship. The fuel tank was more than half full.

"We have enough to get somewhere else."

"They won't want us anywhere else, and then what?"

"They don't want us here, either, son."

"They don't want us anywhere. We have to go."

That should have been on the news:

"All of Earth displaced. No one wanted anywhere!"

Alit's chest was drenched in blood. He and Caretta were fighting about where to go, when a blast hit right next to us. Debris pierced right through the gate (cheap piece of junk) and collided with the side of the ship.

I should have pre-programmed the system to detach the rock from the ring, should there be a violent breach like this. Strand the monsters inside. No matter. Next time. I turned to look at Caretta, whose eyes were glued to the console.

"The fuel."

"Let's go!"

Alit pushed the old man aside and lifted us up and out of the bridge, as the fuel line drained.

Another explosion went off, and when the debris hit the windows, we all instinctually held our breath, as if... well, it was funny, in a way. But the glass didn't crack, and as the fuel continued to flow unused, we started to fall away from the fireworks.

We took turns tending to Covas and Fulgencio, both of them conscious again. I was too afraid to look at their injuries, but from what I could tell, Sylvia had it under control. Caretta held both their hands, as we ripped like a handmade arrow through the atmosphere. The ship shook us like a cocktail, with a merciless hot clatter.

Moments later, we landed somewhere in the vast new ocean. The sound of fire was all around us. A rumble rattling. We panicked, as we realized that we were sinking. Caretta had fainted as we entered Earth and Alit was screaming in his face trying to wake him up.

"Where's the floating device?" No response.

"Ascilogo!" Fulgencio joined in, exhausted but determined to survive.

Covas shook Caretta violently until he woke up. Without saying any words, he sprung up, opened a compartment

409

below the console and pulled a little green lever to release the floating device tucked into the rim of the hatch. The little can turned, sending us all for a tumble to the ground, rolling until the hatch was facing up, on the surface of the water.

For one reason or another, now that we could exit the ship, we chose not to. Covas and Fulgencio had to rest, we agreed. And so we spent the night together inside the tiny ship. We opened the hatch for ventilation and immediately a cloud of gas seeped in, spreading like fire. It seemed toxic at first. A stench we'd never known. Asparagus urine, rotten flesh, metallic, rusty, a mustard gas kind of smell. Had it always smelled that way? Or was it just a result of the recent environmental shift? Anyway, we covered our noses as well as we could and pretended to sleep. I played a game: catch the others looking up at the stars. We mock the idea of being disarmed by them, for fear of sounding like simpletons, but all living things look up—in awe or for mere sustenance. The sun has trained us that way. The real mother of life is the brightest burning fire. And the state of being alive is nothing but a reaction to that heat. Lucky ones we are, regardless of what circumstances destroy us, individually. Surpass the danger and you've carved your part of our name. That's if you're breaking through, not if you're healing. Well, wait a minute, that's the same idea, if you're healing: what needs to be said is that you need rest. No warrior wants to rest. That's a dangerous statement to make in that world. But we all think about it. That's why some of the greatest stories about war times are about quiet moments and "beautiful" things. They're about hope. Hoping to reach peace again. But prolonged peace allows for some to become greedy about their comforts, which in turn creates a deficit for others. It may have started as an extra-hungry friend asking for part of your rations. One imposes on the other. For the sake of peace, the other yields. Generations of this dynamic birth irreconcilable disparity. Eventually it's not voluntary. And war returns again, in one form or another. Our stability is enduring but volatile. But beyond the heat, there's only rocks and darkness. So we make it.

I caught everyone except Sylvia looking up at the deep velvet sky, at some point during the night. Caretta won the tally. Mantis Green was nowhere to be seen, either destroyed or at peace. Yarey could have been any one of millions of dots. Only some of the dim lights from the Marionette broke up the clumpy texture of the new stars. They collected like dust on the firmament. Sticky. Brilliant. I uncovered my face, to relieve myself from the humid heat. All at once it hit me, this air. The salt. The fizz. This planet's wonderful creamy air. None of the stench was there anymore. Only sweetness. No sounds beside the breeze and the gentle lapping of the water around the ship, like popping bubbles. The light rocking, back and forth, made me sigh louder than I intended.

"Son?"

"Yeah… I'm awake."

"Long night, ah?"

I smiled. Earth nights were once unbearably long to me, too.

"Yeah, it feels pretty endless."

"Morning's gotta be coming soon, now, for sure."

"Well…"

Judging by the sky, we were still a few hours away from dawn. Caretta's cheeks dropped an inch as his mouth hung open. Funny guy. I asked,

"Did you sleep?"

"A little. I guess I'll try again."

"Good luck."

We shared a voiceless chuckle and looked up at the sky again. With nowhere to go, we floated there silently with the stars and the faint sounds of the ocean landscape. I must have dozed off out of exhaustion. The last thing I heard was Caretta calling out to his friend,

"Fulgencio…"

The next morning, we awoke feeling like a decade had gone by. Our joints popped and we were parched. Alit had been the first to leave the ship. I could hear him talking to a woman nearby. While Sylvia gathered what we'd brought in terms of food and belongings, Caretta and I helped Covas and Fulgencio get out. We were greeted outside, in the cool blue serenity of the world, by Alit and his new friend Uanamira, a small middle-aged woman with faded hair and a strong face. She gripped my hand with sturdy muscular fingers, ensuring I wouldn't lose my balance, as I hopped onto her little boat.

Uanamira drove us to a little key, one of thousands in the area, where she had brought another dozen people. She offered us fish broth and coconut water, some medical help for our injured friends, and spots on the ground for us to claim.

"Your choice. We're democratic!"

She smiled at me, as she readied to get back on her boat.

The ground felt good on my bare feet, salty and clean. Up ahead, a gradient of warmth revealed itself at the bottom of the sky. The tops of palm trees dotted a wavy line that pointed at some purple hills in the distance. A group of small boats was using the treetops as a guide to get to those hills, where they would find the largest settlement in sight: Esparta Nueva.

A hundred eyes were on us, friendly and otherwise. In the distance, I saw movement in and out of the water.

"Las toninas!" An enthusiastic three-year old came and sat next to me, pointing exactly where I was looking.

"They're dolphins!" She translated for me. It occurred

to me that I'd never seen dolphins in the wild. Caretta would be furious if I didn't tell him, so I told the little girl to point them out to him. There his cheeks went, an inch below his chin. Funny guy.

The dolphins swam next to one of the boats, jumping up playfully. The three-year old came back with something in her hand. A small crab. She asked me to hold him, so I did.

"His name is Patrick."

Patrick's eyes were tiny pellets, but I knew where to look at him and say hello. How can some people insist that animals don't see us? We know that being endowed with senses, we can't avoid looking into other eyes or listening to sounds directed at us. Social animals may be obsolete, but we're more precious than the everywhere cynic illusionists who think themselves transcended animals. We will give our lives for the next world because we've fought to see it.

We breathed the clean, humid air, and were coated in the mineral breeze. The sun was rising as we settled into our little nooks by the sea, indistinguishable from the rest of the debris. As the rays hit my face, I felt worthy. Earth was my home, and I would never apologize for surviving in it.

Farah Ysvette Mourad Vera

PRAYER

To the edge of blue,
where Day 1 and Year 100 are
Alike
Alone
Alive
An elderly green sea turtle moves slowly through the mangroves of a small key off the coast of the remains of Fort Zachary Taylor,
where it was photographed by a conservation group 30 years ago.

The turtle will feed on what it finds in the grove and then swim up and rest on a shady patch of sand.

There it will die on its last day.

For now, a dove will sit with it awhile, as a full moon shines on them together.

The dove will sleep on a nearby branch
And by the time it wakes
The turtle will be gone.

MANTIS GREEN

The dove will fly to another key, where it will be photographed.

The sea turtle will see the moon grow thinner each night, and on the night of the New Moon

The game will end.

And life will have been a fruitful success,

For instinct carried the turtle from egg to mangrove

And as it dies,

It will see the deeper blue before it sleeps.

www.ingramcontent.com/pod-product-compliance
Lightning Source LLC
Chambersburg PA
CBHW030549020726
47494CB00005B/1545